LEAVE BEFORE YOU GO

LEAVE BEFORE YOU GO

EMILY PERKINS

THE ECCO PRESS

An Imprint of HarperCollins*Publishers*

for BRITA

This book was written with the support of the Todd New Writers' Bursary.

This book was originally published in Great Britain in 1998 by Picador.

HarperCollins books may be purchased for educational, business, or sales promotional use. For information please write: Special Markets Department, HarperCollins Publishers Inc., 10 East 53rd Street, New York, NY 10022.

FIRST U.S. EDITION

Library of Congress Cataloging-in-Publication Data has been applied for.

ISBN 0-06-019661-0

00 01 02 03 04 ❖/RRD 10 9 8 7 6 5 4 3 2 1

The searing sound of aeroplanes taking off and landing was the background noise of Daniel's childhood. In his earliest memory he is standing in the street outside his parents' flat, watching a mammoth white jet cruise up and over their outer London suburb, rising, rising until it's nothing but a silver finger pointing an escape route through the smoky sky. Now he is more than twenty-five years older. He's inside one of these big planes for the first time. It's different from how he'd imagined it would be, here in the middle seat in the middle aisle in the middle of economy class. Daniel is hot and uncomfortable and would like another drink. He's been trying to flag down an air hostess but none of them will catch his eye and the 'call' button on the arm of his chair seems to be broken. He doesn't trust his Bloody Mary-ed legs to carry him up the length of the plane to the stewards' little hidey-hole. The headrest in front of him is very close. He's not that tall, average really, but there isn't enough room in here for a six-year-old child, let alone a man of young but indeterminate age like himself. Sweat starts to appear at his temples. London was freezing when they left it but the temperature in the cabin shoots right up and right down every twenty minutes. He takes his jumper off again and folds his arms tightly over his ribs. Jiggles his knees. Two and a half hours into the flight. Nearly ten hours to go. Why are the fucking tropics so many fucking miles away?

A couple of weeks ago, with his friend Richard, Daniel went round to Richard's mate's place, just for a visit. The North London flat had an unholy smell, like someone had vomited in a corner a month before and then someone else had pissed on it and then someone else had sealed all the windows and turned the heating up. Richard's friend was reading the paper at a rickety table. The only other furniture in the room was a couple of chairs and a beanbag. The friend was dressed in a spotless linen suit. He exuded aftershave and good health and his tan was a deep solarium orange. He peered up at them with the reddest eyes Daniel had ever seen.

Richard shook the guy's hand. 'Sticksy, mate. This is Daniel. Bloke I told you about.'

The guy smiled at Daniel without opening his mouth. Daniel nodded at him.

'Sit down, man.' He sounded almost American. 'I'm Sticks. It's very nice to meet you.'

Richard and Daniel sat down at the table. Daniel put his arms on it but it was gluey and he tried to wipe his sleeves without being obvious.

Richard leaned back in his chair and stretched his arms behind his head. 'Seen Seth lately?'

'No way. Guy's a loser man. It's a bad vibe.'

Sticksy talked like a record player at half speed. He rolled a joint with fingers as slow as his voice. 'I was reading this really cool book on body language, yeah? And one of the things uptight people do, right, is they fold their arms in front of them all the time, right?'

Daniel unfolded his arms. He held on to the sides of his chair. Sticksy kept talking. 'And they clutch on to things, right? And what do you think Seth does, man?'

'Yeah,' said Richard, 'I know what you mean.'

'Huh,' said Sticks.

Daniel loosened his grip on the chair. He lit a cigarette
and put one hand in his coat pocket. The kitchen door
opened and a heavily pregnant girl with stringy yellow
hair wandered into the room. Sticksy looked up at her.
'Piss off, darling,' he said, not unkindly.

Her eyes drifted over to the three of them sat there at
the table. Daniel wondered how she could stand the
stench in this place. She smiled at them and Daniel shot
a look at Sticksy before smiling back.

'I said piss off, all right?'

The girl stopped smiling and went back into the
kitchen, closing the door behind her. Sticksy sighed. 'It's
totally bad timing, man, my lady's got herself in the
family way as you can see and, hey, I'm going to stand
by her. I'm going to do the right thing, you know.'

There was a pause. Daniel felt as if it was his turn to
say something. 'Timing?'

'Yeah.' Sticksy smiled at Richard. 'I'm due for my
annual trip, you know, to Thailand and New Zealand.
I'd love to go but I have responsibilities and the nuclear
family's a beautiful thing, you know?'

Sticksy looked at Richard and Daniel with a manly
mixture of pride and regret. Daniel smiled back. Sticksy
lit the joint and passed it to Daniel. The paper was soggy
where his lips had been. Daniel thought it might be
uncool to twist the end bit off. Richard was squinting at
something on the ceiling. Sticksy kept on smiling.
'Thailand, right, is fucking amazing. It's Paradise, man.
You know how in the Bible they have, uh, the Garden
of Eden?'

Daniel nodded.

'Nothing on Thailand. I'm telling you. Beautiful
beaches, endless sunshine, pools, girls, bars, girls. You
name it. Yeah?'

They all grinned. Richard reached over and took the joint off Daniel. 'You know,' he said, 'I heard about this guy in Bangkok who made four thousand US gambling in one afternoon . . .'

'That's nothing, man,' said Sticksy, 'that's nothing.'

' – and then instead of cash, you know what they give him? A fifteen-year-old virgin. His. To do with what he likes. For life. You know what I mean?' Richard looked from Sticksy to Daniel with wide eyes.

Daniel didn't recognize his friend of twelve years in this nodding puppy dog. Still, he felt some response was called for. 'Hmmph,' he said.

Sticksy laughed. 'Life is cheap, man. But in Thailand, who cares. It's heaven on earth, man, heaven on earth. Last time I was there, we were riding these elephants through the jungle – can you imagine that, man, like fucking Tarzan riding these elephants.'

'Cool,' said Richard.

'Yeah, and above the tops of the trees in the jungle, you're up high because you're on these elephants, right, out the top of the jungle you can see *sky*scrapers. Yeah.'

'Great,' said Daniel.

'Hey, but I was thinking of something – what was it?' Sticksy frowned at the table, then looked up at Daniel. 'Oh right, so I can't go this year so I'm looking for someone else to go for me, so will you do it?'

Daniel laughed, a short chokey 'ha'. Sticksy's scarlet eyes didn't leave him. Daniel turned to look at Richard, who was watching him with an unfamiliar, detached expression. He tried the laugh again. 'You what?'

'I asked you if you wanted to go on a free trip to Thailand and New Zealand in my place, seeing as how I can't unfortunately go this year seeing as how my child is on the verge of being born, man. It's a simple question really.'

The smell of the room seemed to have intensified. Daniel thought he saw something scuttle across the floor and under the beanbag. He lit another cigarette. He imagined all of grey filthy London stretching out beyond this flat, this sticky table being the epicentre of the whole stinking creaking mess, the three of them huddled around it like guard dogs or something. He picked up his lighter and flicked it on and off. He remembered Sticksy's body-language book and put the lighter down.

'What's the catch?' He surprised himself with the question.

'Catch?' Sticksy looked at Richard and they both laughed. 'There's no catch, man, it's a fucking beautiful offer, it's simple.'

Daniel couldn't figure out why Richard seemed so unfazed by this. He just sat there, icy as anything.

'I'm going for a piss,' said Sticksy. 'If you can't do it, man, I'll find somebody else, no problem.'

He left in the direction of the kitchen. Daniel turned to Richard but Richard's expression hadn't changed. 'He's mad.'

'Nah,' said Richard, 'he's a good guy.'

'There's got to be a catch.'

'There's no catch. All you do is have a week's holiday in Thailand, cocktails on the beach and as much Thai pussy as you like, then you take a little package on to New Zealand for my friend. It's easy.'

Daniel looked at Richard disbelievingly. He tried to keep his voice low. 'This package right, it's drugs isn't it? Smack. They kill you for that, they fucking murder you.'

Richard smiled at him. 'Mate, this is foolproof. This

geezer's done it ten or twelve times. Nothing's going to happen, no way. It's a fucking doddle.'

Daniel shook his head. 'You're crazy.'

'You're the crazy one my friend if you don't go for this. Get out of London, get to a beach, get to New Zealand – you can bungee jump, man.'

Daniel couldn't believe this. *My friend?* Richard would kiss him on both cheeks in a second and he'd wake up tomorrow morning with half a horse in his bed. 'So why don't you do it?'

Richard laughed. 'Leave work? You've got to be joking. That's my life, mate, you know that. I'm sorted here.'

Daniel frowned. Richard's record shop. He was always holding that one over him, like he'd really achieved success in the industry while Daniel's last job, selling advertising space for a music magazine, had lasted six months. He heard the clank of dishes from the kitchen. The door opened and Sticksy walked back to the table, zipping up his fly. Richard leaned over and hissed at Daniel. 'London's dead for you, mate. You've got debts. It's a lost cause. Don't be a fuckwit.'

Daniel lit another cigarette off the one in his hand. Was this all he had, the time it took to smoke a couple of fags, to decide what he was going to do with his miserable life?

'Well, man,' said Sticks, 'what do you say. Are you up for it?'

He hated things here just now, it was true. He was sick of Richard being so superior and cool. He was sick of the weather and of having no job. His friends, the pubs, the threat of court action over his unpaid poll tax. The way nothing ever, ever seemed to change.

But the main thing was this. Daniel had seen a lot of

movies, he'd read a few books. From these he was used
to the idea that chance events occur, that somebody like
him could be caught up in an adventure, swept away
into a fictional world of fifteen-year-old virgins and
drug barons and bungee jumping. Isn't that what had
just happened to him when Richard called round and
said in an offhand way, Let's go and visit a mate of mine
this afternoon? Another thing was, he'd never been
around junk in real life. His concept of heroin culture
came in Technicolor with the soundtrack available from
a high-street record store. The thought of agreeing to
this proposal was fantastic, from the world of make-
believe. He'd be opening the map and stepping into the
charted dream of fantasy land, Erehwon, the un-real.

Sticks held his gaze. 'There's ten thousand dollars in it
as well.'

Ten K? Daniel's mouth opened. Escape *plus* money?
What he could do with ten thousand dollars. He
laughed. 'Yes,' he said, 'yeah, yeah, yes.' The room
seemed to expand and contract again in a rush.

'Top man,' said Sticksy, and Daniel looked at Richard
and grinned. Richard grinned back.

ONE   It's Richard's grinning face Daniel
can see now, hovering behind his
closed eyes, a great toothy smile like the Cheshire Cat.
He opens his eyes and the same movie about a friendship
between a man and a dog is still playing on the blurry
screen up the front of the plane. He'd kill for a cigarette.
He read somewhere they put stuff in the food to stop
you from shitting. They don't like their clean aeroplane
toilets messed up. That was the same place he read that
if you don't touch your meal they suspect you of
smuggling drugs and search you at customs. He pulls his
jumper up and wraps it around his head like a bandage,
trying to block out the next-door conversation and the
light. They don't let you smoke. They don't let you
take a dump. They don't let you out.

Finally he's at Don Huang airport then on the minibus to Pattaya. Daniel lolls in his seat. In the window his
reflection looks dark-eyed, his thin nose and his high
cheekbones sharp with shadows. It could be any time in
London now. He didn't sleep on the flight. Hasn't slept
much since the visit to Sticksy's. His head knocks against
the bus window in time with the bumps in the road.
There are noisy package-tour lads in the back of the bus.
One pasty-faced guy, the softness in his middle empha-
sized by his towelling polo shirt, is rolling empty beer
cans up and down the aisle and staggering, shaking with
laughter, after them. His three friends entertain themselves with a burping competition. A gay couple across

the aisle from Daniel take photographs of each other. They keep swapping seats so the kit-set suburbs of Bangkok, TV aerials and car factories, appear through the window in the background of each shot. It's hot. Daniel keeps his eyes on his suitcase, slipping around on the seat beside him.

Richard had come around the night before and given Daniel the name and address of the hotel in Pattaya he was staying at. He sat there, in his annoying ginger-haired way, stroking his goatee and almost smirking as Daniel threw T-shirts into his scuffed plastic case. He was giving Daniel the low-down. The picture had altered, just slightly.

'So you don't move, right? Hotel room, hotel pool. Room, pool, room, pool. No night spots for you, matey. No twelve-year-olds popping ping pong balls out their twats. Mr Go Home Stay Home, that's your name.'

'OK.' Daniel was doing his best to ignore Richard's presence. 'Whatever.'

'No, not whatever. No moving, I'm serious. You don't want to go to the beach anyway, it's a fucking toilet. And the clubs around Pattaya are shit as well. Used to be ravers and now it's just sad old krauts. So don't feel as if you're missing out.'

There was a tightness in Daniel's stomach. He went into the kitchen and drank a glass of water. Ran his wet hands over his face and went back to the packing.

'Mate? Don't sulk, mate, this is a fantastic opportunity. Thailand, for fuck's sake. I did you a favour introducing you to Sticks, you could be a little bit fucking chirpy about it.'

Daniel couldn't look at him.

'Ah, fuck it.' Richard stood up. 'So, the guy's going

to turn up with the gear. I'm not sure exactly when but probably your last day. So that's why you can't move, OK? If he shows up and you're not there it's a complete cock-up. It could get nasty.' Richard bent his head around into Daniel's face. 'This is why I'm telling you. You've got to be a bit careful. All right?'

Daniel made himself nod. 'Yeah. Cheers, mate.'

'And listen. You get your ten K when you deliver to the guy in Auckland. He'll sort out Sticksy's payment, his money side of things, you don't worry about that.'

'I get paid in Auckland,' Daniel said. 'New Zealand dollars?' For some reason he'd imagined US dollars when they'd been mentioned before. 'What are they worth?'

'The Kiwi dollar's really strong, mate, it's right up there with the Americans, right up there. So you got me? You know what's going on?'

'Yeah.'

'Good.' Richard paced the room, swinging his arms back and forwards. 'Whoo! You're going to have the best time. Sunshine, pool, sometimes they send a girl to your room—'

'When were you there?'

Richard stopped pacing. 'What?'

'When was the last time you were there?'

'Yeah, OK, this is what I hear, all right. I don't know if your hotel does it or not but Sticks stays at this place every time and he says it's top. Exclusive, know what I mean? Sticks, mate, he's got taste.'

Daniel snorted. He shut the suitcase and looked at Richard's skinny face. He didn't know why he had agreed to do this but he knew that he was glad to be leaving.

'Well.' Richard slapped Daniel on the back and

grinned. He grabbed him and hugged him really hard for half a second. Daniel could smell his friend's sweat. He swayed back towards the wall, his eyes on his shoes. 'Yeah,' said Richard. 'I'm off then.'

Daniel looked up in time to see him waving his way out the door, calling, 'See ya!' He heard him clatter down the stairs, then fainter but echoey from the stairwell, he could hear him say something else, and laugh. Daniel thought of leaning out the doorway and yelling down, 'What?' But when he went to the door, all he did was close it.

Thick hot air, bright light and freighters glinting on the horizon. The package-tour boys surge past Daniel to be first off the bus. He rubs his eyes. Peers through the dusty window at the curving row of palms lining what has to be the beach. Won't be going there.

Early the next afternoon Daniel wakes up from a dream that somebody − Sticksy maybe − is filling his mouth with cotton wool. When he opens his eyes he is surprised to see a wall on his right side, not where the wall usually is in his flat. Then he remembers. The room is cold. There's the gurgle and whirr of air-conditioning. He sits on the edge of the bed with his head dropped forward and wonders what he has done. He doesn't wonder for long. He pulls on his T-shirt and shorts and stumbles downstairs. The soupy air hits him as he steps through the French doors of the restaurant to the hotel pool. It's a smallish, grubby looking thing, filled with pale cloudy water. The white tiles sport the same faint stains as the walls of his hotel bathroom. Daniel holds on to the handrail part of the ladder and dips his foot in. It's tepid.

This is the life, he says to himself as he leans back in a
woven plastic deck chair. There is no breeze. The
poolside pot plants give off a vaguely rotten, jungly
smell. The sky is overcast. Daniel's dream comes back
to him. It had been like a bad trip to the dentist's. His
mouth held wide open while thick fingers of cotton
wool were jammed in. Two lizards pick their way across
the deck chair next to his. The heat envelops him. He
can feel his pulse slow down. A man in a blue cotton
jacket and trousers has appeared beside the thatched
parasol of the poolside bar. From behind the safety of
his dark glasses Daniel stares at the man's face. A growth
or tumour protrudes from the left cheekbone and under
this a white scar runs down to his jaw. The growth is
the size of a satsuma. Bristles stick out of the top. Perhaps
it's an extra head. An undeveloped twin. Perhaps inside
the skin and cartilage is a brain. In between selling
Daniel beers the two-headed barman sweeps the concrete paving blocks, hoses the pot plants with brown
water and stands, swaying, holding a radio tightly to his
ear. Daniel can hear the static. Every time he opens his
eyes Two-head is looking at him.

On day three Daniel wakes up feeling strange. The
surface of his skin is cold – they have the air-con set to
Arctic again – but he also feels hot and nauseous. He
unpeels himself from the bed and looks in the full-
length mirror on his wardrobe door. A lobster looks
back. He is a bright angry pink all the way down his
front except for where his shorts have been. He peers
down at his shoulders. Small white blisters cluster over
them. How did this happen? It's been cloudy since he
got here. He doesn't understand. He moves his arms up
and down experimentally and winces at the stinging

tightness of his skin. He has left his life in London, his
friends, his hang-outs, that bird Fiona who was getting
keen on him, for this. Sunburn and virtual hotel arrest
and a crazy situation he cannot get out of. He considers
trying. Just splitting from the hotel, running away. But
he's skint and he is scared of Sticksy. He doesn't trust
himself to hack Thailand on his own. He walks like the
Michelin man, holding his arms carefully away from his
torso, down to the hotel shop to buy sunburn cream.
Lying on his bed with the heat of the burn throbbing
through him and the cream stiffening in the artificially
chilly air, he thinks about what a fool he's been and he
starts to laugh.

The last time Daniel got this burnt was a few years
ago, one scorching June. He'd gone to visit his parents
for some reason. He remembers the intensity of the heat
inside their small house, the windows closed to keep
traffic and aeroplane noise outside. His mother was pink
and perspiring over a saucepan full of jam, and the
kitchen shuddered under an extra blast of warmth
whenever she opened the oven door to extract a scalding
hot glass jar. There was the smell of sugar, and of the
large wet circles under the arms on his father's shirt. He
tried to watch the cricket on TV with his father but it
all became too much. In the park across the road he lay
sweating on the grass for a bit, an occasional gust of air
giving some relief from the still heat. Planes whined and
roared overhead, their unfelt shadows sliding over
Daniel, over the grass, the asphalt, brick walls, rooftops.
He kept meaning to go back into the house and spend
the day with his parents like he'd promised but he would
imagine the smell of cooking fruit and his father's silence
and his racist newspapers and he just couldn't. He lay in
the park all afternoon. By the time the sun had dropped

in the sky and he could bring himself to consider going inside again he was totally fried. He was so burnt that his mother wouldn't let him go home, she made him sleep in his old bed and stay there, stifling, all the next day.

The tap water he's been drinking has given him diarrhoea. This in itself is grotty enough but he knows, though he's been suppressing the knowledge, that in order to fulfil his part of the deal with Sticksy, he will need free and clean access to that part of his body and he cannot afford for his colon to go spastic. He obtains diarrhoea pills and a couple of paperback thrillers from the shop where he'd bought the sunburn cream, grimacing with embarrassment at the pretty Thai girl behind the counter. He watches eight hours of Thai pop from his bed, the bathroom door open for emergencies. He's grateful that Sticks forked out for a room with its own toilet. From his window down to the pool he can see the other hotel guests sunbathing and knocking back beers. The sun goes down and the flashing red and blue neon of the bars and open-air cafés light up.

Over the next couple of days the sunburn blisters and peels and Daniel is released from the grip of diarrhoea. He ventures out to the empty pool again, covered in factor a million, and spends an afternoon floating in the shallow end and flicking through his airport novels. Two-head sells him beers and they smile at each other.

Something's moving by the pot plants. A brown and yellow snake slides down the trunk of a miniature palm and onto the paving stones. It's about a foot and a half long. Daniel dog-paddles to the middle of the pool and stays there treading water, watching its progress along the side of the pool and over to the outdoor bar. It's

freaky how it moves. He's never seen a snake live
before. Two-head's got his back to it, holding that
crappy radio to his ear.

'Hey!' Daniel feels like an idiot but he's got to alert
the guy. That snake looks lethal. Two-head doesn't turn
around. 'Hey! You!' The snake is almost at Two-head's
feet. Daniel splashes over to the edge of the pool and
hauls himself out. He jumps up and down, dripping.
'Snake!' he calls, his voice coming out high-sounding.
'Watch out!'

Two-head doesn't move. Daniel looks around wildly
for something to poke him with. He grabs the long rake
Two-head uses to clear sticking-plasters out of the pool.
'Snake!' he calls again, as the creature squirms to about
an inch away from Two-head's papery ankle. It looks
ready to strike. Daniel runs at Two-head, brandishing
the rake low in front of him like a hockey stick. The
barman turns, leaps back and crashes into the fridge's
generator. He shouts something Daniel can't understand.
Daniel hops on the concrete, looking for the snake. He
can't see it anywhere.

'What you doing?' yells Two-head.

Daniel lets go of the rake. 'A snake,' he shouts, 'there
was a snake. Right here.'

Two-head looks down to where Daniel is pointing.
'There's nothing.'

'I know, but it was just there, a bloody horrible snake,
stripy, poisonous, it was going to— Really.' He stands
there, all pink and wet, panting. Two-head stares at him
as if he's just tried to attack him. Daniel peels a strip of
skin off his stomach. 'I'm sorry, mate, but there was a
snake there. I thought it was going to kill you.'

Two-head frowns. 'Daniel, please let me explain that
you are advised to return to your room. I understand

you are leaving tomorrow and there should not be any
problems before you go.'

Two-head knows his name.

'Do you understand, Daniel?'

Two-head's in on the whole thing. Daniel's staring at
the guy's tumour. He shakes his head, then nods it.
'Yeah, mate,' he says in a quiet voice. 'Yeah.'

'I call you when your visitor arrives. Probably
tomorrow.'

Back in his room Daniel freaks out. If Two-head
knows the score, who else here does? Has he been
watching the whole time? He paws at his sunburn. Tries
to calm himself down by counting the dead insect stains
on the door. Gives up and flicks through the pages of
the book he's read already, making no sense of the
words.

Eleven a.m. The minibus leaves for the airport at twelve.
He's packed his suitcase, watching from his room as
some obese Germans chuck a couple of local girls in the
pool and jump in after them. A new guy, one he hasn't
seen before, saunters out of the hotel restaurant. A
middle-aged white dude with one of those barrel chests
and the confidence to wear black Speedos. He stands on
the far side of the pool and stares up, straight into
Daniel's window, straight into Daniel's eyes. Daniel is
stuck there. He can't move. He doesn't dare breathe
even. This must be the guy with the package. Oh,
Christ. He looks like the sort who really could make
you do something as well, even if you weren't being
paid for it, even if you hadn't agreed to the deal like the
loser that you were. Daniel's stomach cramps up. Everything is becoming real. There's a knock on the door.

'Hello?'

'Mister Daniel?'

No, sorry, not him, wrong bloke, sorry. 'Yes.'

'Delivery for Mister Daniel.'

Could the guy say it a bit louder, they probably couldn't hear it in Bangkok. Daniel opens the door. A Thai boy, a teenager, is standing there with a motorbike helmet on. He comes into the room and Daniel closes the door. Daniel can't stop pacing up and down the room, shaking his arms about like some crazy dance. He's embarrassed to be doing this in front of the boy but there's so much adrenalin running through him he thinks he might have a fit. He paces over to the window and, yep, there's Speedo staring right back at him.

'This is for you.' The boy holds out a plastic bag. Daniel gives his arms one last shake and takes it off him. It's heavier than he imagined.

'Thanks.'

The boy keeps standing there.

'Uh, thanks. You can go now.'

He shakes his head. 'No, I stay. I stay and my friend takes you to bus stop.'

How thoughtful.

Daniel closes the bathroom door behind him and unwraps the plastic bag. Inside are two large bottles of mineral water and a load of small rubber fingers, more than he would have liked. There must be fifty of them at least. His stomach churns. What if the acid in there eats away at the rubber? Bang, it's all over. He tells himself to be cool, be calm. He lifts the bottle of water to his mouth and starts swallowing. It's like biting off an accidentally big mouthful of something and having to

force it down your gullet. Finger, water, finger, water.
The metallic taste makes his lips curl back and his tongue
burn. He gets through forty and feels bloated. He can't
take any more. The alternative to swallowing them,
though, is too nasty to contemplate. He must have hated
London to put himself through this. Funnily enough it
doesn't seem so bad there to him now. No, right this
minute a cardboard box on Tottenham Court Road
seems like a pretty fine lifestyle alternative. He forces
the last few down, willing himself not to retch. His
stomach is distended. He looks at his sweaty, pallid face
in the bathroom mirror. Drops of moisture cling to his
eyelashes. This is a low point. 'You,' he says to the
mirror, 'are a loser.' Then he grabs his toothbrush from
the side of the basin and goes out to meet his new
friends with a nauseous smile.

Speedo has put a black suit jacket on over his bathers.
There's no conversation on the way to the bus terminal.
They pull up alongside the minibus and, as Daniel is
about to lever himself carefully out of the car, Speedo
shows him a sheet of paper. It has a name and number
on it in childish handwriting.

'Thanks,' says Daniel, reaching for it. Speedo moves
it away.

'Memorize this,' he says in an East End accent so high
pitched Daniel isn't sure if he's heard it right.

'Sorry?'

'Memorize this number,' Speedo squeaks, 'and the
name.' He holds it up again so Daniel can read: TONY.
378 2150.

'Is that a phone number?'

'Rocket scientist, aren't you? It's an Auckland phone

number. Go to the Downtown Centre and call from there. Got it?'

'Yeah,' says Daniel. 'Sure. I've got it.'

Speedo rips up the paper. He leans over, yanks Daniel's suitcase off the back seat and shoves it at his chest. Daniel's almost winded. He shuts the door. The car pulls away.

The airport is an air-conditioned hell. He's desperate for a beer but fears it would be fatal. He stands in front of a magazine rack for what seems like days. A woman comes up and asks if he is intending to buy anything. He moves on. Finds a bin-sized ashtray and chainsmokes, avoiding all eye contact.

'Excuse me, sir.'

Daniel starts, and his cigarette falls to the floor. He grinds it out with his shoe and bumps his leg against a guy in a beige suit and thick Coke-bottle glasses, standing bang up next to him.

'I'm sorry to bother you, sir.' He has a voice like an android.

Daniel nods. It's all he can do.

The guy smiles, displaying a lot of upper gum. 'I couldn't help observing that you seem rather tense.'

Sweat runs down the backs of Daniel's knees. He clears his throat. The guy smiles again. 'If you are a nervous flier there is help available to you. I personally belong to a meditation group called Flying Free. We have branches in many major cities. May I ask your destination for today?'

He's bonkers. Daniel's voice comes out hoarse. 'No thanks.'

Undeterred, the guy passes him a pamphlet. 'You can

conquer your fear. May I recommend you to read this helpful leaflet.'

Daniel shoves it in the ashtray in front of him. 'Go away,' he says. 'Go away.'

The flight's announced and somehow he gets through passport control and the metal detector without being arrested. Any minute he expects to feel a hand on his shoulder or a dog lunging for his leg. He waits for ever in the departure lounge with about sixty other people. A steward with a microphone addresses them.

'Due to unforeseen volcanic ash in the Auckland area, Flight K48 will be delayed for approximately one hour. We apologize for any inconvenience.'

Daniel moves to the smoking area and lights up. His stomach feels enormous. What kind of place is this he's going to, volcanoes blocking off airports? What sort of life is he living? He thinks of Richard and wonders if he actually knows him at all. He wonders if he knows himself. What kind of person he might be. Everything seems mysterious, like something achieved with smoke and mirrors. He doesn't know if he's the rabbit or the hat. The sword or the girl. He feels dizzy.

The plane is delayed three and a half hours and then they're allowed to board. Daniel sits on the plane and it flies through the air. The movie stars human actors and his earphones work. The meal is some sort of reconstituted chicken. It's harder to force down than the condoms were but he makes himself eat enough so they won't get suspicious. He doesn't dare move out of his seat in case one of those things inside him bursts under

cabin pressure. He repeats to himself the number that
Speedo gave him.

'We hope you enjoy your stay in Auckland and apologize for the delay. Unfortunately today is cloudy, also
due to drifting volcanic ash. And due to the current fruit
fly outbreak we will be disinfecting the plane. Please do
not move from your seats while our staff come around
with the spray. This spray is not toxic to humans.'
    After the plane's been doused, he queues with the rest
of the passengers and follows them down the concertina
tubing to the main terminal. The walls, the brightly
coloured carpet, the advertisements for rental car companies all look extremely clean. There are dark green
plants everywhere. It's a science fiction utopia. He and
the others from his flight walk like robots through large
empty rooms towards passport control.

Daniel manoeuvres his way to the middle of the queue,
as though he's done it a hundred times before. His
stomach is heavy. There are five officials at the passport
desks. He prays he'll get the young woman. The
American couple in front of him do. His right eyelid
flickers. A woman in uniform points him towards a
desk. He shuffles over to it. Through the free-standing
wooden door frame in front of him are the baggage
claim carousels. Beyond them he can see daylight.
Freedom. The man behind the desk has a thick policeman's moustache.
    'Holiday is it?' he asks in that swallowed-sounding
accent.
    'Yep,' says Daniel, thinking, Don't sound too English,
they hate Poms.
    The man flicks through his passport. 'Thailand, eh?'

'Yeah,' says Daniel, his pulse thumping.

'How long do you intend to stay in this country?'

'Uh, two months.'

'Who are you staying with?'

'My sister.'

'And her name is . . .?'

'Fiona,' Daniel croaks. 'Fiona Brown. She's, uh, married.'

The guy frowns at him. Daniel attempts a smile. See, he thinks, I'm relaxed. I'm cool.

'Righto.' The man stamps his passport. 'Enjoy your stay.'

Daniel stands there. He tells his arm, pick up the passport. Pick it up, dickhead.

'That's it,' the guy says. He looks at Daniel again, frowning harder. 'Do you have any questions, sir?'

'No. No, thanks.' Daniel goes for the passport and knocks it onto the floor. Bending over is not going to be easy. He looks at the man. The man looks at him. He's wondering whether to squat or bend from the waist when the woman behind him, making ticking noises like she's in a hurry, steps forward, grabs the passport off the floor and hands it to him.

'Excuse me, madam,' the passport official says. 'Behind the line, please.'

Daniel nods to her. 'Thanks.' His throat is so dry it feels as if it might crack open.

He wobbles towards the baggage claim. There's a policeman with a beagle-type dog on a lead. It's sniffing a hippie girl's rucksack. Daniel can hear the dog snuffling and whining, really rooting around in there. The hippie girl's trying to act cool. She catches Daniel's eye. He looks away. Spots his suitcase and heaves it off the conveyor belt. The parcels feel like they're getting bigger and bigger inside of him. A green arrow points to a sign saying Nothing to Declare. He makes for it. Walks through the waiting crowd with his suitcase in one hand and his passport still in the other. No one stops him. No one calls his name. He finds the exit and comes out blinking into the harsh white glare. The world smells different.

TWO Bang! The movie star has been shot in the chest. He falls in an arc backwards, blood geysering out of his designer suit. Kate yawns and presses the light on her digital watch. Ten minutes to go. This is her third murder today. Matinée, five o'clock, eight o'clock. She's persuaded Janice, another usher, to cover the late session for her. A friend of Josh and Lucy's called Lolly or Lally or something is having a volcano party. Kate's a bit nervous. The only thing she knows about Lulu, Lola, whatever, is that she's now going out with one of Kate's exes.

Some kid is causing a disturbance near the exit in the back.

'Hey, you.' She shines her torch directly into his eyes. The kid whines. 'I'll have you thrown out. Stop rolling those Jaffas down the aisle or you give them to me.' She holds out her hand. There's a general 'sshh'. The kid tips the box of Jaffas back and chucks the lot in his mouth.

'Good. Now don't choke.' That boy shouldn't even be in here, it's an R18. A group of girls in the last row have lit a joint. She ignores the sweet smell wafting over the back third of the seats.

The actor springs to life again, reconstructed by the evil doctor. Kate often has to resist the temptation to call out the plot, especially during the fuller screenings. 'He dies!' she wants to cry, or 'They get together at the end!' or 'Don't be fooled, she's the murderer!' A helicopter carrying the famous actor and the evil doctor blows up. The romantic leads embrace as fire from the explosion blazes behind them. Credits roll. The house lights come half-up and the audience start shifting in their seats, standing and pushing each other towards the exits. There'll be a lot of popcorn cartons to pick up tonight. Kate checks her watch again. Twenty minutes to clean this place, get out of her uniform and change before Lucy comes to pick her up.

Somebody's still in their seat. Who would sit through the credits in this kind of movie? Kate runs her torch-light along the seats until it hits the person's face, then she lowers it.

'Excuse me, we're closed in here till the next session.'

The man doesn't move.

'Hello?'

He doesn't say anything. There's a moment when they are both still, her watching him and him facing ahead to the darkened screen. A shop alarm starts up outside and Kate flinches. Looks like a job for Bill from the projection room, if he isn't too out of it. She takes a couple more steps towards the guy. 'Hello? I'm going to have to ask you to leave now.' She strains to make out his face but the lights are too low. His eyes are open though, she can see them shining. 'Right. I'm just going to get the manager.'

Manager schmanager, she thinks, running up the steep steps to Bill's projection box. If this guy's trouble they haven't got a hope in hell of sorting him out. She shakes Bill out of his stupor and pulls him by the arm down into the cinema and to where the man was sitting. The seat is empty. Bill just stands there, head to one side, doped. She runs quickly along the aisles, flashing her torch under each row of chairs. Nothing. He's gone.

Lucy's holding her hand down on the car horn when Kate swings open the passenger door and slides in. 'Sorry,' she says. 'Arsehole day.' Lucy works part-time at a clothing shop and part-time at the Women's Refuge. She often takes a while to unwind. 'Did you see the eruption photos in the paper? Kate?' She glances over from the driver's seat.

Kate's thinking about that guy. There was something about him that disturbed her. 'Keep your eyes on the road,' she says. She smiles, turns the car radio up loud and they sing along.

At the party, Lucy disappears to find Josh. Kate skirts around the crowd, down the hallway and into the kitchen. It's a bit quieter in here but not much. She deposits her and Lucy's bottle of wine on the bench. A boy she doesn't know hands her a glass of something. 'Volcano juice,' he says with a smirk. It's sickly sweet. A girl in plaits appears on the other side of the boy and glares at Kate. Kate drains her glass and refills it from the punchbowl on the table. The other people in the kitchen all seem to know one another. She feels the bass thumping through the floorboards. It's a big room. She looks around, taking in the film posters and prints of African women carrying baskets on their heads. A sticker on the fridge says Free Kanaky. She tops up her glass and squeezes past the punch people into the living room. Lucy and Josh are by the stereo, flicking through CDs.

'Josh's counted three of his exes here tonight,' yells Lucy, 'and so far I've only got two.'

Kate smiles. She's hoping not to even have one. On one side of the room there's a bunch of people she was at university with. The dim light reminds her of the movie theatre and she wonders how much of her life these days she spends in the dark. She leans over to Lucy and shouts. 'I want to dance.'

'Go on then. I'll time you.'

'No one else is.'

'You start.'

Kate shakes her head. 'As if.'

'Go on!' Lucy tries to shove her out into the middle of the room. Kate pushes back. They're both laughing. Out of the corner of her eye, by the door, Kate sees the ex, his arm around what must be the new girlfriend, Leelee, Lala, the hostess. Kate stops hitting back at Lucy and looks in a nonchalant way to the other side of the room, as though she's mildly interested in something happening over there. She doesn't see Lucy give her one more push and loses her balance, her knees unlocking and her upper body falling towards the floor. She sticks her hand out to grab the arm of a couch and braces herself just in time. The volcano juice has flown out of her glass and splattered over the shirt of a girl on the couch.

'Shit, sorry,' says Kate, 'here let me get it — ' She grabs a paper napkin off Lucy and mops at the girl's soaked sleeve. Lucy stands next to her, muttering, 'Sorry,' over and over.

'Don't worry about it,' says the girl. Kate dabs at the sleeve again. 'Just leave it,' the girl snaps. Kate straightens up and surveys the room. For about one and a half seconds, everyone in there is looking at her. She turns to Lucy, who shrugs. They smile.

A strong wind has come up. Rain hammers the car as Josh drives them home. Inside the air-battered car Kate watches the sweep of the windscreen wipers, her head full of punch and music. The yellow glare of the streetlights is comforting through the darkness and the rain. The car coasts through downtown, past the casino. She lurches forward in her seat as a figure runs across the road in front of them, leaning forty-five degrees against the wind, holding his coat collar up over his head.

'Hey that's the guy,' she says, tapping Lucy's shoulder.

Lucy rolls her head around towards her. 'What?'

'The guy from work. The one that stayed.' She slips back in her seat, eyes slowly moving right to left, right to left, with the windscreen wipers.

On the lumpy spare bed at Josh and Lucy's, Kate dreams of Indonesia again. She's been back well over a year, nearly two, but the flowers and the animals still appear every now and then in the night, vivid as carnival masks. Indonesia. The plan had been to get away from Auckland. To get as far away as possible, for as long as possible, possibly for ever. Kate would lie staring at her ceiling and see projected onto it a horizon, a blue sky, a flat sea. She felt her bare feet standing on bare earth. Behind her, a square white hut cast a cool shadow over her back. There was a broom in her hand. She'd wander down to the market later and buy a fish for her lunch, spend the afternoon reading and in the evening walk along the rocky path to her job serving drinks to local fishermen in the taverna. In this way she would grow

peaceful, and old, and she'd get a great tan. Back home
everyone would say, What happened to Kate? Has
anyone heard from her? It seems she's just disappeared.
The whole thing rested on the fact that her absence
would be noticed, that somehow by disappearing she
would remain even more present in people's minds.
Whose minds, particularly, it didn't matter. All right,
her mother's. Her father's. Anyone else she'd ever come
into contact with.

She'd been having this sort of fantasy ever since she
could remember. Sometimes her disappearance would
be caused by death, other times by mortal injury or
terminal illness. She has lain in many imaginary hospital
beds forgiving those who've slighted her and imparting
pieces of wisdom to the loved ones fortunate enough to
hear. Once she put off a potential boyfriend because
after the second time they'd slept together she asked him
if he would speak at her funeral and if so what would he
say. Occasionally the fantasies have taken a violent turn.
She's barely survived a brutal mugging. She's been taken
hostage. She's been shot, usually throwing herself in
front of a bullet intended for somebody else.

Kate did not pretend that there was anything healthy
or productive about these idle thoughts. She knew they
were symptoms of a lack of perspective on the world
around her. Still, she'd found herself in something of a
double bind. The more she felt as if she should be
engaging with the world outside her bedroom, the more
difficult it became to do this. Everything out there
seemed pretty much pointless. More than anything it
was the fact that she was thinking this way that depressed
her. She was disappointed in herself for lacking a mature
and practical outlook on life. Her fantasies were clearly

the creation of somebody who'd never known real danger or trouble. She felt middle-class guilt and she felt guilty for indulging in middle-class guilt. She was in a state of near paralysis. The only thing she could think of was to escape, despite her mother's favourite saying about you can't run away from yourself, blah blah. There had to be some chance, any chance, of running away from herself. And she hoped that Indonesia was it.

So she worked like crazy as soon as she'd graduated, cleaning houses, painting houses, serving behind the counter in an early morning café and at night taking home typing. She had a childminding job on Saturdays, and on Sundays did the double-pay shift at a hotel reception desk. The money came excruciatingly slowly. It seemed that nothing she was qualified to do was worth more than ten dollars an hour before tax.

'You know,' she'd said to Lucy one night over cheese on toast, 'I wish I'd been brought up to be some rich man's mistress. It's only older men who ever dream of paying for anything these days.'

'Well, why should they?'

'I don't know. Guys have more money, on the whole. Don't ask me why, they just do. They earn more, or spend less, or something.'

'Josh is broke.'

'Josh is an eternal student. He'll always be broke because he'll always be going out with you and you're practical enough for two people.'

Lucy skimmed her finger round the top of the tomato sauce bottle and licked it. 'That is a depressing vision of my future.'

'Sorry. But it's true. He won't get his shit together unless he's forced to.'

'You'd be a lousy mistress. They're meant to make people feel better about their lives.'

'I don't have the underwear for it either.'

'Don't think they're supposed to wear much.'

'All that lacy slimy stuff.'

'Spare us.'

'And you've got to be brilliant at oral sex,' Kate mumbled through a mouthful of toast.

'Have you been reading a manual?'

'My mother taught me nothing useful.'

'Don't let's talk about parents and sex. It's too revolting.'

Kate ripped off a piece of handitowel and passed it to Lucy. 'I just can't believe all those men I've slept with and not one of them ever bought me anything.'

Lucy wiped her mouth. 'You're crap in bed, obviously.'

'Obviously.'

There was a pause.

'How many men *have* you slept with?'

'Never counted,' Kate said as if it just hadn't occurred to her. This wasn't true. She didn't keep notches in the bedpost but she knew roughly where she was, numbers-wise, and it was well off the fingers and on to the toes. 'How many have you?'

'Four. Counting Josh.'

Kate groaned. 'Can we not play this game?'

Now, lying awake with drunkard's insomnia at Josh and Lucy's, Kate runs a mental check-list of the people she has slept with. A rough list. Even as an alternative to counting sheep, she can't face going through the lot.

First: meat-headed but good-looking high-school boyfriend. As an introduction to sex and romance he

started off OK. Went to shit when Kate discovered he
had also been taking to bed one of her alleged friends.

Next up, his best mate. Less good-looking than the
first boyfriend. Still, as revenges go, perfectly adequate.

Then the first knowingly meaningless night – a near-
stranger after a party (number one in a series; uneventful
apart from one possible date-rape but then again she
might've been leading him on, she'd had so much to
drink it was hard to tell).

Then a boy met through one of her flatmates. That
lasted for ages. What was going on all those months?
Not a lot, possibly, but they both needed somebody to
spend time with. After two birthdays each they had to
admit to one another that it'd been great to start off but
they had less and less in common and – well, you know
how it is, yeah, really, me too, oh, I'm so glad you say
that – and they walked off in different directions,
mopping the sweat of relief from their respective brows.

After a while, a seemingly standoffish guy who turned
out to be simply boring. Plus he had a habit. He worked
in finance and liked to boast about how he could spend
over a grand a week on smack. It took a while to figure
out if it was the drug talk that was boring, or just him.
Extricating herself was slow and painful.

Back to mindless fun for a bit. Honorary guest in this
category, Kate thinks, twisting now under the sheets, is:
Frank, who's a friend. For a minute she had made the
mistake of thinking something might work out between
them. Only for a minute, though.

And there was a lovely guy she met just before leaving
for Indonesia – her dumb timing – and when she got
back he was engaged to be married to the girl who'd
previously been his ex.

Before that, the requisite flirtation with bisexuality,

with a girl from one of her tutorial groups who was
gorgeous and funny and smart and very out. They got
on really well but Kate could never manage to go below
the waist and eventually the girl got fed up and moved
on. It was kind of a relief at the time, but every now
and then Kate wishes she wasn't so repressed.

And – who else – Frank again, briefly and stupidly,
after Indonesia. Kate grits her teeth at the memory.
Rejection King. She'd walked straight into that one.
Oh, yeah, and him from Lola's party, and – maybe that's
it. That's it? That's it. Up until now.

Back then, before she went to Indonesia, she imagined
that she'd return a different person. She'd pledged to
Lucy that she wasn't going to have any more casual sex.
Sure, said Lucy. Yeah. Right. Then she decided that she
was going to take up a new activity: kick-boxing, or
gardening, or swimming. Instead of any of these, she
took up smoking. From being an occasional social
smoker she graduated to fagging on the afternoon
teabreaks at whatever job she was doing that day, then
on to having a couple at lunchtime, sneaking a puff at
morning tea, finding that the only thing that could get
her out of bed in the early mornings was a cup of coffee
and the first drag of the day. It became common for her
to wake with a sore throat and a burnt taste in her
mouth. On the plus side, she ate less, cried less and had
something to do while waiting for the bus.

'Maybe,' she said to Lucy, 'I'm addicted to this idea that
something's *about* to happen to me. That whatever it is
is just around the corner. The thing that's going to
totally consume me.'

'You think about yourself too much.'

'I know, I know. How do you stop? Thinking, thinking all the time, endless little thoughts passing and disappearing and reappearing, snap snap, like weeds. What am I doing, what's this like, should I be doing this or that instead—'

'Find something you want.'

'I'm a drug addict waiting to happen.'

'Oh, shut up. Stop worrying. Go to Indonesia and get a suntan.'

So she went to Indonesia. Lay on the beaches, climbed a mountain, visited temples, thought about converting to Hinduism, decided not to, stayed for a few weeks in a place not unlike that of her bedtime fantasies. She got calm, she got the suntan, and returned with no greater idea about who she was or what she wanted to do. The dole would have done her head in, so she hunted around and picked an ushering job at a local cinema as the least humiliating of her options. And she's still there. Her mother, who prefers to be known as Ginny, is always on her case about getting a better job. Her mother! She starts, whumped back into the spare room at Josh and Lucy's with a shock. She's supposed to be having lunch there today. Where's her watch? Oh, Jesus. She pulls her party clothes on and splashes her face with water, yells out Bye, and sprints up the road to the bus stop.

'Hoo-hoo,' she calls out, mimicking her mother's greeting call, walking down the shadowy hall to the living room. Her shoes make a knocking noise on the bare floorboards. Ginny is intensely proud of these floorboards, which she sanded and varnished herself. The

interior of the house is a monument to her HRT-
fuelled interest in DIY. The floorboards, a mosaic in the
bathroom, new bookshelves everywhere. She's starting
on the garden next.

'Hello, darling.' Ginny is wearing a full-body leotard
and standing on her head, leaning her legs against the
only living room wall to escape bookshelves. A large
painting of a nude man and a donkey hangs perilously
close to her feet.

'Hi, Gin.'

'I won't be long, love, put some coffee on.'

Eventually Ginny breezes into the kitchen, rosy-faced,
fluffing up her long grey hair. They hug.

'You look great,' says Kate.

'It's my yoga,' her mother smiles. 'It's revolutionized
my life.'

'How's Nina?' Kate asks. Nina is her younger sister.
She hosts a music video programme which is filmed in
Wellington.

'Terrific. She might be getting a transfer up here. I'm
trying not to get my hopes up too much in case it
doesn't happen.'

'And Andrew?' Andrew, her mother's boyfriend, has
been around for seven years but they live apart. Ginny
says she's too settled in her ways to put up with a man's
things around the house. 'I love my freedom,' she likes
to say. 'God knows I deserve it.' That's a reference to her
former life as a housewife with two kids. Since Kate's
father left she's been unstoppable, constantly taking up
new activities. The DIY, yoga, Japanese language lessons,
Mediterranean cooking classes – Kate loses count.

'We're going tramping for three weeks. I thought
you might come and mind this place.'

Kate hesitates.

'You could use my car as well if you like.'

'Thanks, that'd be great.'

'How's work going?'

The trade-off. 'It's good,' says Kate, kicking her heels against the legs of her kitchen stool. 'They're going to make me a manager. Organize rosters and stuff.' This lie takes her by surprise. Ginny doesn't spot it.

'Did you have a look at those brochures from the polytech I sent you? The business courses are wonderful, it's an *international* qualification. Their semester starts in June and you don't want to miss enrolment.'

'No, thanks. Great. Thanks.'

On Monday at the cinema there's sick in the men's loos. 'I'm not paid to do this,' Kate tells the front of house manager, but it's no good. She holds her breath as she scrapes her rubber-gloved hands along the bottom of the urinal, picking out cigarette butts. The Easter holidays, prime movie-going time, are at the end of this week. It would be nice to have a different job by then. Something with some purpose. In her room at home after the five o'clock showing she writes down:

Something political?

With children?

Educative?

Community?

Environment?

She studies the list: a) Political. Apolitical. Is she? Do they have marches against things any more? Her mind goes blank.

b) Children. No. Kids make her nervous and they cry when she picks them up.

c) Educative. She doesn't even know if that's a word.

The problem with teaching – apart from what exactly it is that she would teach – is that it would be likely to involve children. See (b).

d) Community. Nursing homes. She has to admit the thought of Meals on Wheels depresses her. She'll be old herself soon enough, she doesn't want to hang out with a bunch of geriatrics now. Guilt swamps her. There is no doubt that she is a horrible person. But she has good intentions! She will, she must, carry them through. She picks up the list again.

e) for Environment. The thing about recycling is, it's boring. It is a major chore to wash all your tin cans, separate bottles into green, brown and see-through and keep paper rubbish in a bin all of its own. Maybe she should start a compost heap in the back garden. She sighs. The problem is she doesn't know anyone who is both environmentally conscious and interesting.

She flops back on her futon. There's a cobweb in one corner of the ceiling. Perhaps what she needs is to redecorate her room. She likes it so plain though, the futon, her record player and her records lined up along the skirting board, the books stacked against the wall, her clothes out of sight in the built-in wardrobe and nothing on the walls except a print of some Japanese characters. She doesn't know what they mean and she is aware that she's appropriating a culture for purely decorative purposes but she does enjoy the effect. It calms her, usually.

'So get this,' Lucy says later that night. They're sitting on a rug in her small garden, wine bottle and glasses set out in front of them. 'A woman comes in today with her three kids. They haven't been beaten up or anything but they all had malnutrition and they'd been evicted for non-payment.' She lights a cigarette and exhales a stream of smoke into the clear evening air. 'The woman's DPB's been cut off after a neighbour spotted the boyfriend's car parked outside for a whole week and called Social Welfare. I mean, the fuckwit actually dobs her in. A neighbour! And the boyfriend wasn't supporting her or anything, sure he was buying some groceries but they were hardly de facto. Jesus.' Lucy thumps the ground with the flat of her hand.

'What's she going to do?' says Kate.

Lucy shakes her head. 'Go through a bureaucratic nightmare.' She digs at the ground with her lighter. Kate pours them some more wine and swipes a mossie off her leg.

'The thing is we can't spare the beds at the moment and if someone comes in black and blue I don't know what we're supposed to do with these people. Plus the DSW paperwork makes me sick. Sorry, I'm raving. How are you?'

'Oh, another day at the coalface,' smiles Kate, 'helping the people of Auckland enjoy their cinematic escapism to the full. I mean, OK, so it's a retro job and it's kind of cute to be an usher and stuff but really it sucks.'

Lucy laughs. 'The cute quotient's always a good thing to base a career on.'

'I realize that,' says Kate, 'and now that I've done ushering I think I might try for a bunny girl. Or an air hostess maybe.'

'Anything with a uniform,' says Lucy.

'Exactly.' She lights a match and watches it burn for a bit before blowing it out. 'Anything to give myself a sense of belonging.'

★

Later that week Kate goes into town for late-night shopping, to buy her mother a birthday present. She's looking for a book, something on decorating maybe, paint distressing techniques or landscape gardening. Perhaps she could get a tramping guidebook for Ginny and Andrew to take on their hike. She wanders around the multi-levelled downtown bookstore, blinking under the blazing fluorescent lights. Everything on gardening and decorating is too expensive. Maybe a novel? Her mother's into Latin American magic realism. Kate can't remember any of the author's names and the place looks too daunting to ask for help. The travel section seems more affordable – affordable but bland. Perhaps she should go for a piece of jewellery instead. Kate stands between the New Zealand Travel and New Zealand Literature shelves and covers her face with her hands. Just – buy – something, she tells herself. Just go to the shelves, reach out, pick a book and pay for it. Take it home, wrap it, give it to your mother. She takes her hands away from her face and looks around. The bookstore is almost entirely populated by women. Middle-aged women with large flax shopping baskets and chunky earrings; pairs of blue-rinsed, macintosh-wearing old women standing by the greeting cards; women about her age but better dressed flicking through the fashion magazines. Dyke couples in the cooking section, a lone westie girl reaching for a Danielle Steele. Stylie young mothers in the children's department, their toddlers running around barely under control. Where are the men? There's a fat male security guard standing by the door, a man in a suit and tie with a name-tag brooch at the Information desk and that's it. And there's a guy over in the corner, checking out road maps.

Kate goes cold. She could swear it is the one from the movie theatre, the one from the street after that party. She moves closer, running her fingers along the book spines as she passes the shelves. This is crazy. It's unlikely to be him and even if it is, so what? It's not unusual in this place to see the same people day in and day out. She cranes her neck to see what he's looking at. A street map of Auckland. Now that is kind of strange. She's at an excellent perving distance now. He's younger than she'd assumed at the cinema. He's got scraggy brown hair and he's not too tall or too short. An angular face, like a pirate. Dark eyes. Nothing offensive about his clothes either, they don't look as if he got them from around here. There's a decent-looking camera slung around his neck. Kate watches as he folds the street map back up and slips it inside his cotton jacket. She bites her lip. He walks slowly, in a relaxed way, towards the exit. Kate's eyes flick from him to the security guard. She wants him to get away with it but she also wants him to be caught. The guy gets nearly to the exit and then turns, as if he's forgotten something. He walks back to the map racks and picks up an umbrella which is lying next to them on the floor. He swings it under his arm. Kate sees the corner of the map sneak out from his jacket but a second later he's nudged it back in. She can't understand it. The map must only cost about $3.50. He doesn't look as if he's broke. She wonders if the camera was acquired in a similar way. He gets close to the door again. The security guard is checking him out. Kate has an impulse to run up to the guard and distract him, ask him directions or the time. But the guy's through the door and out into the street. He made it. Kate walks quickly to the exit and tries to spot him in the thin crowd of shoppers drifting slowly down the footpath. She looks up the street and down it. She crosses over to the other side and looks there as well. He isn't anywhere.

THREE   After surviving customs Daniel took
a taxi, a yellow Ford Falcon driven
by a man in a bright floral print shirt, to the Downtown
Centre. He didn't notice anything about the suburbs
they drove through except that the streets were wide
and empty and there were a lot of trees. The car's
suspension was bad and his guts were whomping away
like Christ knows what, badoom, badoom, badoom. He
still had the picture in his head of the acid working away
in his stomach, eating through the rubber fingers,
delivering death. He wound down the window and felt
the warm breeze. They drove over a bit of motorway
into the city.

'This is it,' the driver said to Daniel, outside a building
that looked like a shopping arcade. 'Fifty bucks.'

Daniel had no idea if he was being ripped off or not.

He looked around the mall and headed for the men's
loos. He wanted to get rid of this stuff so bad. He
jammed himself into a cubicle with his suitcase and
waited. All that came into his mind was Richard's smirk.
He could hear various men coming in and out of the
toilets. After twenty minutes a new worry entered his
head, that someone might try to open his door. Finally
it was over. He washed everything under the toilet flush
and dried it off with loo paper. Wincing – what if
someone looked under the door – he laid the suitcase
on the floor and opened it. He wrapped the fingers in

an empty plastic bag he'd picked up on the plane and
shoved it under all the clothes in his case. He waited
until the room sounded empty and ventured out of his
cubicle, one hand running over his concave stomach.
The lightness inside him was amazing.

He bought a card at a newsagent and went to use the
public phone. Fear rose up again when he had to speak
and he remembered what he was carrying inside his
case. He imagined himself just blurting it out: 'I'll have
a ten dollar phone card and would you like to buy some
smack?' He picked a telephone at the end of a row,
furthest away from the shops. He stood with his back to
the wall, the phone cord wrapped around his chest, and
dialled the number the bloke in Pattaya had shown him.
That seemed days ago now.

A nasal-voiced girl answered. 'Hiya.'

'Hello?' he forced out, his voice cracking.

'Hello?'

He took a deep breath and imagined that he was the
type of person who did this all the time. 'Yeah, is Tony
there?'

'Tony?'

'Yeah, uh, is Tony there?'

'No one here called Tony. You've got the wrong
number. Byeee.'

'Wait, wait a minute—'

There was a pause, and a tch. 'Yes?' She spoke slowly,
as if he was retarded. 'There's no Tony here.'

'Is this 378 2150?'

'Yes it is.'

'Um – what's your name?'

'Oh, fuck off, eh?'

She hung up. Daniel redialled the number.

'Look, piss off, you, there's a law against this.'

'No wait, I promise, is Tony there or anyone who knows Sticksy? Are you expecting a delivery?'

Now he'd said it. Cards on the table. The girl was silent. 'Are you there?'

'Hang on a minute.'

He waited. He couldn't hear anything at the other end of the phone. His eyes flicked around the terminal. Tourists mainly, generic American couples in matching shell suits. Groups of Asian girls wearing knee socks and pigtails. A black poodle came running up to him and sniffed around his ankles. He kicked at it. 'Fuck off,' he said. A freckle-faced kid of about ten ran over and scooped it up in her arms, giving Daniel a hurt look. Had the phone gone dead or something? Maybe she'd hung up on him again. Maybe she was tracing the call and notifying the police, he'd seen them do that in FBI films.

'Hello?' It was a guy this time.

'Is this Tony?'

'Tony isn't here. I'm his mate.'

'Oh yeah?' Daniel tried to sound tough.

'Yeah. I understand you've got something for us.'

'For Tony. I've got something for Tony.'

'Tony's not around right now.' The guy dropped his voice. 'He's inside. Uh, Sticksy knows about it. He asked me to take care of things while he's out of action.'

Daniel hesitated. Who was to say if the guy was straight up or not? He looked at his watch. Just after five o'clock. Too early in London to call Sticksy. Anyway, he realized, a bubble of near-hysteria rising in his throat, he didn't have his number.

'Where are you?'

Daniel was in the middle of lighting a cigarette. 'The Downtown something,' he said, not thinking.

'Yeah, that's right, Downtown. We'll come and get you.'

'No, don't do that.'

'Yeah yeah, that's the plan. Wait outside the Novotel. Um—' and for the first time the guy sounded uncertain, ' – have the stuff ready. We'll be fifteen minutes.'

The phone went dead. Daniel had a headache. He rubbed his hands through his hair. It was greasy. What was this place? He wanted to offload the junk, get the money and leave, maybe to Sydney or LA. He felt disoriented and out of time. This guy could be a total con-artist. He decided to call Richard.

Twenty rings. No answer.

Ten minutes later Daniel was waiting outside in the shade of the Novotel awning. He stood watching the street, people coming out of offices and shops. The small-town look of the place made him uneasy. He smoked without stopping.

A large, old green car cruised past and reversed up to him. Daniel didn't move. A girl with peroxide blonde dreadlocks and wrap-around shades was driving. A big mongrel dog in the back seat started to bark. The guy in the passenger seat, fat, with John Lennon sunglasses, reached over and whacked it. He smiled at Daniel as he rolled down his window. 'Hi.'

Daniel put his hands in his pockets. His legs were straddled either side of the suitcase. 'Hi.'

'Do you want to get in the car?'

No was the quick answer, but it seemed the only thing to do. He lifted his suitcase and climbed into the

back seat of the car, trying to squeeze up against the left
hand door, away from the slavering dog.

'Hi,' he said to the girl.

'Hi,' she said in that slow nasal whine, and smiled.

'Take no notice of Sharon,' the guy said, thumping
the dog's side with a dull thwack, 'she won't bite.'

Yeah, but what about the dog, he thought but didn't
say. Sharon was dribbling and steaming up the windows
with rotten meaty breath. This was not reassuring.

'So,' the guy said, 'you want some money?'

'Yeah,' said Daniel, 'and the payment's sorted into the
account, right. For Sticksy.'

'Yeah, the payment's under control man. How is the
guy?'

'All right.' It crossed Daniel's mind to double-check
whether or not this bloke was the right contact by
seeing if he knew about Sticksy's baby. He didn't do it.
If he was being strung along, if the guy was nothing to
do with Tony or Sticks, the consequences were too
horrible to consider. He pushed Sharon out of the way
and opened his suitcase.

One minute later he was standing out on the street, a
brown envelope full of one hundred dollar bills in the
suitcase and that plastic bag out of his life for ever. He
banged the car door shut and Sharon barked again. 'All
right?' he asked the couple.

'Yeah, all right, mate.' The guy had his hands pressed
down on the plastic bag and an anxious look on his
pudgy face. The girl was inscrutable. 'Hey, mate,' the
guy said, 'got a ciggie I can bludge?'

Daniel took his pack out of his jacket pocket and
chucked it in the car window on to the guy's lap. 'Keep

them,' he said. 'Cheers then,' and he slapped his hand down on the roof of the car. He was free. He picked up his case and started walking down the street away from them, he didn't know where. When he came to a corner he turned it and did not look back.

Richer than he had ever been in his life, Daniel went into the first Burger King he came to and ordered two Whoppers, King Size Fries and an extra large Coke. He stuffed them in his face. For a second he glimpsed his reflection in the wall-length mirror and was embarrassed for himself. He looked oily and desperate and he needed to shave. Then he thought, fuck it. He was filthy rich and on the other side of the world from anything that mattered to him. And the thing was that nothing there did matter to him, that was why he had left. He put the two thoughts together and the idea flashed into his mind that nothing, anywhere, mattered to him. He shook his head and looked up from his burger at the people eating and talking around him. Despite the food there was a hollow feeling in his stomach. The thought of the money in his suitcase made his fingers go cold. He needed something normal, a bed, somewhere quiet. He lit a cigarette. His eyes fell on a tanned blonde couple wearing purple polypropylene jackets and sharing a Walkman. Two rucksacks were propped up against their table.

'Excuse me?' He waved at the guy, who looked up. Daniel leaned over. 'Hi. Can I just ask you something?'

The bloke disentangled himself from his half of the Walkman. The girl raised her head, bemused. Daniel hoped he didn't look too much like a tramp. 'Hi,' he said, 'I just wanted to ask you, do you know where a backpackers is around here? A b. & b. or a backpackers?'

The couple looked at each other and said words
Daniel couldn't understand. He tried again. 'Youth
hostel? Bed and breakfast?'

The guy's face lit up. 'Youth hostel, ja.' Then he
looked blank again.

'Where?' said Daniel. 'Where is youth hostel?' He
was shattered. Maybe it'd be easier to kip here on the
Burger King seats than struggle with this language
barrier.

'It is in town.'

'Near here?'

The girl nodded. 'Near. This street,' she gestured,
then indicated a parallel street. 'That street.'

'On the next street?'

'Ja,' she said, then something else to her boyfriend.
She took the earphone out of her ear and wound up the
Walkman's cord. 'We go there now.'

He paid the extra for a single room, hauled himself along
the hallway and fell inside. He kicked the door shut
behind him and collapsed onto his bed. Two hours later
he woke up wired. Eight o'clock at night in a city where
he didn't know anyone, falling off the edge of the world.
Ten thousand dollars in his suitcase. Shit. He grabbed
the case and yanked it open. The envelope was still
there. He exhaled. What a moron to fall asleep like that,
the money available to anyone who opened the door.
First thing tomorrow he'd take it to a bank. Daniel sat
back on the bed. Unless the money was tainted, trace-
able somehow. Ah, he didn't want to think about
anything like that. He'd got a thirst on. It was time to
go out.

He showered, shaved and dressed with the envelope
in another plastic bag tied to his wrist so tightly it almost

cut off the circulation. When he looked in the mirror he saw someone different from his Burger King self. A lightly tanned, clear eyed, clean-smelling stranger. Too thin, but he always was. He stuffed five thousand dollars into his underpants and two thousand into each of his shoes, struggling a bit to do them up. A thousand dollars went into his wallet for luck. He was relieved that he didn't have more flashy clothes. Nobody was going to think of rolling him.

So this is New Zealand's biggest city, he thought, walking down the low wide street from the hostel. It felt quiet. He'd have one night here, a decent sleep, then catch a flight to Sydney. 'Catch a flight,' he laughed. The new, rich him could think thoughts like that. He'd hang out on the beaches there for a while, then go to the States maybe, the Caribbean – ten thousand dollars would last a long time. He peered into the small, uninhabited boutiques and cafés lining the almost dark street. Not much here to stick around for.

The first place Daniel hit, he felt his evening was on the right track. Two pairs of girls in their early twenties perched, all shoulders and hipbones and slim brown legs, on stools by the bar. He bought himself a beer with a whisky chaser. It was a new sensation for him, pressing a fifty dollar note into the barman's hand, not worrying whether or not the next round was on him. He finished his drinks and ordered again.

One of the girls was trying to catch his eye. Daniel let her wait for it, glancing coolly around the room before meeting her gaze. She blinked and looked down. She was all right as well, long black hair that she kept flicking

over her shoulder in a pretentious kind of way, and a
clingy little shirt. Her friend was a redhead, a bit sour
round the mouth. Daniel smiled at the pretty one. She
smiled back. Daniel lit a cigarette and turned away again.
One of his favourite albums came on and he gave the
barman a twenty to turn the volume up. The girls started
sort of wriggling around on their stools in time to the
music.

'Hi,' Daniel said.

'Hello.' The pretty one raised her eyebrows. The
plain one ignored him.

'Like a drink?'

'All right.'

He bought them a vodka martini each. They were
working hard at the look. The ugly one was smoking a
long black cigarette.

'What the fuck is that?' he asked.

'It's a fucking cigarette,' she said, still not looking
at him. He figured that she'd got the hump because
she was going to be sidelined for a bit. Well, it was
true.

'What's your name?' the pretty girl finally asked in
that gnarly accent.

'Richard,' he said. 'What's yours?'

'Andrea,' she said. She pronounced it Andray-ah.
'This is Caroline.'

Caroline smiled a lemon juice smile at him. 'Hi,
Dick.'

'What are you up to then?'

Andrea tilted her head to one side. 'Oh, we're just
hanging out, you know, whatever happens. We're
aimless.'

He grinned. 'Me too.'

She flashed her eyelashes at him, mouth bent to her martini glass. 'We're losers,' she whispered.

'Yeah,' Daniel said, 'we're totally sad.'

They smiled at each other. Caroline humphed off her barstool and stomped over towards the loos.

'Your friend's a bit baity.'

'Eh?'

'Your mate, she's a bit pissed off.'

'Oh, yeah.' Andrea rolled her eyes. 'She's on the rag. Where are you from?'

'England.'

'Oh really,' she said, sounding bored in a studied way. 'Whereabouts?'

'London.'

She twiddled the olive on the end of a toothpick before sticking it into her mouth and sucking. 'I love London,' she said. 'It's not as good as New York though. Do you like New York?'

'I hate it,' said Daniel, who'd never been there.

'But the best place is Miami, oh my God, Richard, you have to go to Miami, it's so wild.'

Daniel signalled the barman for more drinks. He smiled at whatever her name was. 'Yeah? Miami.'

'Oh, yeah,' said Andrea. 'It is *so* wild! Great club scene, all the Cuban scene, it's so sexy.' She gave him her anaconda look again. 'But the drug scene is too much, it's out of control there, totally out of control.'

'So where's good round here? This place is kind of lame.'

Andrea looked as if she didn't usually think it was but was prepared to go along with him. 'Yeah, completely. Well, there's—'

The friend came out of the toilets just in time to be included.

'There's a great new bar just up the road.' Andrea flicked her hair and looked at her watch. 'It should be taking off about now. Let's go.'

The great new bar was dark and smoky and the dingy effect was heavily art directed. It was a moviegoer's idea of a seedy bar. Daniel bought drinks for Andrea and her friend and they melted into the crowd. He settled down with a beer to watch a couple of girls playing pool, after putting his name on the blackboard. By the time it came up he'd lost track of how much he'd had to drink. His game was pretty rubbish but the skinny blonde bird he was playing was really giving it some, flirting and carrying on. Sticking her butt way out as she leaned over the pool table. Making sure he had a good view down her top. She beat him and he bought her a drink. They shouted at each other through the music.

'What's your name?' he asked her.

'Not telling,' she said.

He put his arm around her tiny waist and pulled her close to him. She laughed.

She dragged him by the hand out of the bar and down into a side street and kissed him. She drew him to her up against a wall and shoved her hands down the back of his trousers. He dimly remembered the money in his underpants and shifted away from her, out of breath. 'I'm starving,' he said.

She frowned. 'Oh, all right.' She led him back to a taxi rank and they fell into a cab. She told the driver to go somewhere and started crawling all over Daniel, pushing him back into the corner, rubbing up against him and sticking her tongue in his ear. He forgot about the money.

At the restaurant the girl ordered oysters and champagne. 'Oysters!' she shouted, 'Champagne!' and laughed crazily. She lit Daniel's cigarette for him and stuck her hand between his legs. His face muscles ached because of his permanent grin. He didn't know what to say to her but she didn't seem to care. The oysters were ice-cold and lemony. It was like a dream. Daniel suddenly wanted nothing more than to be telling Richard what sort of a good time he was having. Richard, with his pickup techniques of name-dropping C- and D-list celebrities, would be impressed, wouldn't he? It was hard to impress Richard — he made it a policy never to express surprise. But Daniel felt a surge of gratitude towards him. He had to thank the guy!

'Just wait here a minute,' he said to the girl. 'Listen, what is your name?'

'Not telling,' she said again, giggling.

'No come on, what is it?'

'Tara.'

He leaned over and kissed her. 'Tara, I'm just going to make a phone call and I'll be right back. Don't go anywhere, OK?'

She pouted. 'I'll be bored.'

'Won't be long. Promise.' He nearly lost his balance pushing back his chair. 'Just a minute.'

This was what he'd left London for, this was the story he was supposed to have entered. He lurched out on to the street and down past a few closed shops to the light of a newsagents. The glare inside was superbright. He

bought a phone card and some more cigarettes. There
was a phone box halfway back towards the restaurant,
with the usual phone box smell. He punched in Rich-
ard's number, taking two or three stabs to get it right.
At last he got a ringing tone and then a crackle.
   'Hello?'
   'Richard?' he shouted.
   'Yeah? Daniel?'
   It was a fizzy line, with an echo. He couldn't tell if
Richard had finished talking or not. 'It's me.'
   'Where are you?'
   'I'm very far away,' he laughed. 'I'm not in London.'
   'Yeah, I got that. Are you in Auckland?'
   'It's fucking brilliant,' said Daniel. 'You're a top mate,
you know that? You're a really, really great bloke.'
   'Have you seen Tony yet?'
   'All sorted, tell Sticksy all sorted. Listen, I'm with this
bird, right, Tara, she is so hot for it, this place is brilliant.
And I'm fucking loaded!'
   'Daniel,' Richard had his patronizing voice on, 'mate,
have you seen Tony? Sticks called me this morning,
there's some dodgy shit going on, someone Tony knows
is trying to shaft him. You gave him the gear, right?
You gave Tony the gear?'
   Daniel tried to concentrate. Tony was in the clink.
That guy had said. That's why he had taken the gear,
because he was helping Tony out. 'His mate, I gave it
to his mate and they gave me the money.'
   'What?' Richard was almost screaming. 'You gave it
to someone else? You cunt, you were supposed to give
it to Tony, only Tony you fucking idiot!'
   Daniel's eyes focused on the burning end of his cigarette. 'Yeah, Tony,' he said firmly, 'I gave it to Tony.
Tony and his mate. Chill out man, Tony was there.'

'Are you sure? If you've fucked this up it's going to be ugly, mate, you know what I mean?'

Daniel could hear Richard breathing fast. He visualized his weaselly little face twitching, the ginger goatee coming in for some serious fingerwork.

'It's cool, man,' he said. 'Tony's sorted. He's got the—'

Something hit Daniel in the back. He spun around. It was Tara, holding the phone box door open with one hand, jogging on the spot and waving her other arm up and down. 'Come on!' she shouted. 'We've got to go!'

She leaned over his shoulder and slammed down the cut-off button on the phone, grabbed both his wrists and hauled him out of the booth. Before he knew what was happening they were legging it down the road hand in hand. Tara squealed and giggled.

'We did a runner!' she yelled, sprinting ahead and turning backwards to face him laughing. 'Fuck them! Fuck them! Ha!'

She ran out into the road and stood waving at cars until one of them stopped. Leaning in the window, she said something to the driver, wiggling her hips at Daniel who stood shell-shocked on the kerb. She beckoned him over into the back seat.

'I know these people,' she said. 'Hey, guys this is, uh, someone.' She laughed her unhinged-sounding laugh again. 'Hey, someone, this is the guys.'

Daniel nodded at the three men in the car. He felt as if the money hidden inside his clothes was scorching him. What Richard had said about Tony made him feel sick. Tara put her hand on his knee and smiled a fake-demure smile at him. He managed to move his lips into a rough approximation of a grin in return.

★

They piled out on to a fairly well-lit street. Music was coming from a bar at one end of it. Daniel realized it was the pool bar he'd been in earlier, where he'd met Tara. She wrinkled her nose. 'This town is so useless,' she said, 'ah, fuck it.' She hooked her arm through his and they followed the guys across the road and back in. The place was jammed.

'Give us some money,' Tara yelled, kissing him, 'and get me a whisky sour.' Daniel took a bill out of his pocket – a fifty maybe, it was dark and he wasn't used to the look of the notes – and gave it to her. She disappeared. After two and a half whiskys he was pretty sure she'd split for good. Then suddenly she was back again, pressing a pill into his hand.

'Present.' She smiled. 'Come on. I'm taking you somewhere new.'

The casino was the perfect location for Daniel to be. He felt like a rock star, marching in with Tara, who was swerving and whose top kept slipping off one shoulder. They strode through the foyer and past a waterfall and enormous strange pot plants. The lights were yellow and red and how he imagined America. They pushed past people into the main gambling hall, a hangar-sized room full with the clatter and spin of roulette tables and one-armed bandits. There was a strong smell of perfume. 'Blackjack!' shouted Tara. 'Blackjack!'

She applied fresh lipstick while Daniel bought five hundred dollars worth of gambling chips. He gave them to her and she blew him a kiss and tripped off to a blackjack table. In the men's toilets he stacked the five thousand dollars from his underpants on the cistern while he took a leak. There was another four thousand still in his shoes. Enough for a plane ticket anywhere in the world, tomorrow. He was feeling lucky. He felt like living large. 'Yeah,' he imagined saying to Richard, 'I thought, what is life if you can't take a little risk every now and then? So I did it.'

And he did. He took the five thousand underpants dollars and bought chips with them. The cashier looked at his money a bit strange until she heard his accent. He stuffed the chips in his pockets and went scouting around the blackjack tables for Tara. She wasn't anywhere. He did another circuit and still couldn't find her. There was an incident with a blonde woman at one of the poker tables. He walked up and goosed her. She whirled around, not Tara, glaring, and he could see it was going to get nasty so he shoved a hundred dollar chip in her pocket and ran.

He seated himself at a blackjack table and proceeded to bet with two hundred dollar chips as the minimum. The croupier went bust the first three rounds and Daniel tripled his bets to six hundred dollars. He placed all of that on the next game and pulled in a twenty-one. He laughed like Tara. He'd just made nearly two thousand dollars. Time to go crazy. He lost money, made money and lost it again. He cared nothing for the result of each game, except the wins kept upping his high and the losses made him feel more reckless. He took a break and resumed his search for Tara. He ran all over the vast building, up the down escalators and down the up ones, wheeled around mezzanines looking down to the foyer for her yellow hair, burst into two private dining rooms and had doors slammed in his face, circled couples and wove between drinkers in three bars looking, looking, but he could not find her. In the loos again he took the money out of both of his shoes. He did a quick count. Four thousand dollars in cash and four thousand in

casino chips. He was so rich he wanted to laugh and
laugh.

Back at the blackjack table Daniel placed five five-
hundred-dollar bets and lost two and a half thousand
dollars in a row. People grouped around the table
watching him but he didn't care. He bet one thousand
on the next game and won it back. Then one thousand
on the next, and the next. He couldn't stop winning.
He'd stopped doing the calculations of whether he was
breaking even or not. He felt powerful for one of the
few times in his life. He bet a thousand dollars on an ace
and pulled a two, then bought a four, then a ten.
Seventeen. He bought another card. It was a four. He'd
made ten thousand dollars. He was shaking all over and
the room was too hot. He scooped up his chips and
took them to be cashed.

He caught the lift to the top floor bar and ordered a
round for everybody there. For himself he bought a
bottle of Stolichnaya and two bottles of tonic and sat by
the window, drinking steadily, looking out at the small
gold lights of the city and the cranes by the wharf and
the raindrops that had started to hit the window.

Daniel woke up in the youth hostel with a blinding
headache and no recollection of how he'd got there. He
lay still, fighting the cramps in his stomach. It came into
his mind that the last thing he did before unconscious-
ness struck was put the nineteen thousand dollars,
wrapped tightly in a plastic bag, underneath his pillow.
He slowly drew his hand out from between his legs and
reached under the pillow for the bag. He felt only the
pillow and the sheet. He patted around on top of the
pillow and felt nothing. He heaved himself into a sitting
position and twisted round. The pillow lay there, flat

and stained with something beige. He hurled it across the room and knelt on the bed, shoving his hands down the length of it between the mattress and the wall. He could not feel the bag anywhere. He jumped up and dragged the bed out from the wall, hit the floor and squirmed his way under it. Nothing nothing nothing.

He searched the rest of the small room, throwing his suitcase from one corner to another, lifting all his clothes and shaking them, looking in places too small for the money to be, in shoes, in his trouser pockets, between the pages of a magazine. He went through his clothes again. His jacket was damp along the shoulders. Last night's rain. In the pocket he found three fifty-dollar bills and some loose change, all that was left of the first thousand from the night before. This made him pause in his frenzy, and the pause made tears rise in his throat. He shook the pillow and ripped the sheets off the bed. Flipped the mattress over. Leaned against the wall by the bedroom door, reached across and tried the door handle. It was unlocked. He must have left it unlocked.

He wondered if his memory of leaving the money under the pillow was false. Perhaps that was from the first time in the room, when he'd slept for two hours? No. That time he'd crashed without doing anything to the money. It must have been last night. Couldn't there have been something else he'd done with it? Left it with the casino cashiers to look after? Stashed it in a hidden place somewhere else? He slid down the wall till he was on the floor and sat with his knees drawn up to his chest, hitting the sides of his head with his fists. He couldn't come up with anything beyond fragments of sitting in that casino bar until somebody shook him awake and then – it was raining – he got a taxi – where did he go in the taxi? – he couldn't remember it. He did remember walking into his room and collapsing on the bed, didn't he? Waking up dehydrated and checking the money was still under the pillow? Did that happen? Did he remember it? Did he remember what happened to nineteen thousand dollars?

Daniel plagued himself with questions and came up with nothing. It was not possible that the money was gone. He retrieved his cigarettes from where he'd thrown them and lit one up, nearly gagging as the smoke hit the back of his throat. He caught his reflection in the mirror. There was something like a bruise on his neck. A love-bite. He searched his mind for some comfort and thought of Richard. He couldn't ring him now. To his alarm Daniel thought he might be about to cry. The idea of that jolted him out of his passivity. He had a bit of money, probably enough to stay on in the hostel a few days and keep some for food. He had to get some breakfast. He had to find a job. What he really wanted to do though, more than anything, was go and see a film.

FOUR On Easter Sunday Kate takes the bus around to Josh and Lucy's for dinner. She tries to pick a seat without chewing gum stuck to it. The floor is littered with tinfoil chocolate egg wrappers in purple and silver. When they were kids Ginny would organize an Easter egg hunt around the garden. Their eggs were always hollowed-out real-life eggshells, painted with whichever style Ginny was studying by correspondence that year. Russian doll decorations were a recurring favourite. Kate had loved them, but of far greater value in the playground were enormous hollow Cadbury's eggs with a little plastic bag of chocolate buttons inside. These could be made to last a long time, and Nina had had one friend – that short girl, Shannon – who could nibble at hers with excruciating control until August, when it was powdery and stale, but still chocolate.

Shannon also owned a doll with enormous eyes and luscious auburn curls and a hoop dress made of green satin. She was on a musical stand and when you wound her up she would rotate slowly to the sound of Green-sleeves. In her left hand she held a parasol. Kate can't remember Shannon's last name but she can remember every detail of that doll. Nina had wanted one desperately. She pestered and pestered Ginny for two Christmases and birthdays running, but Ginny was resistant to the idea on the grounds that the doll was excessively frilly and Nina would be better off with a beginner's chemistry set. Eventually their father came through and brought one back from a business trip to Sydney. This doll had black hair and a red dress and the tune she spun to was Camptown Races. She was altogether sexier than Shannon's doll, but by that time Nina had fallen out with Shannon because she'd tried to steal a friend off of her. In a moment of unusual intimacy, she confessed to Kate that she'd gone off those stupid dolls anyway. Still, she took the opportunity to display the doll in Show and Tell that week. The rumour went round Standard Three that Shannon thought Nina was a spoilt brat. Nina stood outside the school gates holding her superior doll and, as Shannon walked past, announced in a loud voice that jealousy gets you nowhere. In the resulting fight, the doll's head was smashed and Shannon sustained a nasty kick to her shin. She limped conspicuously for three days afterwards and the whole of Standard Three had to sit through a special assembly on violence in the playground.

Nina has arrived in town this morning to take Ginny up the coast for a couple of nights as a birthday present. Kate imagines them sharing a bottle of wine on the hotel verandah and admiring the sea view, as she lets herself in Josh and Lucy's front door and calls out Hello. Tilly's sitting on one of the orange chairs Josh found on the side of the road last week, a magazine in her lap. 'Hi, Kate.' She smiles her toothy asexual smile. If she was an animal she'd be a chipmunk, or a little furry dog. She has kind brown eyes. 'How are you?'

'Hi, Tilly. Yeah, good. You?'

'Good, thanks. Lucy's in the kitchen.'

Kate wanders through and kisses Lucy on the cheek. 'Nice apron.'

'Cheers. Josh likes it with nothing underneath.'

'So that's why the windows are steamed up in here.'

'You all right?'

'Yeah. This smells great.' Kate peers at the stove. 'What is it?'

'Paella. I have no idea what I'm doing. Can you pass me that—' she gestures vaguely.

'Who else is coming?' asks Kate, passing the pepper grinder.

'Frank and Ben.'

'Oh.'

Once Lucy tried to set Kate up with her brother Ben. He's a sweet guy but he's kind of dorky. He has an enormous Adam's apple. Kate can't imagine what he looks like naked. She tries to act normal around him but she's hypersensitive to any show of interest on his part. Maybe Tilly will be a good buffer. She might fancy him, she's been single for long enough. Lucy's theory is that Tilly's a closet dyke. No one can remember the last time she had sex, it's true. So. Lucy and Josh, Tilly, Ben, Kate. And Frank. Kate exhales and tells herself she's absolutely relaxed about seeing him, that their flings, pre-Indonesia and post-Indonesia, were ages ago. Everything's perfectly civilized between them now.

Josh bangs through the back door, wine bottles clutched under his arms. 'It's boiling in here. Hi, Kate. Red or white?'

'I know it's boiling,' says Lucy, 'I'm cooking, all right?'

'Hey, guys. I brought you a pineapple.' Kate hands it to Josh.

'Excellent,' he says, and raises a winged eyebrow. 'You know Ben's coming tonight.'

'Shut up. Come and talk to me and Tilly. Lu? Yell if you need a hand.'

Lucy looks up darkly from the paella. 'I hate Martha Stewart.'

Kate drinks two large glasses of red wine fast as Tilly tells them the latest thinking on her thesis topic, the death of Captain Cook. She prefaces eighty per cent of her sentences with, 'My supervisor says . . .' It amazes Kate to think that Tilly will soon have the word Doctor before her name.

'I always wanted to be a pirate,' says Josh. 'Rum, dead men's chests—'

'Sodomizing the cabin boy—'

'Golden treasure, that sort of thing. Do you think they still have them?'

'I doubt it's that glamorous any more,' says Kate.

'Oh, it never was.' Tilly leans forward. 'Most of them died of scurvy, they'd go all bruised and then their brains would rot. My supervisor says the only difference between pirates and colonizers was the pirates had more respect for indigenous cultures. They didn't integrate as much as the whalers, though. My supervisor says being eaten by cannibals was probably one of the nicer ways to die if you were a pirate.'

'I bet you were one of those girls at school camp who liked to tell ghost stories into the night,' says Kate.

Tilly blushes. 'It's true. I'd hold a torch up under my chin and go on for hours.'

'I don't get girls.' Josh lights a cigarette. 'I mean, ghost stories? Why weren't you masturbating over a biscuit like us members of the stronger sex?'

'We do that now,' says Kate. 'We were saving it.'

There's a knock at the door. 'Ah,' says Josh standing up, 'the Scoutmaster.'

'Sorry, Tilly,' mutters Kate. 'I don't know why I said that.'

Ben stoops into the room, lamplight glinting off his glasses. He's wearing a navy shirt buttoned to the top and has had a haircut since Kate saw him last. The skin around his ears and neck looks red and exposed. His trousers are pulled up high on his waist.

'How are things with you, Kate?' he says in his impossibly formal deep voice.

'Fine.' She smiles up at him brightly. He's so tall. 'Yeah, OK.'

'Any new movies you can recommend?'

'Not really. The holiday stuff's rubbish. Unless you're in the mood for that.' She doesn't imagine Ben's a popcorn kind of guy. He nods as if she's said something very serious.

'Sometimes,' he says slowly, 'rubbish can be just what one needs.'

'Yes,' says Kate, repeating her effortful grin. 'How's the agency?'

'Not bad. It's hardly finding a cure for cancer.' Ben clears his throat, then, as if it's a line he tosses off at parties, 'I'm just an advertising whore.'

Kate winces. It's not right for him to say anything remotely sexual. She coughs out a laugh. 'It must be quite fun though.' *Quite fun?* Is this her new way of talking?

'Not really,' he's saying. 'I'm doing a campaign for dog food at the moment.'

'Oh.'

'I've got used to the money, that's the thing.' Ben

shifts his weight in an embarrassed way. Kate wonders
how much he makes and how difficult it would be to
hang around with a bunch of advertising whores. Her
neck hurts from staring up at him so long.

Lucy yells out from the kitchen. 'Ben's going to
Vanuatu next month.'

Ben ducks his head. It's sweet how he blushes easily,
thinks Kate. Tilly's like that too. They could be the
bashful couple. 'Vanuatu's supposed to be beautiful,' she
says.

Tilly turns towards them. 'There's been a lot of
political unrest there recently.'

Ben's nodding. 'Yes, it's no longer dangerous from
what I can ascertain but yes, there's been an understand-
able public outcry—'

'Yes,' says Tilly, her brown eyes honed in on Ben,
'government corruption.'

The front door opens and slams. Frank. Kate's up out
of the couch and into the kitchen like a rocket. 'Can I
give you a hand with anything?'

The paella looks fantastic, yellow with saffron, full of
succulent pieces of fish, tiger prawns and scallops.
Somewhere in the years Kate's known her, Lucy's
learned to cook. Occasionally they go together to
Seamart. It's wild in there, huge tanks crawling with
crabs, great piles of spiny swordfish, slimy sheets of
squid. Mountains of mussels and oysters. Fat red-eyed
cod, whiskery catfish, a lone grey octopus. The air is
moist with spray, there's the sound of water dripping
and the endless, deep smell of salt and scales. They love
Seamart. Sometimes they'll make a special trip for no
reason, and spend half an hour inspecting the tanks with

the other shoppers, marvelling at all the ugly and beautiful things from the sea.

'How's my lipstick?' Kate's finished setting the table.

'Fine. Go on, go back through.'

She braves the living room. Frank is sprawled out on the floor, lifting a cigarette slowly to his lips. Kate kicks his skinny legs lightly as she steps over them. 'Hi.'

'Hiya,' he says in his slightly camp drawl. 'How you doing?'

'Good. You?'

'Great.'

'Cool.'

Josh stands up. 'Who'd like more wine?'

'Yes, please,' booms Ben. 'Marvellous.'

It's pretty in the kitchen with the candles lit and flickering as a draft comes through the window. The six of them are squeezed around the square table, legs bumping underneath it. Kate gives up trying to tell if it's Ben's shoe or Frank's that's pressing against hers. She passes bread diagonally across to Tilly. 'Where did you have Easter last year?'

'Taupo.'

'We used to go there when we were kids. Did you do any sailing?'

'Too cold. Did your parents have a bach?'

'We'd go camping. Or no, sometimes we borrowed someone else's. They had a little P-class too.' Frank is showing no interest at all, just sitting there forking food into his mouth. 'We capsized once.'

'Can you swim?'

'Yeah.' Kate remembers the moment when the boat keeled over. She can see grey waves and a charcoal sky, her orange life jacket, strands of hair, like seaweed, floating in front of her face. But she also remembers standing on the pebbly shore with a group of adults, watching a child being lifted out of the water. Was that her? Was she watching from the beach or was she the girl in the water, spluttering and choking, her wet hair falling over a grown-up's shoulder as he picked her up in a fireman's lift? She can't remember if Nina was there – she can't remember which girl she was.

'We were in New York last Easter,' Lucy is saying. 'Just popped over for a few days, as you do.' She turns to Josh. 'How did we ever afford that?'

'I embezzled funds from the station and you sold your body.'

'That's where I'll be next week,' says Frank. 'No, week after.'

Everybody looks at him. 'What for?'

His nose seems extra-long and his eyebrows are extra-arched. He looks pleased with himself, as if he's got a secret. Kate hates this ability of his to simply ignore a question. Josh gets up to change the music. 'I didn't realize you were going so soon.'

So soon? Since when? Maybe she's been told about this and deliberately forgotten it. She catches Lucy watching her.

'It's been brought forward.' Frank yawns. This is another tactic of his, acting blasé, as if everything bores him. Even in bed he was like that, slow and languorous, hooded eyelids fluttering at the crucial moment and neck stretching back in an intensely private way.

'Are you going with work?' says Tilly. Kate's relieved that she doesn't know about this either, that she can get the answers for questions Kate doesn't want to ask.

'No, I've quit work. I'm going to stay there for a while.'

'Who with?'

'My friend Diane.'

Oh, *Diane*. Diane the *actress*. Blonde, leggy Diane with the rich father and his apartment in the West Village. Diane who says, before she tells you anything, Oh, listen to *this*. You're going to *love* this. *Neat*. Kate rips off a piece of bread.

'Fantastic,' she says. 'What are you going to do out there?'

'Just hang out.' Frank bares his teeth into something like a smile. 'Be a kept man.'

'I recommend it.'

Lucy thumps Josh's arm. 'Hey.'

'Have you ever been supported by anyone?' Kate turns to Ben. 'A woman you were living with?'

Ben shakes his head. 'No—'

'There,' Kate says to the others. 'Don't you feel emasculated?'

'I've never lived with anyone,' he continues, 'a partner I mean. Well, I asked my last girlfriend but she didn't want to.'

Kate shuts her eyes. 'Thanks, Ben.'

'Have you ever? Lived with anyone?'

'No,' says Kate, 'no, I haven't, I've never wanted to, really.'

'Ever?'

'No. Well, maybe once. Anyway, I never have.'

A group survey on cohabitation would put her, Ben and Tilly in one camp and Lucy, Josh and Frank in the other. She doesn't need this sort of demarcation. What's something else they can talk about?

'I've always lived with my girlfriends,' says Josh.

'That's because you're a lazy sod.'

'Cheers, darling.'

'It's true!' Lucy looks around the table. 'You're totally slack.'

Josh leans over Ben to kiss her cheek. 'But you love me.'

'Get off.' She wipes her face, laughing. 'Clear the table or something. Christ, you're neither use nor ornament.'

Later, over more wine, Frank favours Tilly with his best smile. 'So, how's life at the ivory tower?'

In the candlelight she glows a warm pink. 'My supervisor says my thesis might be published.'

'Did they eat Cook after they killed him, or what?'

'Well, it's contentious. He was dismembered—'

Josh groans. 'Do you mind?'

'Don't be a pussy,' says Frank. 'Cannibalism's fascinating.'

'It's gross.'

'Yeah, but if you had no choice,' says Kate, 'like that football team.'

'That was a great movie.'

'Yeah,' says Ben, 'but they were dead already. It would be different if you had to actually kill someone.'

'I didn't see it.'

Kate steals a glance at Frank. He's looking at her in that predatory way. The football plane-crash film had been on at the cinema she worked in while they were having their second short affair. She used to sneak Frank in and they'd make out in the back row. He was like that, always running his hand up under her skirt in public, half-undressing her in taxicabs. Irresistible Frank. No, she tells herself now, lips pressing hard against the rim of her wine glass. Don't even go there.

'If we were on a life-raft,' says Lucy, 'who'd get chucked overboard first?'

'Me,' Ben says immediately. 'My skills as a copywriter would be fairly expendable.'

'You could eat me,' says Tilly, 'uh, you know what I mean. High percentage body fat and that.'

'Til, you're not fat.'

'I am,' she mutters.

'Anyway, you're the most likely navigator, with all your Captain Cook know-how. Josh'd get chucked. He's useless.'

'Yeah.' He yawns. 'Besides, once you'd hurled me to the sharks you'd probably land on a desert island or something. Like, I would have been bad luck.'

Lucy laughs. 'No one's suffering from high self-esteem this evening I see.'

'So, Frank,' says Kate in a quiet voice while the others are talking, encouraged by the way he keeps staring at her, 'how long are you going to New York for?'

But Josh overhears. 'Make it a while, eh. We need someone else there we can stay with. And Ben if you settle down in Vanuatu we can come and crash in your bungalow or under your coconut palm.'

Ben looks disconcerted. 'I don't speak any French.'

'Most of them speak English,' says Tilly. 'And their local village language. There's about a hundred and fifty of those, and French, and sometimes they'll speak another village's language as well.' She looks around the room, her eyes bright. 'They put us to shame.'

'I can speak Pig Latin,' says Josh.

'You'd suit Vanuatu, Ben,' says Kate. 'Thatched South Sea villages, a safari helmet – colonizer chic.'

Lucy leans back in her chair and lights a cigarette.

'God,' she exhales. 'Everyone's going away. No one we know is in the same place, any more.'

Is he, isn't he, is he, isn't he. Yes he is. Frank is definitely going to make a play for her and she is definitely going to turn him down. There are many good reasons to turn him down, thinks Kate as she helps Lucy wash up while he and Josh lounge about in the sitting room, getting stoned and playing obscure records. For a start, he's got a new girlfriend. Correction – girlfriend. She's not his 'new' girlfriend because Kate's not his 'old' girlfriend. She never achieved girlfriend status, not that she was after it. Plus, he just wants one for the road before he heads for the States. Wants to feel he has a girl in every port. Well, she's not going to let him have the satisfaction. But is she cutting off her nose to spite her face? It's months since she's gotten laid. What a nightmare though if she gets all emotional about him just when he's going to leave. It's the sort of stupid thing she'd do as well, fixate on Frank because he's leaving the country and there's no possibility of real intimacy. She wishes she was the kind of person who instinctively knew the right thing to do and didn't have to have this endless back-and-forth second-guessing herself all the time.

'So,' says Lucy, 'you think Tilly's having sex with her tutor, by any chance?'

'Don't talk to me about sex.'

'Are you going to do it?'

'Do what?' Kate squeezes more detergent into the sink and runs the hot water.

'It.'

'No.'

'Oh, go on.'

'No.' She flicks a soap bubble at Lucy. 'I'm not going

to have some tragic last fling with Frank just so you can get your vicarious kicks.'

'You're no fun. It's so boring being in a couple and only ever having meaningful sex.'

'What are you guys up to tomorrow night?'

'I'll probably send Josh out for takeaways and videos. Want to come over?'

'Uh – I don't know, maybe I should try and have a life— Oh, OK, sure.'

Frank stands in the kitchen doorway, jingling his car keys. 'Want a lift home?'

It's cool outside and the sky is streaked with iron-grey clouds. Beyond them the grey is darker, milky, impenetrable. Frank's car is parked up the road. Kate keeps her eye on the edge of the kerb as they walk towards it, trying to stay in a straight line.

'I saw you in the street the other day,' says Frank, his voice surprisingly low in the quiet night air.

'Did you?'

'I was in my car. I tooted.'

'Oh. I didn't hear you. Where was I?'

'In town. You were crossing the road. It was late-night shopping.'

'I don't shop.'

'I know. I tooted twice.' He's standing close enough so that she can smell him. When they first knew each other he used to smell faintly of sandalwood. Now his scent is something altogether more chemical.

Kate looks up at the sky. 'No stars,' she says.

'Josh,' Lucy says while she's eating breakfast and he's packing together his Scalectrix set to take into the radio station, 'have you seen all that stuff in the paper about the Pill?'

'What about it?'

'How they don't know if it's safe, it leads to thrombosis or heart disease or cancer. And it's worse if you're a smoker.'

He looks up from his model cars. 'How long've you been on it?'

'Six years, maybe seven.'

'Maybe you should go off it then.'

'But what about contraception? Condoms are awful.'

He stands behind her and kisses her neck. 'I could cope. I could get a vasectomy.'

She laughs. 'Yeah, right.'

'Well, I could. We don't want to have a baby.'

'No. I suppose.'

'Do we? Nah.'

The telephone rings. Lucy smiles. 'That'll be the phone.'

Cycling in to work, she remembers how her cousin had come back from overseas with a Scottish husband and a fully-formed baby. Watching them walking out of the brown double doors at customs and through to the arrivals lounge was like seeing a person who looks a lot like someone you know, but hang on, it can't be her because she's with a strange bloke and they've got a kid. Lucy hadn't been able to shake the feeling that her cousin had nicked the baby, snatched it out of a passing pram or borrowed it from a friend and refused to give it back. Two years ago the cousin hadn't been pregnant, she hadn't even met this guy or begun to think about getting married and having a child. And Lucy and her

close friends follow the minutiae of each other's lives in
real time, there's nothing major that any of them don't
know about the others. If Kate met someone and
decided to have a baby, Lucy would be so present
through the process it would be as if it was happening
to her, too. Every thought, every made and un-made
decision, every abandoned plan, is shared. Well, that's
what she thinks, anyway. But a baby— Maybe it would
be easier to be like her cousin, to disappear from view
until you'd actually got the thing, and then to return
like a person in a movie whose life has ceased to exist
once they're off the screen, but with all the necessary
plot developments having been made.

A car brakes suddenly and honks. Lucy swerves out of
the way. What if she was pregnant? she thinks. What if
she was a mother, with another human life to worry
about? Most of the people she knows have enough
trouble taking care of themselves. She's seen from the
refuge how hard having children can be, and how
having a man around doesn't make it any better if he's
useless. What sort of a father would Josh be? A risk. But
she loves him, she's still in love with him, even if he's a
kid himself sometimes. If only she could get pregnant
accidentally, she thinks. Accidentally on purpose. Oh,
she doesn't know. Perhaps it's only because they've been
together five years and it seems like there's got to be
some development, a next step, something new. It's
hardly fair to have a baby just because your relationship's
hit a plateau. But she sees pregnant women everywhere
these days, and she's been looking at children in a new
way. It makes her laugh, how the clichés are coming
true for her. Maybe they're all just victims of biology, in
the end. She chains her bike to the fence outside the

refuge and walks straight through the hall to the back
garden where three new kids are fighting in the sandpit.

Next time Kate sees Frank is at his going-away party.
Talking to him while Diane's watching is kind of fun.
It's hard to hear so they have to lean right in close to
each other's faces. She can feel his breath buzzing on her
cheek.

'Hey,' he says, 'I think I saw one of your flatmates
out last night. With another man.'

'Out where?'

'Some club.'

Kate smiles. 'Some club? Are you frequenting gay
cruising spots these days? Which one was it?'

'Which club?'

'Which of my flatmates.'

'The blond one.'

'They're both blond.'

'Blond leading the bland.'

'Watch it.'

'So which one's the shagger and which one's the
shagee?'

'I don't know. Why do you want to?'

'Well, it's interesting, isn't it. Which one's the leader,
which one's the girl.'

'Jesus, Frank. Penetration doesn't equal humiliation,
you know.'

'Yeah, you say.'

Kate eyes him up and down. 'There's a lump in your
leg.'

'Uh?'

She points to the bulge down the side of his trousers,
just above the knee. 'Yesterday's knickers?'

If it wasn't for the sudden twitching nerve under his eye, she'd guess he was completely unfazed. She doesn't, obviously, know that he's thinking, I've had my cock in your mouth. 'Men don't wear knickers, Kate. We wear boxer shorts. Excuse me just a minute. I'm going to the loo.'

His composure staggers her. The effort it would take to remain that controlled. Something must have made him become like that. She finds Lucy in the bedroom, skinning up.

'Lu?'

'Mn?' She looks up and smiles. 'Have you checked this room out since Diane's been on the scene? Apart from when you came back here and shagged the other night.'

'I didn't shag him.'

'Just testing. Get a load of that lot over there.' She nods her head towards the mantelpiece. 'I think they're hoping that people will see.'

'Oh my God.' Kate picks up a rubber G-string between two fingers and dangles it out in front of her, at arm's length. 'I didn't know Frank was into this stuff.'

'Well, somebody is.'

'Thank Christ I didn't come back with him. I'd frighten small children wearing something like that.' She sits down on the bed next to Lucy. 'Wow. I'm so repressed.'

'Me too.'

'Why do you think Frank's a control freak?'

Lucy lights the spliff and passes it to Kate. 'Why's anyone? I don't know. He likes to be elusive.'

'Yeah. I think I'm kind of bored by it.'

'Only because you were burnt by it.'

Kate narrows her eyes against the smoke. 'Maybe. Well. You've got to learn somehow.'

Later, they're lying on the bed, the door closed to keep out the noise. Lucy has ransacked the pile of sex toys on the mantelpiece and is wearing a see-through, holey bra over her T-shirt. 'What about,' she says, 'if Frank had some embarrassing childhood experience, something really mortifying, and that's why he's so determined to be cool now?'

'Maybe he was a total nerd.'

'Maybe a friend of his went round to his house and discovered kiss-marks on the mirror where he'd been practising how to kiss and then told everyone. That happened to me. I just about died.'

'How old were you?'

'Twenty-one.'

'Ha ha.'

'Twelve or something.'

'The first boy who kissed me did it on a dare.'

'No.'

'I know. It took me a while to recover.'

'Have you ever seen photos of Frank when he was at school?'

'Don't think so.'

Lucy rolls over onto her stomach and gives Kate a sideways smile. 'Shall we have a look?'

When the door swings open they're sitting cross-legged in the middle of Frank and Diane's bedroom, Lucy in the T-shirt and cut-out bra ensemble and Kate wearing a moustache, coat and bowler hat she's found in the wardrobe. On the floor in front of them is a pile of Polaroids and snapshots, scattered face-up and face-down like a game of Memory.

'Jesus *Christ*,' Lucy's squealing. 'He's – oh my God –
you never told me that—'

There's a bang as the door slams shut. Diane is in the
room, her face white. Kate and Lucy freeze, mouths
open, two fairground dummies midswivel as if someone's cut the power. Then Kate, fatally, starts to laugh.
'Sorry,' she's saying as they try to sweep the photos
together, 'I know it's not funny, sorry—' She's still
saying it as she's handing Diane back the hat and
struggling out of the coat, 'Sorry,' hiccuping with
laughter while Lucy asks Diane to help her unhook the
bra, 'Not clever,' as they're being herded through the
party and out the door like a couple of shoplifters,
'Terrible thing to do, sorry, sorry—'

'We're making a habit of this,' says Lucy as she and Kate
begin the trudge home.

'We'll stop being invited. I guess we won't be going
to the airport to wave them off.'

'Me and Josh are supposed to be minding Frank's
apartment while he's away. Some deal Josh's jacked up.
He's probably going to use it as a love-den.'

'Ha ha. Isn't Frank subletting it?'

'They don't need to. She's bought it for him.'

Kate whistles. 'I'd put up with a few compromising
poses myself if someone was going to buy me a flat.'

'Yeah, well I don't think she's going to be in a hurry
to give us the keys now. Unless . . .' Lucy reaches into
the waistband of her trousers and pulls out a small square
photograph. She studies it under a streetlight. 'Nasty
outfit. Do you think we could threaten her with sending
it to Reader's Wives?'

★

It's good that Frank's leaving. There's no getting away
from him or any other part of her history, here. Kate
wonders if there's anywhere she could really leave herself
behind. She remembers a time in Indonesia when she
was staying in a youth hostel, just before she'd had to
sell her Walkman. She shared a bunk room with three
other girls. Two of them were Irish and the other one,
a girl with long red hair in the ubiquitous tiny braids,
was a New Zealander. One night it was just the two of
them there, lying in the close heat on opposite top
bunks. They smiled at each other in an awkward way.

'This is like being in prison,' said Kate. 'From the
movies, anyway.'

'What are you in for?' asked the corn-rowed girl.

Kate thought. 'Treason.'

'That's a hanging offence.'

'Yeah. You?'

The girl lit a joint. 'Armed robbery.'

'A bank?'

'Diamonds.'

'What's your name?'

'Jemima.'

Kate grinned. She looked like the doll off *Playschool*,
as well. 'I'm Kate.'

'Hey—' The girl propped herself up on one elbow.

'Mm?'

'Is it all right if we don't do that thing of whereabouts
at home are we from and who do we know and all that
till we find out that we're actually cousins?'

'OK,' said Kate. 'We'll remain anonymous.'

'Good.' The girl sighed and rolled over onto her
stomach. She reached out to pass Kate the joint and
took a mouthful from her water bottle. 'You know, this
terrible thing happened to me last week.'

'What? Were you mugged?' Please don't say raped thought Kate, that's the one thing she was really scared of here.

'No it's—' She sighed again.

'You don't have to say.'

'It's sort of funny in a way. I was on Saronde, up in North Sulawesi, have you been there?'

Kate shook her head. 'No.'

'It's really beautiful.' Jemima laughed. 'Like everywhere here. It's a tiny island, probably only takes about twenty minutes to walk around the whole thing. I'd gone there to think about something—' She held her hand out for the joint and Kate passed it back. Jemima took a drag and frowned. 'I'm here to think about something, this is what this whole trip was about, get away from home and get some space, just hang, not have any pressure— '

'I know.'

'Do you?'

Kate shrugged. 'Maybe.' She wasn't in the mood for a problem competition.

'Anyway I had this big decision to make, and I was standing on this white sand beach at the edge of the water. It felt amazing, just rippling over my toes. The same temperature as the air. Everything felt perfect. The sea was a silvery colour right out to the horizon, where there was a black line – and then the sky was dull too, but pearly – It was like a kind of no-space,' she said, 'like limbo.'

Limbo. Kate felt as if she was a permanent resident there. She didn't have her feet on the ground, as Ginny kept telling her, but then her head wasn't quite in the clouds, either.

'Limbo.' She says it out loud.

'Yeah, like floating. And I decided' – the girl rolled her eyes – 'I was about to make my decision, and then I hear this voice going Jemima! Jemima! And you know, it's got to be me, right, because it's not that common a name. The only other Jemima I know is the doll from *Playschool*.'

'Me too.'

'I can't believe it, but I turn around and coming towards me over the sand on this isolated, completely remote beach, is my fucking parents' next-door neighbour. That brought me right down.' She laughed. 'Talk about how low can you go. It was hell. There's nowhere to go. Just nowhere.'

'Did you make your decision?'

'Nup.' Jemima balanced the roach on the edge of her bunk. 'I put it off.'

Kate stands still for a moment in her mother's dark hall, overnight bag on the floor by her side. The house stretches out big and empty in front of her. Its everyday smell of dusty rugs and Ginny's hand lotion seems stronger. There was a film starring Audrey Hepburn that Kate often thinks of when she's in a dark place alone, about a blind girl who smashes all the lights when there's an intruder in the house, placing him and the audience in the same position as herself. Kate feels for the light switch. Just before her fingers touch it and flick it on, filling the hall with light, there's a bang. She stands frozen in the yellow hallway, mouth open. A door? A window? Furniture? The house creaking?

Taking a deep breath, she starts down the hall, past the living room and into the kitchen, turning all the lights and lamps on as she goes. She takes a rolling pin out of the kitchen drawer and clutches it, feeling

ridiculous, as she moves on through the bathroom, spare
room – they get the all-clear – and up the hall to her
mother's bedroom. She's treading as quietly as possible
in case she misses anything else. As she approaches the
closed door of her mother's room, there's another bang,
a smacking sound like wood on wood. She flinches. It's
hard to tell what direction the bang came from. Was it
behind her somewhere in the rest of the house? Outside
maybe. Or ahead of her in this room? Trying not to
think, she flings open the door, bashing it flat against the
wall like in a police movie.

Ginny's bed, dressing table, wardrobe – open, desk. It
surprises her how familiar, how normal it all looks. She
walks slowly up to the bed and bends down, her
breathing shallow, to check under it. Dust, a paperback.
No intruder. She mentally checks back. That's the
whole house. Every room lit, every room unoccupied.
It was the wind. Or something. She walks back through
the rooms looking behind curtains, under the couch, in
the broom cupboard, anywhere. Her grip on the rolling
pin is slippery and loose. Her bag still sits by the front
door, lumpy and motionless. It makes her uneasy, as if it
might develop a life of its own, somersault heavily down
the hall towards her.

'Hi!' she calls out to her flatmates. 'It's me.'

Mike and Toby are in front of the television, takeaway
containers between them. The stilled image on the
screen looks pink and vaguely obscene. 'What's that?'

'Dirty night in. Aren't you staying at your mother's?'

'No.' She smiles. 'I'm going to bed. Not too much
screaming, please.'

★

A couple of days later, she visits Lucy at her Saturday
job in the wanky clothes store. 'Here, doll.' She gives
her a Styrofoam cup of coffee.

'Thanks.'

'You look like an evil twin has taken over your
identity.'

'It's the make-up. And this stupid dress. I've been
invaded by a bodysnatcher.'

'Has Josh seen you like this?'

Lucy makes a face. 'Don't. I think he likes it.'

Kate paces up and down beside the clothing racks,
flicking the coat-hangers with her fingers. 'Do you read
in here?'

'I try. Mostly I can't concentrate on anything except
a magazine. These clothes cut off the blood flow, stop it
reaching the brain. Hey, I called you at Ginny's this
morning but you weren't there.'

'Couldn't do it. I've got to go tomorrow and water
the plants. They've probably all died.'

'Perhaps,' says Lucy, 'you wanted, subconsciously, to
kill them. Hm?'

Kate holds up a long skinny dress. 'Why do we do
this?'

'What, even look at clothes we couldn't fit one of
our arms into?'

'No, apply our armchair psychology to everything.
Can't I just be a crap gardener?'

'I guess. All right, in this case the cigar can be just a
cigar.'

'Oh, thanks,' says Kate, 'saved from confronting my
inner demons for one morning.' She glances at her
watch and groans. 'I've got to go to the cinema. It's too
nice of a day to be inside. Maybe I should be saving to
go away again. Oh, what am I saying, it'd take me ten

years at this rate.' She laughs. 'I'm going to change my name to Mona.'

A couple walk into the store. Lucy assumes a bland smile. The woman takes a bundle of outfits into a changing cubicle and the man pulls a wallet out of his jacket pocket.

'Listen, I'd better run,' Kate whispers.

From the changing room the woman calls, 'Barry! My head's too big for my body!'

'Eat something then,' murmurs Lucy, her porcelain expression unchanging except for a wink at Kate as she hoists her bag over her shoulder to leave.

'Oh, I forgot to tell you, Doctor,' Kate whispers. 'Not only can I not sleep at my mother's house, I can't even eat the food there.' She raises her eyebrows and grins. 'What do you make of that, huh?'

'Come back here,' Lucy calls after her. 'You need help.'

Josh has driven over to Frank's place to get the spare keys. The hallway is piled high with boxes. 'Hello?' he calls out. 'Frank?'

'He's on the roof.' Diane wafts past him, a scarf tied around her head in a stylish, protecting-my-hair-but-really-it's-for-effect kind of way. Josh holds out a beer to her but she's tripping down the stairs, a load of rolled-up posters under her arm.

'Hey, man.' Josh sticks his head out the trapdoor that opens on to the roof. Frank's stacking plastic chairs up against a corner.

'Hiya. Got a ciggie?'

Josh clambers out and holds out his packet. 'Do you want a hand with this?'

'Nah. Diane's got it under control.'

They wander to the edge of the roof and survey the
suburb, a mix of orange tiled and corrugated iron
rooftops, the odd concrete apartment building like this
one dotted down by the water. The sky is a bright steel
blue. Josh passes Frank his lighter. 'So, New York.'
  'Yup.'
  'What airline?'
  'Virgin.'
  'Nice one.'
  Josh isn't sure whether or not to mention the scene
between Diane and Lucy at the party. Would Frank be
offended? It's hard to say. 'You going to catch up with
Michelle while you're there?' Michelle is one of Frank's
exes. 'Is she still hooked up with that loser, what's his
name?'
  'I think so, yeah. Yeah, that loser with the fifty K
American salary.'
  'That's right, the rich talented good-looking loser.
She still with him?'
  'Yeah, yeah. I might call her up. Diane'll really love
that.'
  'Bit insecure?'
  Frank lowers his voice. 'Just a bit. That young girl
thing. Michelle's sister's there as well.'
  'She's quite a babe.'
  'Yeah, for sure.' He grabs a manky broom from off the
rooftop and starts sweeping leaves and dirt into a pile.
  'Listen,' says Josh, 'I can do all that shit once you're
gone.'
  'No, it's cool. So why're you so keen to look after
this place anyway, you getting stuck into someone round
here or what?'
  'Yeah, right. No it just makes sense, you know? It's
no hassle for me to keep an eye on it.'

Before he says goodbye, Josh flicks his ash over the side of the building. 'So, ah, don't forget to leave your passport behind.'

'And take half a kilo of cocaine with me, yeah.'

'And eat a massive steak before you go. They put stuff in the food to—'

'Stop you taking a dump, I know. I thought I'd try and miss the plane as well.'

'Just remember to be really insulting to the customs officer at JFK. Hey, have you got a map? I'll show you some of the places you've got to go. When are you off?'

'This evening.'

'Really? I thought you weren't going till Monday.'

'No, it's today.'

Frank has told everyone he's leaving a couple of days after he actually is. That way, he'll be gone before they expected, and they'll miss him. Then when he comes back, he'll tell them to expect him a week or so before his real arrival date, to get them into a state of anticipation. Part of him knows how sad this self-packaging is, but he's compelled to do it. He never much trusted that people would find him interesting without that extra effort at control on his part, without that unreliable spin. One of the major reasons he's looking forward to living in New York is that there he'll be able to start a whole new season of inventing himself. Nobody can pin him down. And that's the way he likes it.

Tilly sits in the library trying to concentrate. It's not easy because across the other side of the table a girl with wispy blonde hair is crying. She's said, Are you all right? feeling stupid because the girl so patently wasn't, but the blonde had simply shaken her head and blurted, Yes, thanks. She was amassing a little pile of damp tissues besides her pile of books on Ancient Rome and wouldn't stop sniffing. The graduate students really should have better facilities, thinks Tilly, as she grips her forehead with one hand and draws ballpoint doodles with the other. Still, it's not as though she's reading the latest theory about Cook's alleged deification, or even browsing through a facsimile of some whaler's diary of the time. She's trying to compose a letter. A love letter. *Dear Oscar.* No. Too intimate. *Oscar.* She loves his name. So manly, so – statuesque. *Oscar. Just a brief note to let you know how much I appreciate your support.* Hardly attention-grabbing. *Oscar. I've never done anything like this before* – oh, everyone says that. Why is this so difficult? She's used to writing thousands of words a day for heaven's sake. The blonde girl gives an especially wet snuffle and Tilly looks up sharply. *Oscar. Would you like to share a drink with me this Friday?* But if he says yes she'll be crippled with anxiety and have to bear the responsibility for them both having a good time. Better just to give him a hint and let him do the asking, surely. Oscar. Oscar, Oscar, I'll be your Tosca. No no no no. No. *Oscar – thanks for all your advice this week – hope to see you at the Freedom & Modernity conference this weekend –* aargh—

FIVE   Daniel has got to find a job. He has
enough money left for three more
nights at the hostel, not counting food. Or two nights,
plus food. The thought of imminent homelessness
stops him sleeping. He lies awake wondering how
he wound up in this situation. Ever since he made
that unreal decision, back in London, to be part of
Sticksy's deal, it's as though he stepped out of his life
and into somebody else's. There is too much noise in
the hostel but it doesn't make a difference to him.
He stares at the ceiling, feeling his eyes burn, trying
to think of any job he might be able to do, anything
at all.

The first place he tries is an expensive-looking restaurant. A girl in an oversized white shirt and a black tie
comes to the door. Her hair is pulled back so tight in its
ponytail it looks as if her features have been dragged
halfway up her head. She eyes him doubtfully and asks
for a phone number. He doesn't want to admit he hasn't
got one.

'We'll call if anything comes up,' she's saying in a
pained way.

'I can come back,' says Daniel. 'I can phone or
something. Is there a manager?'

'She isn't here.'

Someone yells from the kitchen. The girl twitches
towards the sound. 'Don't phone, we'll call you if

anything comes up.' She struts away without asking for
his number again.

The next place is a parcel courier company, a red
Pegasus logo emblazoned over its orange brick exterior.
He waits in a dry-aired reception room that smells of
new carpet. There's a copy of Courier's Express on the
smoked glass coffee table but he can't bring himself to
read it. The receptionist, a spotty girl with a slight
overbite, finally gets off the phone.

'Can I help you?'

Daniel explains that he's looking for driving work.

'Right. Well, we don't do the hiring here at Central,
they take charge of that from the Southern office?'

'Oh. Where's that?'

She chews out several words Daniel doesn't understand. Place names or directions, he couldn't tell. 'I'm
sorry?'

She repeats the gibberish and sits picking a spot on
her chin, staring up at him with gimlet eyes.

'Are you sure there isn't anybody here I can see?'

'We do all the hiring from Southern?'

Daniel stares at her. She stares back. He wins. She
drops a bitten finger down on to a button on the
intercom speaker sitting by the desk. There's a hissing
noise.

'Ray?' She doesn't take her small green eyes off of
Daniel's. 'Ray?'

A burble in the hiss.

'There's a gentleman here looking for work as a
driver?'

Daniel pulls himself together. Make an effort, he
thinks. Do you want this job or not? He lowers his
eyelashes and smiles at her. She averts her gaze and a

hand flies up to cover her blemished chin. 'Can you see him now?'

More hiccuping sounds from the intercom. She switches it off and looks again at Daniel. 'Ray's out the back? First door on your right?'

He treats her to a real smile. 'Thanks.'

She jerks her head away. Jaw jutting and her fingers pressed over her mouth, she nods her acknowledgement, waiting for him to go.

Ray's room is almost identical, only smaller. He has a moustache. 'Do you hold a current international licence?'

This reminds Daniel of passport control. He feels his stomach tighten up. 'No,' he says. 'Got a UK one though.'

Ray frowns. 'Not much we can do mate till you get yourself an Enzed licence. Call the MOT. Then call me back.'

Daniel stands there.

'The Ministry of Transport, mate. They're in the book. OK?'

'Thanks,' says Daniel. 'OK'

The third place is a bar that isn't hiring. The fourth is a café with a Help Wanted sign in the window. They need to see his work permit before they'll even talk to him. The fifth place, Daniel walks in and walks straight out again, followed by catcalls from the brawny lesbians behind the counter.

And so it goes on. He treks back to the hostel that night slightly stunned that he hasn't found himself employment. He'd assumed it would happen in a day. He was prepared to do anything, after all. Well, he wouldn't let himself be discouraged, he'd just try again tomorrow. And in the meantime, get some sleep.

He could sell the camera. He should sell the camera. He knows this but he doesn't want to do it. Even though he didn't pay for it, even though he only picked it up the other day, he feels it's been his for years. It was the first bit of shoplifting he'd done in ages. He and Richard used to play at it, tiny stuff when they were younger, magazines and beer and packets of crisps inside the full-length coat. One day they went into an electrical appliance store to watch the music videos and when they went to leave Richard said hard in Daniel's ear, 'Go on, move,' and they got through the doors and belted down the street, Richard clutching his side as if he had a stitch. Daniel didn't know why he was running until they stopped by the playgrounds and Richard, breathless, drew a brand-new Walkman out from underneath his jumper.

Richard was in his mind again when he'd walked into the department store the day after he lost all the money, before the job-hunt had started in earnest. Daniel had been torturing himself with imagining the things he could have bought, if only. New clothes, CDs, a plane ticket. There wasn't a lot to tempt him in the department store, though. It was like something out of the nineteen sixties. Painted old ladies with enormous hair moved behind counters as though they had been entrusted to look after something extremely important. Japanese tourists holding duty free cards wandered amongst the glass display cases. There was the smell of talcum powder and forgotten cardboard. Daniel felt as though nobody could see him, that he'd brought with him a ghostly cover from the outside world, a mantle that rendered him invisible. He drifted into the electronics section and peered through the glass at the calculators and digital organizers and radio alarms. Prices were written in ink on small paper squares next to each object. It all seemed expensive, even after his rough conversions of dollars into pounds. His fingers left smudge marks on the bench-top. This didn't surprise him. Daniel didn't ever feel quite clean. He measured himself, against most of the people he met, as vaguely dirty in comparison. A few people were grubbier than him – Richard for instance was covered in a sort of clammy film that never went away. And Sticks. He was as sludgy as they come.

Out of the corner of his eye Daniel saw it. It wasn't the latest, not even digital, but it reminded him of the camera he'd had at art school. He picked it up, weighed it in his hand. It occurred to him that this was the first time since then that he'd held a camera. Five years? Six? Longer. He threaded the strap through his fingers and hung it around his neck. It felt good. He lifted the camera to his face. The man behind the counter came into focus. He was demonstrating a video camera to some myopic old boy, both of them bending over it close. Replacing the lens cap, Daniel stepped away from the counter and turned his back, the cloak of invisibility still around him as he walked towards the exit, his only traces the fingermarks smeared on the glass.

Four days later he has spent all his money. He's managed to stay on at the hostel because they've got used to his face and are probably assuming he'll settle up soon. Still, he has to sneak past the administration office when he

LEAVE BEFORE YOU GO 87

leaves in the morning and returns at night from another
fruitless day of job-hunting. Now he doesn't know how
he's going to eat. The bad dreams that fill his nights
have begun to encroach on the daylight hours. He sits
on a bench by a waterfall that looks like a giant urinal
and reads the paper he fished out of a rubbish bin. Sits
Vac is pretty slight. He marks a couple of possibilities
with his thumbnail and takes the paper with him to a
phone box.

He emerges five minutes later, the last of his phone
card used up and still unemployed. This feels like what
they call the end of the line. He stands outside a café,
staring at the stacks of coffee cups and piled-high pastries
through the window. The hardest thing about applying
for café work is having to go into these places with their
smells of coffee, hot milk and fresh bread.

'Sorry.' The girl behind the counter shakes her head.
'There's nothing at the moment. Hey,' she says as he
turns to go, 'didn't you come and ask a couple of days
ago?'

'No,' he says, looking her right in the eye. 'That
wasn't me.'

God knows who it is by the time he meanders back
towards the hostel that evening. He feels dizzy in an
almost pleasant way. It's a bit like being stoned. He
rounds the corner into the hostel's street and sees a
marked car parked outside the building. A little closer,
he can see that the markings say Police. He stops
walking. The policeman in the passenger seat looks up,
directly at him. A leaf falls from a nearby tree to the
ground. Another policeman walks out of the hostel door
and down the concrete steps towards the car. A normal
car drives past slowly, windows down, music blaring.

Daniel turns on his heel and walks quickly back down
the street, around the corner, around the next corner he
comes to, so on and so on in an unthinking zigzag
through the city.

He wanders like this for hours. Night falls, he wanders,
people go to dinner and meet in bars, he wanders, the
movies come out, he wanders. Buses stop running,
nightclubs close, couples wait at taxi ranks, he wanders.
Street cleaners brush the streets. Commercial cleaners
come and go from office blocks. His legs shake, his feet
are numb, he still wanders and wanders. The sky begins
to get light. First there's an almost imperceptible fading
of the indigo night. Then it's like in the movies when
black and white brightens into colour. A fresh blue
appears, washing the streets with an eerie glow. The
streetlights die out. He finds himself outside Central
Railway Station, staring up at its big broken old clock.
He walks through the gates and over the scarred slate
floor, through the empty, echoing station. There's a
smell of pigeons that reminds him of something – oh.
London. He might sit down for a minute, just here, just
leaning against this wall for a minute, because his legs
are quite sore and it'd be good to have a bit of a rest.
Just here where it smells of home and the floor is so
clean and cold. Just to have a think about what he's
going to do next.

When he wakes up it's to a clicking, rustling noise. He
opens his eyes. The station is full of people's legs walking
past him, in front of him, over there by the ticket booth,
coming from the platforms, going out the large entrance
doors. He moves his hands down to feel his own legs,
to bring them to life, and something flutters out of his

jacket sleeve on to the floor. A five dollar note. He
picks it up and jams it tight into his pocket. Standing
slowly, he realizes most of the commuters are openly
staring at him, as if he is a freak, a rarity. Well, he can't
blame them. He must look fucking rough. On the way
to the massive doors, not knowing where he'll go once
he hits daylight, he passes a photo booth. He glances at
the silvery mirror on the outside but cannot focus
enough to see his reflection there. To the right of the
booth is a wall of lockers for luggage. Seeing it gives
him an idea.

Sorted. Sort of. He snuck back to the hostel and made it
to his room without anyone getting a look at him,
stopping on the way at the bathrooms to splash his face
with water. Inside his room he slammed everything, his
few items of clothing, the stolen camera and the street-
map of the city, into his suitcase. Then he heard
footsteps clacking along the linoleum hall and froze.
They slowed down past his room and he could barely
breathe. He decided not to risk going back that way so
he chucked his suitcase out the window and jumped
after it, stumbling and twisting his knee a little bit as he
hit the ground. Yeah, he thought, this is just like a
movie. Only there are no guns. He got the suitcase back
to the railway station without getting caught up in a
high-speed car chase, or being seduced by an under-
world spy. Once his case was stashed in one of the
station lockers, he relaxed, as if it still contained heroin
and he had to get away from it. He left the station for
the second time that morning, feeling light-headed and
free. Now he's got nothing left to lose.

★

The railway station five dollars goes on coffee and a hunk of bread at some grungy café. He shoves the food down, his guts aching. His head aches too, either from the dark purple walls or the killingly loud guitar crashing out of the speakers. More luck — someone's left half a pack of Bensons on his table. He lights one and sifts through a pile of brochures. Fringe theatre advertisements, leather and tattoo shops, tarot card readers, piercings, the usual neohippie junk. Daniel blows out a thick stream of smoke, burns his tongue on the bitter coffee. He's stopped worrying about finding a job, or even where he's going to sleep that night. Nothing really matters. He's simply here in this moment, in this café, smoking this cigarette, breathing. The thrashy guitar screams to a halt and a song like he's never heard before fills the room. The woman's voice is sweet as anything, but not sugary, almost painful running up and down and around the minor notes.

Daniel reaches out to the waitress as she carries a stack of dirty plates past him. 'Excuse me. Do you know what this song is?'

She puts her head on one side, concentrating. Her dark curly hair reminds him of that girl Fiona. 'Nah,' she says. 'No idea. They might say in a minute.'

Daniel's confused. Then a DJ starts talking. The guy sounds really young. He sounds really stoned. Student radio.

'Hey, Josh man, listen to this.'

A skinny boy with an elongated face and tawny hair flicking up over his ears spins around in his chair, mock-DJ-style, and shoves a tape into the archaic stereo system in front of him. With a flourish he presses the play button. Josh closes his eyes, leaning in the door-

way, and nods slowly. Over the speakers a girl starts
singing, breathy and shy at first. The music changes
and her voice gets edge, builds, rages. It hurts to listen
to it.

Josh shudders. 'Man.' He stares wide-eyed at the boy.
'Who dumped her?'

'Dunno man. She's that westie chick.'

'Which one?'

'Uh—' He checks the tape. 'The young one.'

'Who's she with?'

'That guy Simon I think, with the tattoos, have you
seen him around?'

'What label.'

'Oh.' Skinny boy wrinkles his nose and bares his teeth
in concentration. 'Uh—'

Josh rubs his hand over his eyes. 'Does it say on the
tape?'

'Green Dog!' shouts the boy.

'OK, put it on the playlist.'

Grinning, Skinny pockets the tape and shuffles out of
the room like a lounge singer, breathing, 'Excellente,
excellente,' to himself. Josh winks and cocks a finger at
him.

'Excuse me.'

Josh starts and spins on his heel. Whoever saw him do
that, he hopes they recognized the ironic intent. The
intruder is a bloke about his age, not anyone Josh has
seen around here before. It must be raining out. He
doesn't look too good.

'Yeah?'

Daniel shifts his weight from one foot to the other.
'Is this the student radio station?'

'Yeah, it is.' The guy's English, or Scottish maybe.
Josh backs into the room. Daniel follows him.

'I was wondering, is there anyone here I can talk to about doing some work? Here?'

Josh sits down and motions for Daniel to do the same. Man he looks rough, smacked out or something. Skinnier even than Skinny.

'I'm Josh.' He sticks out his hand.

'Daniel.' They grip hands and nod at each other.

'Where you from?'

'London.'

'Oh yeah?' Josh nods again. He picks some cigarettes up from the table and shakes the packet at Daniel. 'Don't know whose these are. You want one?'

'Thanks.'

They light up. Daniel looks around the room. Hessian covered partition screens divide it up into three parts. The one they're in is like a makeshift reception, with a low table and plastic seats on either side of it. At one end of the room is an aluminium-framed window. Through the rain-spattered glass he can see clouds, and a palm tree of some sort, wet and swaying.

'What sort of work?'

Daniel shrugs and smiles. 'Anything really.'

'What's your experience?'

'Ah, been in a couple of bands. I used to work in a record shop, ah—'

'Done any radio work before? Any DJing?'

'Some DJ stuff, yeah.' Daniel blushes. He almost feels too desperate to lie. 'Yeah, in London. Done some clubs.'

'The thing is—'

There's a knock on the door. Three girls walk into the room.

'Hi, Josh,' says the one with the shaved head.

'Hi, Lee.'

One of the girls is extremely fat. She bulks into the space between Josh and Daniel. Her leggings are ruched up towards her inner thigh and the jersey she's wearing is misshapen and baggy in the front, under a huge shelf of bosom. 'We've booked this room for the Women's Show meeting.'

The guys exchange glances. Daniel stands up. The third girl, a blonde who looks about fifteen, smiles at Josh. 'Hi,' she whispers.

'Hi, Mary,' he says, and smiles back.

The fat girl plonks herself down in Daniel's vacated chair and begins rifling through her satchel. Calf muscle bulges through a hole in the seam of her leggings. She catches Daniel staring at her. 'It's Wimmin's Hour,' she says, emphasizing the 'i' sound in a pointed way.

'Come on, mate, I'll buy you a beer.' Josh steers Daniel out of the room, leaving the bald girl rearranging the chairs into a circle and the fifteen-year-old smiling after them.

The student bar is murky. It smells of old beer and sweat.

'Listen, I'm sorry, I haven't got any money—'

'I'll get these. Don't worry about it.'

The beer sloshes around Daniel's near-empty stomach, its bitterness abrasive and numbing at the same time. He notices Josh watching him and tries not to drink so fast. Josh buys several packets of crisps. He's strangely touched by the English guy's scrawny build, his bony hands and dark tired eyes. 'The thing is,' he starts again, 'nobody really gets paid here.' He smiles. 'I mean I do, I'm tragic enough to still hang around with kids and play at being the station manager. Some of the DJs do as well, but otherwise . . .'

'Mostly students?'

'Yeah, completely.'

'All right then.'

'But I mean, if you've got DJ experience—'

Daniel takes a mouthful of beer. He's sorted out the
music for a couple of friends' parties, nothing more than
that.

'Yeah,' he says, 'I have. I helped set up a pirate station
back in London. I've worked some clubs as well, easy
listening mostly—'

'Oh, yeah?'

'I mean it's a while since I've done it but I'm sure it'd
all come back.'

'Right.' Josh studies Daniel's face. He doesn't know
whether to believe him or not. 'Well, I'm sorry, eh, but
there's not really much going at the moment anyway.
You could give us your phone number though, and—'

To his utter horror Daniel feels his throat hardening
with tears. He clenches his fists under the table. The
danger subsides. 'These bands I was in, yeah, they were
pretty serious. I do know music, you know, the London
scene and that.' He wipes his hands on his jeans and
leans back in the chair, hoping for a confident effect.

'Yeah? Well perhaps we can work something out. I'll
have a look at the schedule, let you know.' Josh says this
as if it's the last word on the matter.

'OK, thanks.' Daniel exhales. He hopes this bloke
will stick around for a bit, it's just good to talk to
someone. He's been lonely.

'Where are you staying here?'

'I've been at a youth hostel – yeah.'

'Have they got a phone there?'

'No.' He thinks of that police car outside, the single
oak leaf twirling slow-motion to the ground, the police-

man looking up from his paper at Daniel as the other
one comes out of the hostel door. His bag of clothes,
everything he owns, in the locker at the railway station.
People use those lockers if they're catching trains, if
they're going somewhere. Where does he think he's
going, and with what? He stares at Josh. The guy's about
to finish his pint and leave him here.

It's never referred to again, the fact that Josh saw
Daniel break down at this point. It shocked and embarrassed them both. Josh had only seen men cry twice
in his life, if you didn't count on the rugby field. Once
was his brother when he failed School Certificate and
the other was that time his mother left home for a
month. His father was standing in the hallway facing the
closed front door, late one night, and Josh had come
down the stairs and startled him – he'd turned around –
Josh saw his terrible face. And now this, the time when
Daniel loses it. He's twisted sideways in his chair, hand
over his eyes, shoulders contracting every few seconds
and an intermittent choking sound coming from his
throat. Josh reaches across the table and sort of nudges
his arm.

'Sorry.' Daniel chokes again. He wipes his nose with
the back of his wrist and rubs his eyes like a sleepy child.
There is something very young about him, thinks Josh,
though they're probably the same age.

'All right, mate?'

'I'm really sorry.'

'Don't worry about it.'

'It's been a fucking weird few weeks.'

'Listen.' Josh checks his watch. 'I can't be fucked
doing any more work. You want to come back to my
place for a few beers? My girlfriend's at work,' he adds,
just to be clear.

'I – I can't.'

Josh shrugs. 'OK'

'The thing is—' Daniel flushes. 'I'm skint.'

'Don't worry about it,' Josh says again, and smiles. 'Beers are on me.'

When Lucy gets home from work she finds a drunk Josh and a drunker stranger drinking in her living room. Half of Josh's CD collection is scattered over the floor. The two guys gaze at her from their orange chairs, glazed and sheepish. She stands and looks at them, knowing she could go one of two ways here. She decides to laugh.

'Hi.'

'Hi, Lu. Uh, Lu, this is Dan. Daniel.'

'Hi.'

'Hi.'

'Beer?'

'Thanks.'

Josh staggers into the kitchen. Lucy and Daniel are left looking at each other while he crashes about. She tells herself that it's not her living room, it's their living room and that Josh can bring home whoever he likes. 'Do you work at the station?'

'No. Um—'

'Daniel might have a job there,' says Josh, coming back through with three beer bottles clutched between his knuckles. He holds one out to Lucy. 'We're going to sort something out.'

'That's nice.' She feels like a social worker in her own home.

'How's the battered wives' club?'

'Do you mind?' It's no use, she's in a foul mood. Josh

and this random bloke are going to think she's an uptight cow. They're probably right.

After a few beers, though, she is sorry for her earlier grumpiness. Josh is sweet really, he made them pasta, and that stray dog boy is all right even if he and Josh were rambling about stupid music all night long.

'I'd better go,' says Daniel, 'what's the time?' He doesn't know where he's going to – the railway station most likely. Sleeping rough doesn't seem so bad right now. He'll sort something else out tomorrow. 'Is it late?'

'Nah, we started early. Stay here if you like. We've got a spare room.'

Lucy tries to raise an eyebrow at Josh without Daniel noticing. He notices. 'No, it's OK I'll head off.'

'Where to? The hostel? It's too far to walk. I'll drop you off.'

'You will not,' says Lucy.

'I'm fine to drive.'

'Yeah, right.'

'It's my car.'

'And when it's your licence that's revoked it'll still be your car but you won't be able to drive it. And you can forget taxis because all your spare cash will go towards the fine and you can forget me chauffeuring you round because I'll be too busy saying I told you so. That's assuming you get breathalysed before you actually kill anyone.'

It's hard to say who is the most embarrassed – Lucy for her outburst, Josh for appearing hen-pecked in front of Daniel, or Daniel for being the cause of the row. He stands up. 'Really, I'll be fine. I've got a street map. Uh, thanks for everything.'

The phone rings. Lucy and Josh glare at each other. She straightens her shoulders and picks it up.

'Hello?' in a voice that betrays nothing. 'Ben, hi. You booked your tickets yet?'

Daniel hovers by the door.

'I'll see you out,' says Josh.

Ben is wittering about the aeroplane food benefits of flying as a vegetarian – 'but even better, I think, is vegan. Do you say vaygan or veegan?' – when Lucy hears the car rev up and gun down the street. Her eyes narrow. 'Cunt.'

'Pardon?'

'Nothing.'

Josh knows he's in trouble. Edging open the front door he makes up his mind. He won't be pussy-whipped. He's not going to stand for it. Lucy's reading in bed, a dangerous look in her eye. He sits on the corner, his head turned to one side so he doesn't breathe alcohol fumes over her.

'Two teenagers were killed by a drunk driver last night.'

'Lucy, listen—'

'Who's your new friend?'

'Well. I.' He lowers his voice. 'I feel sorry for the guy.'

'Josh.' Lucy puts her book down and folds her arms. 'Why are you whispering.'

'Well, this is the thing. Uh. He doesn't have anywhere to stay.'

Lucy groans.

'I mean, he was going to sleep at the train station.'

'Where are you hiding him? In the car?'

'Well, is it OK?'

'You have to make up the spare bed.'

'Sure.'

'You're still a cunt for driving.'

'And you live with me so—'

'That makes me a cunt's cunt, I know.' Lucy fails to keep the smile off her face. Josh crouches down beside her so he's in the line of the smile, then stretches forward to kiss her cheek. 'Huh,' she says. 'Now fuck off and do your good Samaritan number, I'm going to sleep.'

Kate catches up with the latest. 'What, just like that?'

'Just like that. I mean, it's not enough' — Lucy stretches the phone cord, pushes the common room door shut and speaks as quietly as possible — 'not enough that I work in a bloody women's bloody refuge all day, now my home's a refuge for stray bloody men.'

'Do you think that's why he did it?'

'Maybe.'

'What's this guy like?'

'Christ only knows.' Lucy's voice rises. 'We don't even know his last name.'

'Jesus, Lu, he—'

'Could be an axe-wielding psychopath, I know.'

'Can't you put your foot down?'

Lucy sighs. 'He's got nowhere to go. We've got the spare room.'

'That's my room.'

'You've been usurped.'

'How long for?'

'Till he gets some money, I suppose.'

'Hey, Lu—'

'I don't know.'

'You don't know what?'

'If he's what you'd call good looking.'

'Well, is he my type?'

'You mean selfish and manipulative? Can't say yet. He doesn't talk much.'

Daniel never has talked much, not even when he was a teenager, not even when he first fell in love. His first serious girlfriend was called Cath. Her overriding trait was in fact a lack of seriousness, although this wasn't apparent the first time he saw her. He was on the tube, seventeen years old, going home to his south-west London suburb from his summer job at the record shop. It was a Friday.

What would usually happen on a Friday is that he'd get home, walk into the kitchen, open a can of baked beans. He'd eat it standing up trying to avoid being touched by his mother's flabby arms as she fussed around him and blathered on about, Why don't you heat it, shall I make you some toast? Then he'd shut the door to his room and lock it with the metal hook. She didn't like the hook either. What if you have a complete collapse in there, she'd say, we won't be able to get in the door. It was years since he'd looked her in the eye, she'd got used to that, but this latest trick of his, not talking to her at all, still hurt. She supposed he'd soon get his own place. It'd be a relief, it really would. She'd only have one silent man to deal with instead of two. For now, the only noise Daniel'd make would be music coming from his room. The young mother next door would complain again. Daniel could be found standing on his bed playing air guitar, eyes shut, the single light bulb sending warmth to his face like he imagined it would feel from the blasting stadium lights. Fluff on the

stylus became the roar of the crowd. They wanted him
– oh yeah – he bent one knee and gave it the full
winding motion, full of emotion, thrashing the crowd
into a frenzy – and the needle would hit that scratch in
the record, bounce and twitch – it was no good, it was
over.

Then he'd slap on some aftershave though he only
needed to scrape a razor over his top lip twice a week.
Richard and whoever else'd be down the pub. They'd
drink until closing time and go for a kebab, stagger
around, maybe go to a club or chase up some girls or
back to a mate's if his parents were away. Sometimes
they'd go drinking in another part of London, but then
you had to wait hours for a night bus and Daniel hated
them, hated the urine and vomit and stares. The truth
was he didn't feel safe on a night bus, he felt sort of
frightened. One time he'd been threatened with a knife.
So he'd go through the usual palaver trying to persuade
Richard and whoever else to stay local for the evening.
More often than not it worked. Daniel would wake up
on Saturday morning with his sweat-stained T-shirt still
on, glue in his ears and a taste like sulphur and ash in his
mouth.

The Friday he met his first serious girlfriend was different. He saw her as soon as he squeezed into the carriage.
She was sitting down on the edge of a double seat. Her
facial features were small and hard. She had the look of
someone concentrating on music but she wasn't wearing
a Walkman. Daniel didn't know why he stared at her.
No good reason except she was the only other person
under thirty within sight. Then two stops later another
girl pushed her way through the crush, saw the mean-

faced girl and squealed. Daniel watched, fascinated by
the way the seated girl's face broke open into a wide
smile. She became electric with life, laughing and
chatting to her friend, and he felt somehow cheated. It
wasn't fair that this charge of energy hadn't happened
earlier, hadn't been for him. He looked at her teeth and
mouth moving small and precise and knew that he
wanted to have that effect on her. He wanted to change
her from closed to open like that. He wanted those
glittering eyes focused directly onto his.

Something, it's impossible to say what, was smiling on
Daniel that day. Just before the next stop the girls stood
to leave. He felt a pang of desperation. It crossed his
mind to follow them out, but then what? He wasn't that
much of a freak, not then. Later, he'd think nothing of
following a girl out of a supermarket or a nightclub or a
movie theatre. Once he did that even after he'd bought
the ticket but the anonymous girl in question wasn't
having any of it. She gave him the brush-off and he
missed the first fifteen minutes of *Blade Runner* – *the
Director's Cut* for nothing. Seventeen-year-old Daniel
was not capable of that. He looked on at the girls
hoisting their bags over their shoulders and standing
right next to the doors – the hard-faced girl was
bouncing up and down on the balls of her feet – in
something very close to despair. And then there was the
announcement. Due to a security alert passengers were
requested to alight from the train and make their way
out of the station as quickly as possible. They were asked
to please use the usual exits – replacement buses would
be available from outside the station. Daniel managed to
keep up with the two girls as they jostled through the
suits. He nearly lost them on the stairs – there they were
– sprinted after them up the escalator and then a miracle

happened. The hard-faced girl, the one he liked, turned
to him as she was about to go through the ticket stile,
stuck one bony hip out at an angle and said, 'Do you go
to our school?'

Later, she told him that she knew he didn't go to their
school but she wanted to talk to him and couldn't think
of anything else to say. She knew that he wanted to talk
to her too so it didn't matter. She told him she liked his
looks and that they were meant to be together because
it was on the underground that she'd broken up with
her last boyfriend. He was older, he was a trainee
stockbroker in the City. They'd had a brilliant time, he
was always buying her things and that. Then they were
on the tube one day, they'd been shopping or something, she couldn't remember, didn't matter, and it was
a Saturday and it was really packed with all the shoppers.
They were trying to fight their way on to the carriage,
had to get back for the football or something stupid, and
he got one leg on the train and started going on in this
nerdy grown-up voice, Could you move along the
carriage, please, could you please move down. He
sounded a right git and at first she thought he was
joking, taking the piss, but then she looked at his face
and saw he was serious. And that's when she knew she
had to dump him. He was just too uncool.

Daniel lived for two years in awe of this girl. The first
time they met up by themselves he held his hand out to
her and she flicked her ash into his open palm. This
short hot gesture sent a shock wave through him. She
wore little white shirts and jeans and sandshoes with no
socks. Her hair was cut in a no-haircut sort of a way
with a long fringe that sometimes covered her eyes.

They hid behind the strands of hair, straight and dark with glints of yellow light. Daniel was in love. The first girlfriend introduced him to cigarettes and vegetarianism. She listened to girly punk music. She liked to say she read Russian novels but every time Daniel saw her open her second-hand copy of *Anna Karenina* it was to the same place. Before she'd read half a page she would interrupt herself, light another cigarette and let her gaze drift off into space. They spent a lot of afternoons in her parent's bed. More than once they were woken up by the sound of her mother's key turning in the front door lock. She didn't seem at all concerned by their flushed faces and rumpled school uniforms. She called her daughter 'my little sister' and wore much the same clothes. The mother played French records and smoked a thinly rolled mixture of tobacco and marijuana. The only food in their fridge was the occasional limp celery stalk or tub of mouldy cottage cheese. There's nothing for me to rebel against, the first girlfriend complained to Daniel. She lets me do whatever I like. The only way I could get through to her would be if I turned really square. She shuddered, in a theatrical way.

Daniel had been wary of letting her come to his parents' flat. He thought it would be likely to put her off, the flat and his parents. The first time she visited he met her at the newsagent's on the corner. Standing in its chill, meat-smelling shade, he just about lost his nerve. All the way along the littered street, past the drycleaner's and the pebble-dash wall of the post office, he was on the verge of bottling out. It was with great reluctance that he took her hand and led her up the flimsy carpeted stairs to his parents' wood veneer door. But, 'Cool,' she said as they walked in, 'it's so *authentic*. Hey. Is that a

door snake? Oh my God.' She fingered the edge of the
doily covering the television. 'This is so – *real*.' Her eyes
narrowed, glittering behind her fringe. 'Let me see your
room.'

It was after they'd been going out nearly a year that she
discovered a pile of his dad's anti-immigrant pamphlets
in the cupboard where the videos were kept. One of
them had a swastika on the front.

'Fuck me. What is this?'

'Oh. Uh, my dad—'

'These are his? Your father's a fascist?'

Daniel had never thought of it quite like that. He'd
never thought of it much at all. Apart from the pamphlets, politics didn't really enter the house. His father had
made a hobby of bigotry the way some men made a
hobby of model-making and, like some men, he preferred to guard his hobby jealously, away from the
domestic sphere. Racism created his social life, his
definition of self. It became a great deep hole in which
to pour all his miseries and confusion. It did not make
him articulate. It did not even make him loud. 'Fascist'
seemed so dramatic, so shiny-leather. Daniel found it
hard to equate with his saggy, stick-legged father. But
he supposed that she was right, that that was the word.

'Well, uh. Yeah.'

'Oh my God. We've got to get you out of here.
Come and stay at mine.'

He didn't know if he wanted to or not. She moved
closer towards him and pushed her lower body into his.

'Daniel? Does your father know any genuine skin-
heads?'

★

So the first girlfriend taught him not just to ignore his parents, but to despise them. She also taught him not to for God's sake mention anything about his homelife in public. More than once, though, at her mother's house, he overheard her telling some visitor an embellished version.

'Daniel's father's high up in the BNP. *Really* bad. They were trying to recruit Daniel. He stood up to them of course, took a couple of kickings too.' She'd shake her head, eyes sharp like jet. 'He was on the front line.'

He didn't correct her. He never corrected her. He hardly ever spoke.

It was the first girlfriend who talked him into applying for art college. She was convinced that he would succeed, what with his background and his looks. When the only place he got was at a small school up north it took them both by surprise.

'I can't believe none of the others wanted you,' she said, her face hard, hands on her sixteen-year-old hips.

'I can't believe that one did,' said Daniel. He paused. 'It means I have to leave London.'

She looked at him as if he was thick. 'I know it does. Well, you have to go. You've got to.'

'What about—'

'Oh, I'll be all right. I'll be fine. I'll just get another boyfriend.'

Daniel had laughed but it wasn't a joke. On a Friday night, three weeks before he was due to go, he waited outside the record shop for her to meet him as she always did. When, after an hour, she hadn't shown up, he telephoned her house. Her tone was the vocal equivalent of that pinched, shut expression he'd seen on her the first day.

'Sorry. There's someone here. Give me a ring tomorrow maybe.'

Look, she said to him finally, a few days later, she didn't want to be alone. He was going away – what about her? Was she just supposed to pine for him? No, Daniel wanted to say, and Yes, but again he said nothing. He collected his clothes and his records from her mother's house and never went back there. He was glad to be leaving now, glad not to have to witness his first girlfriend walking around the local shops with the student teacher he'd heard she was seeing. And glad to be leaving the home that oppressed and disgusted him. As well as the relief, though, he felt mostly confusion. Confusion about the first girlfriend and whether he'd hurt her or she'd hurt him. Confusion about the course he was starting on and if it was anything he really wanted. And more than anything, confusion about exactly who he was now supposed to be.

That first night at Josh and Lucy's, Daniel has trouble sleeping. The sshh of wind through the bushes outside reminds him of camping holidays with his aunt and uncle when he was a child. Their lightly breathing bulk silhouetted against the canvas in the early mornings when he'd crawl out of his puptent, escaping its rank smell and warm air, looking at their tent and wondering what he would find to do that day. Sleeping under canvas always unnerved him – the thin tenuousness of the layer between the unsuspecting sleeper and the wide

world of nature. Something of this exposed feeling has
been with him since arriving in this country. The tall
downtown buildings seem flimsy, fragile, as if a storm
could flatten them or an earthquake shake them effort-
lessly into the sea. There's something about the wooden
homes of the suburbs, as well, that makes it easy to
imagine them slipping back into a gully or collapsing
inwards like so many houses of cards. There they stand,
separate and alone on their little plots of garden. There's
space around everything here, the buildings, the people,
the hills, the clouds. People sit two seats apart on the
buses; they pass one another with no danger of colliding
on the wide footpaths. These footpaths, and the roads,
sit lightly on the earth, as if they've just been painted
over the land and could be peeled off at any time. It's
very far from the flat he left in east London, the footsteps
on the ceiling and music through the floor, the trains
beating past the window, the street of people with funny
shuffling walks. He feels released, somehow, from the
crush of the tube and the exhaust fumes and the beery
salty pubs, from the wall-to-wall clubs with their constant plunges in and out of darkness, from the queues at
the supermarket, the confusion of magazines and newspapers and community rags at the newsagent's. He's
been flung out of this clutter, he's lost everything at last,
the process of shedding is nearly complete here in this
sparse, reduced world.

'Stay if you like,' Josh tells him in the morning. Lucy's
long gone to work. 'I mean, you don't have to leave.'

　　'Thanks,' Daniel says, 'but I can't.'

　　'Where are you going to go then?'

　　Daniel shrugs. 'I might be able to get a job today,
then I could stay at the hostel again.'

'What if you don't get a job? You've got no money,
have you?'

He shakes his head. 'That's the thing, I couldn't pay
you any rent.'

'Ah, fuck that. Come in to the station, have a look
around. I'm sure we can sort something out.'

'Really?'

'Look, would you stop worrying.' Josh burps, to show
he isn't only a soft bastard. He grabs the car keys from
the table and stands up. 'Are you coming or aren't you?'

SIX   When was the first time we met?
Kate imagines herself wondering
later. Maybe she and Daniel will say that to each other at
some random point in the future. Maybe they'll tell the
story of their meeting to friends, to their children even.
Kate projects herself twenty years forward, pretending to
cast her mind back to the late nineteen nineties. Yes, she
thinks, seeing herself Ginny's age only better looking and
more wise. Yes, in those days she'd been mucking
around doing nothing for too long, before she really
discovered where she was going. It was just after Daniel
had arrived – the end of a hot wet summer – oh, not hot
by today's standards. And back then you could still go to
the beach. That's right, they first met through Lucy
and— Who was that guy she used to live with? Josh, yes.
That's when it was. On that picnic.

Come round. That's what Lucy had said. Come round,
we're going on a picnic. Is that new guy there? Kate
asked. Do I need to shave my legs? Jesus, said Lu, do
what you like. He's not a honey. Right, thought Kate,
but you think Josh is a honey. So. She wore jeans.

'Hi,' she called. 'It's me.'
The door was open. She swung into the living room,
calling Hello-o. 'Are you in the garden?' she said, turning
in a circle. As she completed the revolve a figure appeared
in the doorway to the kitchen. She looked at it.

'Hi,' it said, seeming to shrink back into the other room. 'They're at the shop.'

'Oh. I'm Kate,' she called after it, but it had disappeared into the kitchen. She swayed a little bit on the spot, unsure whether or not to follow. It looked like the guy from the bookstore, the guy from the movie theatre, the shoplifter, the weirdo. As she took a step towards the kitchen he came back out. Definitely the same man. Skinny, brown hair, eyelashes. In his hand was a newly lit cigarette.

'Hi,' she said again. She found herself smiling. He sent a half-smile back before his eyes skittered away to the middle distance. 'You know,' she ventured, 'I've seen you around.'

He didn't say anything, just took a drag on his cigarette. Then he shook his head. 'I just got here.'

He had one of those English voices that New Zealand indie bands used to try to imitate when Kate was at high school. 'Well, I've seen you,' she said again. 'Downtown and stuff. In that bookshop.'

Something crossed over his eyes and then he shook his head again, looked up and smiled at her. 'I don't go to bookshops. Not much of a reader.'

'When did you get here?' She had to keep the annoyance out of her voice.

'Just a few days ago.'

'But—'

'Hi, hi.' Josh and Lucy pushed through the door with plastic bags full of groceries. 'Hi, darl. We've got a feast. Have you guys met? Daniel Kate Kate Daniel. OK let's get in the car. Hang on, I've got to get some knives. Oh there's one, sticking out your back. Ha ha.' Etcetera. It was the Josh'n'Lucy show.

This is weird, thought Kate. She knows something

about that guy Daniel that nobody else knows. Does he know that she knows? Does he recognize her? Is he lying? He was behaving as if he'd never seen her before in his life. It made her feel invisible. Part of the wallpaper, a ghost, a hidden camera. She was absent to the room, in a fog, helping Lucy pack paper plates and make a thermos of tea, nodding to something Josh said in a distracted way, her eyes in the same distant trajectory as the stranger's.

'Hey, Josh,' Daniel said, 'someone called Mary phoned. Just a few minutes ago.'

'OK,' Josh said. 'Thanks.'

'Who's Mary?' called Lucy from the kitchen. 'Your new girlfriend?'

'Ha ha,' Josh called back. 'She's the new, ah, weather thingy.'

And then they were piling into the car and ready to go when Lucy remembered her cigarettes. As she opened the driver's door to go back into the house, Josh jerked his head towards her and said, 'Be quick, I don't know why the fuck you can't just get some on the way.'

She walked around the car and bent down to his window. 'Relax,' she said. 'There's no rush.'

As she sauntered towards the house, Josh mumbled something like, Oh for *fuck's* sake. Kate didn't know where to look when, just as Lucy disappeared through the front door, he slammed his fist down on the car's horn.

What Daniel would remember about meeting Kate was the experience of sitting with three people he didn't know in a car. The feeling of being picked up like a toy and tossed from child to child, looked after but never really looked at. He was a lost soldier that had been found on the pavement and then popped into some kid's pocket, taken along for the ride. That Kate girl freaked him out a little bit. She gave the impression that she might find it interesting to take him apart if she got him away from the other kids, to see what he was made of and how exactly he worked. This was something he wanted to avoid. They, of course, wound up sitting together in the back seat of Josh's car, the picnic basket and a folded-up rug between them. Lucy drove, fast. 'Yell out if you see any speed cameras.'

'You could always slow down,' suggested Kate.

'It wobbles under one-twenty.'

'Speed freak.'

'Hey, uh.' Daniel cleared his throat. 'What's bungee jumping like?'

'Dunno,' said Josh, 'never been.'

'Nor me.'

'Me neither.'

'Oh,' Daniel said.

'A guy from the station did it and burst all the blood vessels in his eyes.'

Daniel tried to picture this but it was Sticksy's eyes he saw, half closed but not blinking, smoky and mean. His top lip went cold. There was something bad about the Sticksy situation. Daniel knew it was irrational but he was frightened of being tracked down.

'Apple?' Kate was holding one out to him, a small smile on her face, almost a smirk, her eyes very green. A rectangular block of sunlight slanted in through the car window, across her face and down her shoulder and arm, lighting the skin up a pale bright yellow. Hair, eyes, skin, fruit – she was a green and gold corner flashing under the shadows of the trees they were racing past.

'Thanks.'

She smiled again, showing her gappy teeth, and turned
to look out the window.

'Yes, thanks, Kate,' said Josh, thrusting his arm back
over the passenger seat.

'Oh, sorry.' She shoved an apple into his hand in an
over-energetic way. 'Lu?'

The motorway took them past flat-housed suburbs, a
glimpse of grey water, the peculiar wide low vista of
Auckland, scattered under its sprawling sky. Daniel
gazed out the window at the freshly washed view and
tried to think of nothing, only sometimes looking down
at Kate's knee swaying with the movement of the car,
towards him, away, towards him and away. Lucy turned
off the motorway. The interior of the car darkened as
they drove slowly along the twisting road cut through
dense layers of native plants. Sinuous vines were
wrapped tight around parched white tree trunks, enormous ferns fringed the road, broad-leafed palms and
scrubby bushes pushed up against each other towards the
small shafts of light. The green was not an English green,
not soft and reassuring. From the lowness of the car he
could no longer see the sky, just green filling the
window frame, an emphatic, deep navy-green broken
only by the bone and charcoal bark of the trees.

They drove in silence for about ten minutes, up a slowly
graded hill, around its curved side and out of the
thinning bush. Houses appeared at intervals, wooden
and broken-looking, just visible through the sparse trees.

'You could get a place out here,' said Josh, 'be at one
with Nature.'

'No, thanks,' Daniel said, and tacked a laugh on the end to disguise how frightening he found the idea.

Kate pointed to a dog kennel. 'How about there?'

'Or there?' Josh gestured to an orange plastic skip turned over on its side.

'Maybe I'll just sleep in the bushes back there.'

'Winter's coming. You could build a bivouac.'

'A what?'

'It's a shelter thingy.'

'A shelter thingy?' Josh half-turned back towards Kate. 'Girl Guide were you?'

'Got kicked out of Brownies.'

'Nobody gets kicked out of Brownies.'

'I set fire to the mushroom.'

'The sea!' Lucy said, her first words in nearly half an hour. They all looked down between their hill and the next, to a triangle of silver that grew larger as the car began its descent towards the beach. Daniel could see the water darken and swell, buckle and break on to sand that was black as asphalt.

Surf. Dark sand. Dense bush. It might just have been the steep incline and the bumps of the unsealed beach road that made Daniel feel queasy. But it might not. As they clambered out of the car, clouds melted away from the sun and they stretched, turning closed eyes towards its heat. Daniel stood a few feet away, staring at the slam and suck of the sea. This place was like a black and white negative, like another planet.

They spread a tartan rug over a sheltered spot by the dunes and unpacked the food. Lucy lay back on the sand, arms over her head.

'This makes you believe in God, doesn't it,' she said to the sky.

'No,' said Josh.

She swivelled round towards Daniel. 'Were you brought up religious?'

His mother had gone to church every Sunday, and sometimes he used to hear her mumbling prayers behind her closed bedroom door. 'No,' he said after a bit. 'Not at all.'

'Me neither,' said Kate, passing around sandwiches. 'At primary school we had to draw God once. I had such a clear idea of how I wanted him to look, all misty and old, like a cloud. He came out looking like Santa Claus.'

'Remember that time I had Christmas in Tokyo?' said Lucy. 'With Ben? This department store had a massive decoration of Santa on a cross. Crucified.'

Josh yawned. 'It's commercial bullshit anyway, isn't it.'

'Yeah, you're right. I'd better not give you any presents this year, we don't want to corrupt—'

'Hey, did none of us grow up religious?' Kate asked, moving her gaze away from Daniel.

There was a pause. The waves sounded like traffic. 'I went to Carols by Candlelight once,' said Josh.

'Me too. No, I'm thinking of Bonfire Night.'

'My mother was a Catholic,' said Lucy, 'but not very seriously and then Dad left her, so . . . Divorce kind of put paid to that. I believed in God for a while though, when I was a kid. I wanted to be a nun.'

'Really?' asked Kate. 'A nun?'

'You might as well be a nun, Kate,' said Josh. 'Poverty and celibacy being your strong points.'

She threw a plastic cup at his head, still looking at

Lucy. 'What do you mean you believed in God for a
bit? Why stop?'

Lucy wrinkled her nose and pursed her lips to one
side. 'Oh, I don't know.'

'And you don't believe in anything now?'

She lit a cigarette. 'I suppose something. Not a
Christian god, or any organized religion kind of god.
But a greater power. Of some sort.'

'Yeah,' said Josh, 'money.'

'Why are you such an arsehole today? No, it's— I
don't really know how to talk about it. Some kind of
cosmic force, some pattern – it sounds crap I know.'

'Yeah,' said Josh, 'it does.'

'I believe,' Kate intervened, 'that we're all controlled
by aliens. We're an alien experiment that's gone horribly
wrong, and they're sitting up there on the Southern
Cross having a great bloody laugh at us.' She made a po-
face and put on a cod English accent: 'Are those
Earthlings still alive? Goodness me.' Then, 'Sorry,' she
said to Daniel. 'I don't know why but aliens in the
movies always talk like that.'

He thought about it. 'We're the villains, I suppose.
You know what I mean?'

'The great colonizing bastards,' said Josh.

'Do you believe in anything then?' Kate was still
looking at him.

He shook his head, smiling. Jesus, she thought, he
looks amazing when he smiles. Like he could get away
with anything. 'Science,' he said, 'DNA.'

'There's got to be more to it than that. Doesn't there?
I mean, we can't only be these little atoms or molecules
or whatever just mindlessly reacting against each other,
just chemistry—'

Josh snorted. 'Science major?'

'OK, I don't know the right words but don't you think? There has to be something else?'

'This,' said Lucy, nodding towards the sea. 'I don't want to sound like a hippie, but all of this, maybe there's God in this.'

'God's Own?' said Josh. 'More like, God knows.'

When it got colder they went for a walk. Lucy and Kate headed off down the long stretch of beach towards the blowholes, Josh and Daniel trailing after them. Nobody else was there. Kate dragged a stick of driftwood behind her. After a while she stood still near the water's edge, digging a small hole with her stick. She watched it fill from the bottom with seawater, scraped the burial mound beside it back in and stirred it again, like a six-year-old preparing mud pies. Lucy held three shells in her hand, an orange one striped with cream, a pale blue spiral and a fragment of mother of pearl, like a fingernail. In the clothes shop she worked in there were shells and stones lined along a mantelpiece as decoration. It was in fashion to collect objects from your Sunday forays into Nature and display them in a whimsical way in your home. It was supposed to say something about you and your lifestyle. Lucy dropped the shells back onto the sand and continued up the beach, seeing feathers, pieces of worn glass, shells, wood. A sand-lined plastic bag blew over her feet and she bent to pick it up. Kate ran over to her.

'What's that?'

'Bit of rubbish.'

'Eco-warrior.'

'I know, I know.'

'Josh is in a good mood.'

Lucy sighed. 'I don't know. I think it's the job. Maybe he's premenstrual.'

'It's nice out here.'

They walked slowly, looking out to the horizon, a black line between the pearly sea and the darkening sky. Josh and Daniel caught up with them, struggling against the wind that had suddenly come up from every direction. Kate jumped up and down on the spot, her hair blown all over her face.

Racing towards the caves, sand rising underfoot, a wall of dark rock rushing into vision, the blasted hole in the wall like a promise and beyond it the crash of water, more water, lifting to smash against the cave's inside and drain away. A moment's silence – waiting – and the mass of trapped water hurled against the rock again, as if to beat its way out. Out at sea the surface of the water was stretched taut, heaving up towards the mottled, bruise-coloured sky. There was going to be a storm and it was going to be brutal. Now they could all see it, a blurred wall of rain moving solidly, swiftly into shore. The four of them looked at each other and a current of adrenalin raced between them like electricity. Kate felt Lucy fumble for her hand. Josh had a cigarette halfway to his lips and Daniel – Daniel's face was open, alert, alive – when sheet lightning whipped across the scene and caught them, frozen in a photograph that burnt this image into each of their memories for ever. A wave flared up and cracked against the cave like a starter's gun. They turned and ran over the unsteady sand into relentless bullets of rain.

Something strange happened that night. Maybe it was considered strange only by Daniel. He didn't like it. They were taking turns in the bathroom, showering to get warm. Lucy was in there and Josh had just run

through to the bedroom to dress. A bottle of red wine
sat in the middle of the living-room floor. Kate sat next
to it, an old jumper of Josh's pulled over her knees, her
hair darkened from the rain. She nodded along to the
music on the stereo. In the quiet bits they could hear
the slow drum of water on the corrugated iron roof.
Daniel lit a cigarette. He wished she wasn't there, he
didn't know why. He just didn't want – to be presented
with a package. The room smelled of wet wool and
smoke. His eyelids felt heavy. His neck was bending
slowly forward when the phone rang, startlingly loud.
What time was it?

'Get that?' shouted Josh.

Kate and Daniel looked at each other. She moved her
arm as if to get up but he was already there.

'Hello?'

A pause.

'Hello?'

The line was silent. He thought he heard a fizz, the
light crackle of a long distance delay. He held the
receiver to his ear for one more second then quickly put
it down. Kate was watching him from the floor. He
shrugged, tongue pressed hard to the roof of his mouth,
arms hanging by his sides in an uncomfortable way. He
was acting natural. Behind him, Josh balanced on one
foot, pulling on his socks.

'Who was it?'

'No one. Crank call.'

'Oh.' The corners of Josh's mouth pulled down.
'Well, they'll ring back. Or they won't.'

And then Kate had gone on to talk about something
and Lucy got out of the shower and got dressed, and
Daniel took his towel from where it lay crumpled on
the spare bed and locked the bathroom door. He stood

under the water and could not get warm. The noise of
the rain combined with the shower and covered the
sound of his voice saying, softly, 'Oh fuck. Oh fuck.'
'Oh fuck,' over and over while he leaned his head
against the tiles and rolled it from side to side. The water
ran cold. 'Oh fuck,' muffled into his towel. 'Oh fuck.'
He dragged the bunched-up towel down his face, under
his chin and held it to his throat. His head was fuzzy in
the steamed-up mirror. 'Richard,' he said, then, 'Tony.'
Then, 'Fuck. Sticks.'

The distraction of Daniel's arrival on the scene has not
helped Kate sort out her lack-of-career troubles. Not
that she fancies him or anything, but it's something new
to think about, the mysterious stranger. Her job still
sucks but she can't seem to concentrate on what she
might do instead. Besides, Janice has come back to work.
It's nice talking to Janice, a large teenage girl who often
does the same shift at the cinema as Kate. She's back
after a three-day absence. She'd gotten into a fight, had
a couple of ribs cracked and her jaw knocked out of
whack. Kate's listening to the story as they change into
their bumpy-textured pink polyester uniforms. Janice
talks without hardly opening her mouth. It's not just
because of the jaw – this is how she talks normally,
mouth ajar, head tilted back a little. It gives her a sneery
look.
    'So I've got to eat through this straw? Like only soups
and that. McDonald's thick-shakes I'm allowed but they
hurt my teeth. Too cold.'
    'They're made with lamb fat,' says Kate.
    'No bull? Yummy though. Anyway, that bitch that
come at me's still in the hospital I think.'
    'Janice. No way.'

'Oh, not from me,' she laughs. 'She walked right out into the street and this car run her over. She's all right. They put a plate in her head.'

'Oh my God.' Janice's huge pink hands doing up the plastic buttons on her uniform look meaty and very capable. 'How'd the fight start?'

Janice tchs out a breath. 'She reckoned I was gawking at her boyfriend. As if! Only because he was such a dog.'

Kate thinks of a question she's never asked Janice before. 'How old are you?'

'Seventeen nearly. In June.'

'Oh.'

Janice smears on frosted blusher and brushes her feathered hair. She catches Kate looking at her in the mirror. Janice is one of those girls who'd be on the top netball team at school, fast and solid with a chest pass that'd come at you like a cannonball. One of the girls who'd play touch rugby as well, only 'touch' would mean 'shove face down in mud'. She'd have a couple of friends just like her. They'd lean against the low, pitted stone wall of the school gates, smoking Winfields within full view of the teachers, taking one last drag and chucking the butts behind them without bothering to look. Then they'd step, as one, on to the school grounds with a noisy, public exhalation of blue smoke, Come and fucking try it on their faces. Kate had been at school with girls like that. She knew to stay on the right side of them.

'So what happened? Did she just come up and thump you, or what?'

Janice shook her head in a proud, bored way. 'Nah. She come up to me, right, and starts yelling. All this bullshit? About I'd better keep my eyes off of her man,

and I was asking for it, and all this.' She giggles. 'Do you
think we've got time for a fag?'

The black digital clock with white numerals flips over
from 10.28 to 10.29. 'Yeah, sure. Go on.'

Janice lights a ciggie and Kate hauls herself up to sit
on the table, swinging her heels. Janice's already small
eyes narrow. 'I mean she was screaming, right, just about
going to burst my eardrum—'

'Hang on where was this?'

'Where?' She looks at Kate as if she doesn't want any
interruptions. 'Muzza's.'

'Is that a club?'

Janice's chin juts forward. 'Yeah,' she says with a rise
in her voice, as if she can't believe Kate has to ask.
'Downtown?'

'Anyway, so—'

'Anyway.' Janice takes a suck on her cigarette and
blows the smoke up to the ceiling, jaw sliding from left
to right and back again as she does so. 'She was really
giving me a pain, right, I mean, stupid cow. So I says to
her, if you don't shut your stupid face I'm going to shut
it for you. And she says,' Janice mimics the girl's scared
high voice, 'Don't you threaten me bitch, my boyfriend's got a knife, he'll fucking do you – so I slap her
one across the face right, to belt her up. Then' – Janice
smiles again – 'I tell her her boyfriend's a fucking homo
and he'd better watch out because Ray's going to get
him—'

Who's Ray, Kate nearly asks, but stops herself.

' – and she's screaming at me all the time, then she
pushes me so I give her a really good shove against the
wall and then we're having this massive scrap.'

'What about her boyfriend?'

Janice looks at the clock. 'Ray got on to it. Took the guy outside. That's when the stupid bitch runs after them and under the car.' Breath escapes from between Janice's teeth, like she's trying to titter. 'It was bullshit about the knife anyway. He didn't have one. So.'

It's after 10.30. They quickly grind their cigarettes out and run up the stairs to the confectionery booth. As she's loading popcorn into the machine Janice says to Kate, 'Hey. She was asking for it, eh.'

Kate nods. 'Yeah,' she says. 'I know.'

And she stands in the half-night, half-day usher's area with her torch, showing the few viewers in, and then waits at the back of the cinema, her eyes on the wavering screen and her mind on the stranger.

Not everyone is pleased to have the distraction of Daniel in their lives. When Josh lets himself into the house, wincing as the front door slams behind him, he is surprised to find Lucy reading in the living room.

'I thought you'd be asleep.'

'Couldn't. Where've you been?'

'Oh, this gig on the Shore. New garage band.'

'Oh. I was kind of in the mood for going out tonight. Any good?'

'Bit shit. You didn't miss much.' He sits down on the couch. 'Good evening?'

'I've been here all night. With him.' She jerks her head in the direction of the spare room.

'Oh, yeah.'

'Josh, he's a bit weird. I mean he's fine, but—' Lucy tucks her feet up underneath her. 'Is he any good at the station?'

'Well, ah. He hasn't actually done anything yet. Just

been cruising around, getting to know everyone, seeing how things operate.'

'So he hasn't been DJing?'

'He was going to the other day.'

She raises her eyebrows and nods, waiting.

'And, uh, the equipment broke down before he started, remember I told you, we were off-air for half an hour. Had to get Mike to come in and sort it out, and once he was there he just started his show early.'

'Oh.'

'But you know, he's done it before in London.'

'He says.'

Josh laughs. 'Why would he make it up?'

'I don't know. Do you want a cup of tea?'

In the kitchen, they whisper. Daniel's room is right next door. Josh stands beside the open fridge, staring into it.

'I was thinking,' Lucy starts, 'that maybe he could stay at Frank's.'

'Why?'

'What do you mean why? Frank's apartment's completely empty. And we live here.'

Josh starts to move things around from shelf to shelf. 'I don't know, Frank doesn't know him, maybe we shouldn't put a stranger in there.'

'But he's a stranger living with us. What's the difference?'

'Well, you know, here we can get to know him, check out that he's OK'

Lucy hands Josh a cup of tea, an incredulous expression on her face. 'I'd rather he was not OK at Frank's place than not OK here, if he's going to be a nutter.'

'He's not a nutter. He's broke and we're helping him out.'

'So why can't we help him out by letting him stay at Frank's place? Frank gave you the keys, he entrusted it to you—'

'Exactly—'

'So don't you think that if a guy is safe enough to stay here, he's safe enough to stay there? Frank'd be pleased to have someone in there, looking after it. It's perfect.' Lucy says this as if that's the end of it.

'I don't know.' Josh takes a sip of tea and puts the mug on the bench. He turns back towards the fridge.

'Why not? You're mad if you can't see it's a good idea. What could possibly be the problem?'

'Why don't we just wait till he's got some money and he can get his own place.'

'Because Frank's is free and it's there. I don't understand you. Besides, he has got money to buy food and everything. And he went to the pictures the other night so it's not like he's on the bones of his arse.'

'Well, I gave him some money. A loan.'

'What?' Lucy forgets to whisper.

'He asked if I wanted to buy his camera. You know, that thing means a lot to him. His father gave it to him before he disappeared.'

'His father disappeared?'

'I couldn't— It's an advance. Because he will be working at the station.'

'You hope. You don't even know if he's any good. What are you doing, buying a friend?'

Josh shuts the fridge door, hard. 'Look. If you were doing this for one of your neurotic girlfriends you'd be being a fucking saint, helping womankind, being so holier than thou about it, what's wrong with me helping out this guy? What is so fucking wrong with it?'

'Why are we having a fight about this?'

'We're not having a fight.'

'Yes we are.'

'All I'm saying is, the guy needs a break, and I can give it to him. That's all.'

'Right, because he's walked in here with his London accent and his hard-luck story when he could be anyone, any kind of freak—'

'What about those freaks you work with all day? Those poor-me women who haven't even got the sense to pick a guy that's not going to shit on them?'

'Hang on, Josh, I don't think we want to go into this—'

'Oh, sorry, you wouldn't, because you're always right. Lucy is right about everything, I forgot that. Lucy knows best for everyone around her and don't dare disagree or—'

'Are you drunk?'

'No. Have you got your period?'

'Fuck you.'

Something makes them both turn towards the door. It's Daniel, clearing his throat, hovering in the doorway. 'Sorry. I just came to get some water.'

Lucy pulls at her earlobe and watches, jaw clenched, as Daniel walks to the sink and fills his glass. Over his shoulder Josh glares at her.

'Uh,' says Daniel, 'while we're all here I should say, I was thinking maybe I should start looking for a flat, you know what I mean, by the time I find one I should have a job, or I could sell my camera—'

He must have heard them. 'No, don't do that,' says

Lucy. 'It's fine for you to stay here, stay as long as you need to.'

He shakes his head. 'I'm in the way here, I don't want to intrude.'

'You're not,' says Lucy, 'really. I'm going to bed,' she says without looking at Josh. 'Night.'

So the next day Daniel broaches it again. He takes a cigarette from his packet and offers one to Josh. 'I think Lucy'd rather have the flat to herself, don't you?'

Josh sighs. 'Thanks. I guess.'

'That's cool, I'll start looking tomorrow—'

'You don't need to.'

'But if—'

'A friend's place is empty. You can stay there. And there's no rent.'

'Are you sure?'

Rubbing his eyes, Josh smiles. He flicks his lighter and bends his mouth down to it. 'Yeah,' he mumbles through the cigarette. 'But listen, if you're going to move in there there's something I've got to tell you.' He looks around the studio and jerks his head towards his office. 'Come in here.'

So Josh lets him in on his secret. It doesn't shock Daniel. No more than he shocks himself. Deception and detachment are − were − two of his specialities. He trained himself up in them when he should have been training as an artist. He did have initial enthusiasm for the art college course. And then he had begun to attend fewer and fewer classes, for reasons that he still didn't understand. His work held up OK compared to the other students', though he couldn't take it all as seriously as they did. There was a particular group of girls who

hero-worshipped one of the sculpture tutors in an embarrassing way. The tutor was an androgynous-looking
woman whose lectures blahed on about something called
queer theory. Daniel could barely get his head around
it, and he suspected that nobody else in the class could
either. They just learned some of the jargon and chucked
it about here and there in conversation, in an overly off-
hand fashion. Four or five of the girls took to dressing
like this tutor. They sat together in the café or slouched
outside lecture halls in a severe uniform of work jeans
and boots offset with skimpy T-shirts. When it got
colder they wore jumpers that looked synthetic in a
studied way. The work they produced became uncan-
nily similar in style to the wax sculptures for which the
tutor was mildly famous.

In those strange months when he was dropping out of
art college, Daniel went through a stage of having sex
with so many different women that he lost count. He
couldn't say which came first, his slacking off or the
sleeping around. Early in the second year the students
were asked to decide what they wanted to major in. In
the other students there was a shift in gear, a new
attentiveness, a hint of ambition. Daniel found himself
staying in bed. Absences were noted.

A meeting was called by his photography teacher,
who wanted to know why he hadn't completed the
latest assignment. Daniel sloped in to college at two in
the afternoon and sat in the tutor's office rubbing sleep
out of his eyes. The room was beige and tiny. Stacks of
paper on the desk and a cluttered collage of Polaroid's
on the wall to the right of it made the office seem even
smaller. The other wall was covered by a man-size
cibachrome print of three orange squares. They

reminded Daniel of the square holes running down the
side of a strip of film. He wondered what the point of a
photograph of photographic material might be.

'What do you think about that?' asked the lecturer, a
man in his fifties with a ravaged face and bored eyes.

Daniel turned towards him, then back to the picture.
'Well,' he said in the quiet voice that came out of his
mouth during seminars or tutorials, 'I can understand
what it might be saying, but—'

'What might it be saying?' The lecturer's eyes were
magnified by his glasses. They stared at Daniel in a flat
way.

'Well. Maybe. Oh, I don't know. I'm not sure if I see
the point.'

'Ah.' The eyes snapped downwards to focus on a
manila folder with Daniel's name written across it. 'I'd
like to have a little chat, ah – Daniel, if you don't mind,
about your attitude.'

He'd emerged from the room an hour later with a
killer headache and a confusion about photography he'd
never felt before. It was then, it must have been, that he
took himself to the local pub. Not the student bar but a
place nearby where it was considered cooler to hang
out. He'd gotten talking to one of the sculpture tutor's
disciples, a good-looking girl called Ange. That evening
she was wearing the regulation asexual workgear but
she'd added a touch of lipstick. Daniel bought her a pint
although she was already drunk.

'Where are your friends?' He'd never seen her out on
her own before.

'Fuck them,' she growled. 'Silly cows.'

It took a while for her to slur it out, but there'd been
a fight over whether or not a certain theorist was

inconsistent and whether or not that was actually the whole idea. Daniel went to the loos and she followed him in. They'd tried to have sex there but Ange kept losing her balance. Back at his place it was easier. Ange lay back on the bed, out of it. Every now and then she'd come to and indulge in a Hollywood semblance of wild sexual fervour. Daniel found this, while obviously a put-on, quite endearing. Still, when she staggered out of the flat into the wan early morning light he did not open his eyes.

He never tried to see her again, though by the way she acted especially indifferent to him in class he knew she'd be up for it. And that had been the start. Another girl from the pub, another one, another one, a woman from the takeaway up the road, two girls at a concert one after the other, someone he picked up on the train back to London one weekend. In toilets, alleyways, his room, their rooms, movie theatres, stranger's flats with the party going on a wall away and, as the summer holidays approached, in the park. With condoms, without condoms, pulling out, staying in. Girls who were on the pill or struggled with a diaphragm or said they didn't care. Happy girls, sad girls, local girls, southern girls, students, barmaids, a mother of three. And to all of them he lied.

He was an orphan, he explained, or his parents were loaded but had chucked him out of home, or he was brought up by his grandparents because his mother was too young to care for him. This was the first sex he'd had in three months, six months, a year. He was in a band, he was leaving for Africa with his father in a month, he had a blood clot moving towards his lung and they'd given him till next winter at the outside. When he spoke, if he spoke much at all, lies fell out of him like toads falling from his lips. At the start he told them his name if they wanted to know, but stopped after a piece of graffiti appeared at the bus shelter down the road – FUCK DANIEL IF YOU WANT SCABIES. It was inevitable, he realized, that some of them would know each other, and that they'd talk. After that he started using different names and going clubbing in the seedier places on the edge of town. It was impossible to believe that every girl he met was taken in. There were those that went along with it. There were those, probably, that lied right back. Girls who came on to him – it did work both ways – recognized his detachment, his mean streak, and it operated like a small strong magnet. There was no point, they knew, offering up a phone number or suggesting a second night. They'd met someone like him before. They knew the score.

The score, for Daniel, wasn't always sexual pleasure – sometimes he would fake it – but there was a moment that he unconsciously sought, that kept him keeping on, that every now and then he achieved. He'd be looking at the face of whatever strange girl he was with, staring at her face as they fucked each other, studying her from this closest most intimate vantage point – and he would think to himself, I don't know this person and she does not know me. That thought comforted him. It was as if by engineering these encounters he maintained control over the trouble that he felt running in his veins every day. He chose this, so it could not frighten him. Emptiness looked him straight in the face. He stared back.

Classes continued without him. Project assignments came and went that he knew nothing of. Tutors, lecturers, heads of departments and finally the dean all left messages at his flat. Would Daniel please return this call. Would Daniel please come in for a chat. Would Daniel confirm his space allocation for the end of year exhibition. The notes lay around the house until his flatmates binned them. After a while they stopped bothering to write them down.

It had to end. He was failing his course — had failed it already. He'd made up his mind. He would return to London and find a job, it didn't much matter what. One incident had jolted him. He'd been using the men's public loos in the park after an encounter one evening. The toilets stank of ammonia and excrement. Daniel was at the sink scrubbing his hands more than was necessary. Through the chipped dull silver of the basin mirror Daniel saw a man come in to the toilets. The guy was cruising, it was obvious. He was older than Daniel, with blond curly hair like a baby's over his leathery face. What difference, Daniel suddenly wondered, between an anonymous girl and an anonymous man? He didn't know what to do, what signal to give or words to say. He turned round at the sink to face the stranger. The man looked back, and smiled. Daniel did not.

Afterwards, at his flat, he couldn't sleep. He turned on the radio and listened to the top 40 countdown. The afternoon didn't mean he was queer. There was a novelty factor to it, that was all. But now he knew he could stand in the public toilets and pick up a guy as easily as he could pick up a girl in a bar — more easily in fact, much more easily — what would that do to him? Would his encounters double, now that he had both genders to choose from? Limits he'd always thought existed suddenly meant nothing. He could become consumed by sex. It would be possible for him to live that life and no other. It was a long time before he slept.

He found someone to take over his flat, arranged to stay with Richard in London, bought a train ticket and left before the end of year show. He abandoned his uncompleted artwork, his few friends and many acquaintances, his promiscuity and his fear. London, the ex-council flat he moved into, the part-time job on a music magazine, Richard, plans for forming bands, buying CDs and going to gigs – all these things filled his hours so completely that he no longer had to think about what he might do or might be doing.

SEVEN   It was one of the last warm days of the summer. The air had a softness that made you think this weather ought to be savoured, that very soon, tomorrow even, you'd walk out your front door and have to stop, go back inside for a jacket or a thicker top, maybe change your shoes. People lingered at outdoor café tables and paused, fanning themselves, at the traffic lights, as if to convince themselves they were ready to change with the season, as if to say I'll be so glad when this heat is over. Kate was happy, and she didn't know why, and she didn't care that she didn't know. Maybe something smelled like Indonesia. Whatever it was, she stepped lightly out of the Post Shop. It was crazy, she thought, how sending a card that would reach her Australian step-brother in time for his graduation could give her such a sense of control, of purpose and of moral surety. Her pleasure in this small act was a sign of an inactive and formless existence. Even so, this didn't unduly worry her. Again she marvelled at her capability for blithe carelessness, her insouciant, youthful laugh in the face of her meaningless life. Perhaps it was hormonal.

She turned a corner and was immediately knocked in the back of the shoulder by a large piece of wood. Twisting round she saw it was one of a pair of stilts, and that there was a man on the top of it. Around his neck he was wearing a small placard that swung and bounced as he moved. Bumping into Kate had made him lurch

forward and as he pulled himself back to regain balance
he shouted down at her 'Watch it stupid.' Then he
loped away. Kate blinked. More people, mostly walking
on their own legs, were brushing past her, talking
amongst themselves. Some of them had linked arms and
every so often a pair of people would be carrying a
banner that ran the width of the street. Kate couldn't
make out what the demonstration was for or against.
Abolishing the minimum wage? – they'd already done
that. Privatising electricity? – that too. Slashing benefits,
selling off forests, disempowering the unions – there
didn't seem to be anything left to protest against.

She stood to one side and watched as the people
passed, remembering various marches Ginny had
dragged her on, balancing on the shoulders of some
bloke with a beard as they all chanted about South
Africa, or nuclear testing, or saving the whales. Her
mother would go braless for the day. There'd be jugglers
and dogs and men in floppy orange hats. They'd march
for a bit and then sit down in the road outside the Town
Hall. Kate and Nina and the other kids ran around
playing chase. One of the mums would pass round
muesli bars and apples and the grown-ups would share a
couple of bottles of beer. It was like a picnic, but with
the police watching. There were speeches you could
never properly hear over the scratchy loud-hailer system.
After a bit everyone pulled themselves up and straggled
off to their vans and station wagons. They'd go back to
some friend's house and the grown-ups would continue
talking over more beer and wine. Two or three of the
mothers would produce a huge salad, one of the boys'd
get in trouble for throwing dirt at one of the girls, the
fathers would stand around the barbecue turning chops
and sausages over on the grill.

The day after one of these, Ginny's most conservative
friend had spotted her in the paper, laughing underneath
a banner that said, IF IT'S SO SAFE TEST IT IN PARIS.
The straight friend visited that afternoon and said Ginny,
my phone's been running red-hot with people asking
me if you're some kind of radical. Oh for goodness sake,
Ginny had said, Look at me. I'm not exactly Patty
Hearst. And radical she certainly wasn't. They were
liberals, most of that group, but then they could afford
to be. Once the kids got older a lot of them would be
sent to private schools. The parents didn't want strip
mining on the Coromandel because they knew people
with holiday houses there. Still, Kate could tell that the
allegation she was some kind of urban guerrilla pleased
her mother. She retrieved her old beret from the dress-
ups and wore it the next day, her hair hanging long and
dark beneath it.

These people look different, thinks Kate, and it's not
only the fashions. When she was a kid everyone seemed
more relaxed and more certain about what they
believed. Maybe it was because they'd started off as poor
students, with cheese on toast and red wine and Joan
Baez and naked two-year-olds running round, and
ended up with swimming pools and superannuation
plans and tennis club memberships. Whatever it was, in
those days her parents and their friends had appeared
confident, clear about right and wrong, free from
political doubt.

Sure there were arguments, raised voices over the
breakfast bar or a scene that ended in someone storming
off the verandah to sulk in the gloom of the living room,
but these were only, as far as Kate could remember,
disagreements between people who held opposite
positions anyway. Kate's father, who believed firmly in

individual rights, would disagree with Ginny's brother, an environmentalist who advocated a ban on car driving and compulsory return to the push-bike. A wealthy friend banged on about overseas investment and Ginny said she didn't see why they should sell any of their beautiful country to foreigners at all. Nobody occupied the middle ground, nobody admitted to doubt, there was no grey area.

The ugliest splits were over playing rugby with South Africa. Everything came to a head when Ginny's brother's girlfriend was arrested for running on to the pitch at one of the games. Kate's father said That was it, it was bloody irresponsible behaviour, and took it as a personal affront that Ginny wouldn't condemn her for it. In fact, Kate realizes now right there on the street, her mouth opening, it was just after that that he left for the first time, the Trial Separation that was presented to Kate and Nina as a long business trip, though they knew precisely what was going on. Funny, she thinks, the demonstration still marching slowly past her, that even then he didn't make any attempt to see them, that even then they were packaged up with Ginny as her daughters not his, as lives only accidentally attached to him, as incidental.

All of a sudden it feels as though she's being pushed into the concrete wall behind her by this stupid crowd, that she's got to get through them and get home, clean her room, do her laundry or something. It's harder making her way across the street than it looked as if it would be. Two enormous men block her way then a woman elbows her. This is ridiculous, there are never this many people on marches, they look so angry. Now there's shouting, the disjointed yelling of an unrecogniz-

able chant. She's swept along in the crowd a little way
down the street, walking in time with a middle-aged
couple who are red in the face from bellowing. Behind
them is another man on stilts, dressed in a long black
cape and mask and carrying a noose. The executioner.
It must be against nuclear testing. Then Kate sees a
placard with a man's face on it, black and white like a
police mug-shot. It is a police mug-shot. It's that guy,
that child molester from up North, the one who's on
trial at the moment. And the words of the chant become
clear. This isn't a demo against job losses, or to save the
environment, or to prevent further welfare cuts. It's the
Hang Him High crowd, the Eye for an Eye crowd, Life
means Life. Kate renews her attempt to reach the other
side of the street. This is one mob she doesn't want to
be part of. She shunts the middle-aged couple out of her
way and cuts through as fast as she can to the opposite
footpath. She stops to breathe. And through the protes-
ters, back on the side of the road that she came from,
she sees Daniel, leaning against the same wall she'd
leaned against, watching the march.

'Hey!' she shouts out, 'Hey!', but her voice is puny
against the now feverish screaming of the crowd. She
lunges into the mass of bodies again, keeping him in her
sights – he's got something around his neck too – for a
second it looks like another, smaller noose like the one
carried by the hangman – but it's his camera. He raises
it to his face, masking himself, and another figure pushes
past Kate, blocking her view. When she can see again,
he isn't there. Oh, there he is, along the street a bit, his
angular shoulders sidling along between people by the
kerb. The crowd is thinning out.

'Hey!' she shouts again. 'Daniel!' and he turns his head

round towards her, but there's a tall blonde girl with dreadlocks in the way – Kate bounces up and down, waving, trying to be seen – slips past the blonde and watches as Daniel starts to take off down the street, elbows and knees slicing through the demonstrators, women jerking their heads angrily towards him as he pushes past. Kate stands confused for a moment, then starts to run after him.

Around a corner she slows down, looking around her. Where's he gone? She didn't imagine him. Did she? There's nobody there but a couple of Saturday afternoon window shoppers and three kids sitting on a public sculpture, covering its surface with red marker pen graffiti. She thinks about going up to them and asking if they've seen anyone looking like Daniel, but it's too crazy. Like wandering around a movie set with a crumpled-up photograph in her hand. Have you seen this man? Disappearing Dan. She supposes now she's meant to flop wearily down on a park bench, and some old codger in a raincoat will come up to her and say without moving his lips, 'Follow me.' Down third-world alleyways, past chickens and drying washing and suspicious-faced women, to a room with a single over-head fan and a suitcase and – what? This is idiotic. She's going home.

'Hey,' says Daniel, at her left shoulder. 'Kate. Hi.'

She turns to look up at him. 'Hi.'

'What are you up to?'

'I . . .' She doesn't want to say, I was calling your name. I was running after you. 'I got caught up in the lynch mob. I don't agree with them,' she adds, just in case.

'Yeah, me neither. I saw that movie, about the death penalty. It's terrible.'

'Yeah.' She nods. Please don't let him be thick. 'Is that your camera?'

He hesitates, then says, 'Yeah I brought it with me. Managed not to lose it so far.'

You nicked it, she thinks.

'I know I should have sold it when I was skint,' he says, stroking the lens cap. 'But I couldn't do it, you know what I mean?'

He definitely nicked it. 'Do you do much photography?'

'I studied it at art school.' He clears his throat. 'Do you want to get a coffee or something? Do you have to be anywhere?'

'No,' she says, 'nowhere at all.'

'It's funny,' she says later at Lucy's. Josh is out, and she's told the story in great detail except for the bit about her chasing him. That was over an hour ago and now she feels the urge to talk about it again. 'It's funny,' she says as if it has just occurred to her. 'You know I bumped into that guy Daniel.'

'Mn,' says Lucy.

'Yeah, well I don't know. It was just really nice, to bump into somebody and have it be somebody new, you know what I mean?'

'Mn,' says Lucy. She doesn't say, That guy Daniel says You know what I mean.

'And I was in this really good mood anyway for no reason, and I didn't know where I was going or anything, and then I bumped into him and he didn't know where he was going so we just hung out together.' She smiles. 'It was kind of a coincidence.'

Lucy shuts her eyes. The C word. Why is it that women are so in love with the idea of coincidences

peppering their lives, spicing them up with extra meaning, making a chance encounter with a bloke out to be
fate with a capital F? She heard it from the women at
the refuge all the time. If they were talking about how
they first met someone, there'd always be some com-
ment like, It was amazing, he was wearing a green
sweatshirt just like mine, or When I found out his name
was Mark I couldn't believe it – that was my first
boyfriend's name, or The numbers in his birthday add
up to the same as the numbers in my daughter's. They'd
clutch on to these talismans, these omens, as proof that
they were right to be with the man, that they hadn't
made an error of judgement or been duped. And all it
did was make it harder to let the man go. Lucy doesn't
believe in coincidence and she doesn't believe in fate.
What she looks for are repeating patterns, as if the years
are wrapped in one great spiral, and she has to be extra
vigilant to avoid the mistakes her mother made, or the
fuck-ups of her own younger days.

Five minutes pass. Kate looks up from her magazine
again. 'So that Daniel guy's staying at Frank's.'

'Yup,' says Lucy.

That's pretty weird, Kate thinks. How she used to
have a thing with Frank and now this guy Daniel's
staying there. She's been naked in that apartment. She's
had sex in it. When Daniel told her he'd moved in
there, she'd tried to drop hints that she knew the place
in detail – intimate detail – without coming right out
and saying that she'd slept with Frank. She didn't know
why, but she felt sort of proprietorial about the apartment. And she'd wanted him to guess about her and
Frank without her having to be crass and say it. God
knows why. It wasn't as if he was going to be impressed

by this. But she'd hoped so, somehow. That it would
prove her sexual attractiveness to him. How gross. She
groans.

'What?' says Lucy.

'Nothing. You know, that guy Daniel was saying this
afternoon that this place is really like Britain in the
nineteen sixties. I hate it when people say that.'

'Mn.'

'You know, what do they mean? Nineteen sixties,
what does that even mean?'

Kate lets go of her magazine. It splays on the floor
with a quick rustle. She gets up and makes them both
another cup of tea. Lucy stretches and rubs her eyes. As
Kate places the mug down beside her she says, 'I thought
that was pretty rude. What Daniel said. He'd get on well
with Frank, it's a shame they didn't meet. Do you know
if he's seen much of the country, Daniel? Has he been
south?'

Lucy closes her book. 'Kate.'

'What? Oh, OK.' She sits back down and slaps a hand
to her closed eyes. Through clenched teeth she asks,
'How many times did I say his name?'

'In the last twenty minutes? Four or five.'

'God. OK. That's it, I promise.' She retrieves her
magazine and they read silently for a bit.

'But listen,' she says, 'I don't fancy him. Really. I just
don't.'

She doesn't fancy him, really, she just doesn't. That must
be why, when a week later Josh suggests that she
borrows his car and takes Daniel for a drive down the
island, go on holiday for a few days, she thinks, What a
fucking brilliant idea. She doesn't say this, no, she says,

Oh. Really? Well I am owed some time off work. Do you think? Does Daniel want to? Are you sure you won't need your car?

'Look,' Josh lies, 'I never use it. It'd be good for Daniel to get around a bit. And he can't drive, apparently.'

'Oh, so cheers. I'm the chauffeur.'

'Well, only if you want a break. It's up to you.'

Kate is so into this idea that she doesn't stop and think, why is Josh doing this? That doesn't occur to her until much later. It occurs to Lucy, though, and she asks him.

'So, uh, Kate says you've offered to lend her and Daniel the car for a few days.'

'Mm-hn.' A pause. 'Yeah, well, I thought it'd be good for him to see a bit of the country.' Another pause. 'And, uh, I'm hoping this job will work out for him at the station but I need to speak to Fraser first, I've sort of got to give him the push and I don't really want to do it.'

'Is he bad at his job?'

'Yeah, he is. But I hate the idea of sacking someone.'

'Be careful. You don't want to get taken to the Employment Tribunal or whatever it is.'

'I know.' He sighs. 'I've got to sort it out. So it's a good idea if Daniel's not hanging around there for a while.'

The thing is, when you suspect someone's lying to you, or at least not telling you the full truth, it's really hard to call them on it. Even if they are your boyfriend of five years. So Lucy drops it. Whatever Josh's reasons are, she thinks, they can't be that bad. After all, she knows him. As well as you can know anybody.

★

So. Kate's lying by pretending not to be interested in Daniel. Josh is lying about his reasons for getting Daniel out of Frank's flat for a bit. And Daniel is lying about being unable to drive. Of course he can drive. It took him a couple of tries but he's had his licence for nearly ten years. Still, when Josh first said Take the car for a road trip if you like, Daniel answered, Sounds great, but—

'What?'

'Don't have a licence.'

'Oh.'

The lie happened before Daniel knew it was going to. As soon as it was out of his mouth he thought how stupid and pointless. That it would be an annoying pretence to maintain. But he was hoping Josh would offer to come too, be in control, show him around. Mostly guys take road trips in pairs. It'd be better that way. Still, there was no question of asking. 'So. I guess not.'

Josh thought. 'What about Kate?'

'What about her?'

'She can drive. You want to go with her? You know she's after you.'

'No.'

Josh smiled. 'Mate, she's up for it.'

Daniel shrugged. 'She's all right.'

'Her sister's all right as well. You could pay her a visit. She's a bit of a cunt though, Nina. Jump up and down on your balls.'

Now Daniel smiled. 'I can handle that.'

'Well,' Lucy says to Daniel when he's visiting that night, 'you'll have an excellent time. Are you going to the South Island?'

'I don't know,' he says. 'What's it like?'

'Beautiful. Beautiful but empty. Speaking of which,
are you going to stay with Nina while you're in
Wellington?'

'Who's Nina?'

'Kate's sister.'

'What's she like?'

'A bitch princess. Don't tell Kate I said that. She
hasn't quite figured it out yet.'

Kate wakes up early on the morning they're supposed
to leave. Being up when it's still dark outside reminds her
of family holidays. They'd leave at five in the morning
'to beat the traffic'. Her father was obsessed with traffic.
He considered himself a faultless driver and was almost
fetishistic about his car, lavishing it with care and attention on the weekends he was home and not working at
the office. Open road journeys were a special challenge
to him. He was forever experimenting with new routes.
If he could knock ten minutes off the travel time without
exceeding the speed limit his mood of triumph would last
the entire holiday. If, however, they got stuck behind a
truck on a winding gorge road, it was best to duck out
of his way for the rest of the day. The early starts were
his idea. Kate was always the last one to crawl out of bed,
giving herself only a few minutes to pull on clothes she'd
laid out the night before and shuffle out to the car, where
she'd lean her head against the cold window and try to
fall back to sleep. Nina would have showered and eaten
breakfast and probably helped Ginny pack sandwiches.
Food was the only thing that could cheer their father up
if a section of motorway was closed for improvements.

★

In the car, Nina and Ginny talked in high, bright voices
about who might be there again this year and what
developments there'd be to the campsite and remember
that party when Beverly Bevan tripped over backwards
and collapsed on the dip table? Yeah, Kate'd think in
her grizzly half-sleep, the same party where Nina pashed
Damien Bevan in front of all the younger kids and let
him put his hand up her top and had to wear her one-
piece the rest of the holiday to hide the love-bites on
her stomach. And where Jamie Grimshaw picked his nose
and ate it because Tamara Savadan told him to. Those
parties were what Kate dreaded most about the holidays.
Families from all over their suburb would relocate to
the campsite for three weeks in the summer and everybody had to host a barbecue or a drinks party or, if they
had a yacht, a yacht drinks barbecue party. And while
the grown-ups stood around drinking and flirting and
dancing in embarrassing ways, the kids would be under-
going growing-up rituals in the games room on the
camp compound. Spin the bottle. Truth or dare. That
game someone's older sister thought up where you went
round the group one by one, telling people what you
least liked about them. This game was still etched in
Kate's memory. She was 'moody', 'too boyish' and 'should
grow her hair'. The worst anybody said about Nina was
that they were jealous of her ability to tan so easily.

On the way back to their tent Ginny and Nina would
chatter about who'd said what to whom. Nina had a
knack of getting indiscretions out of Ginny because she
asked questions in a very respectful voice. She was
fascinated by the machinations of the adult world. In the
electric light falling through the pines from huge metal
campsite lamps, Kate could see Nina's mind working,

putting pieces of information together, making sense of
what Ginny told them and what she left out. This
knowledge gave Nina an edge over the other children.
And they knew, just quietly, that the edge was there. If
a girl secretly suspected her mother of having an affair,
she didn't want to get on the wrong side of Nina.
Information could spread amongst the children like a
virus, and if it was known that all was not well in your
four-to-six-person tent, a subtle form of ostracism took
place that it was impossible to combat. The kids operated
out of fear. Any threat to the security of family life was
ignored in the hope that it would go away. If Nina, of
course out of great concern, felt it necessary to discuss a
person's problems, then that person, as the carrier, had
to be ignored as well.

By fourteen Nina was the undisputed social queen of
the campsite kids. She did everything first but was never
called a slut like the other girls, not even behind her
back. Her hairstyles were imitated, her clothing, her
mannerisms. At least three boys would chase her every
summer and she'd always pick a different one. Kate
watched, and became adept at brushing aside any
thoughts of comparison. She refused to think about the
differences between her bad bushy haircut and Nina's
shoulder-skimming flip, between her burnt nose and
shoulders and Nina's dark even tan. Kate wore the
school regulation swimming costume while Nina had
saved her babysitting money to buy a hot-pink bikini.
Kate hung out on the edges and tried to avoid the other
weirdos who wanted to be her friend; Nina was pursued
by everybody. She still is.

★

Neat, thinks Kate, rummaging for a jumper in her messy shelves, how I thought I'd done such a good job at not feeling inferior yet I can remember every sodding detail from those summers. Images flicker in her mind: a man's crimson neck above a turquoise polo shirt; a bowl of salad falling, slow-motion, carrots and radishes and lettuce spilling over the pale pine deck; lumpy-armed women smoothing oil into their shoulders and nodding to each other as if at some secret. Brett Chee pulling Tamara's bikini bottoms down whenever she tried to get out of the surf. Lane Bevan's red face as he explained to the group the meaning of the word 'come'. The doorbell sound of her mother's voice; Nina's effortless swallow dives at the public pools; her father's stubborn silence at the wheel of the car or back in the tent or anywhere there weren't at least two other men. The deep lines that ran from the corners of his mouth down his chin.

Trying to be quiet in the living room, she dials her mother's number. Andrew answers and she blinks to clear out the picture of both of them in bed.

'Mum? Sorry to call so early.'

'That's OK.'

'I'm going to Wellington for a couple of days, just thought I'd let you know.'

Ginny yawns. 'That's nice, darling. Are you staying with Ninie?'

'Yeah, I called her last night.'

'Are you driving?'

'Yeah, I've borrowed a car.'

'Well, be careful.'

'I will. Is everything OK?'

'Oh, fine, yes lovely. Oh, I can hear the tui singing outside. All right, darling, speak to you soon.'

Ginny reaches over Andrew to replace the receiver. He's reading a novel, glasses perched at the end of his nose, face rumpled and unshaven. She snuggles into his warmth. After a minute she says, 'I hope Katie's going to be all right.'

He looks down at her over the rim of his glasses. 'Why?'

'Oh, I don't know. You can't run away from yourself. She just seems to drift around.' Ginny laughs. 'Where did I go wrong?'

He smiles and kisses her hair. 'Your Katie'll be fine.'

Ginny stretches her arm round to squeeze him. She loves the slept-in heat of his skin through his soft T-shirt. 'Do you promise?'

Smiling, she slides back into sleep, as he grunts and turns another page of his book.

EIGHT Lucy's right about Nina. Her theme music is the soundtrack from the movie *Jaws*. Dum dum dum dum. Dum dum dum dum, etcetera, etcetera. It's in her pulse, in her alpha and beta brain waves, in the rhythm of her breath. It plays, sometimes silently, sometimes with the volume of a thirty-piece orchestra, under whatever she's doing – driving, talking, shaking someone's hand before a meeting. It plays when she's in her flat alone. It doesn't stop when she's asleep. In her REM moments it gathers force and momentum – *dum* dum *dum* dum – while she is dreaming. You don't want to know what Nina dreams. No need to dive into those dark and shark-infested waters. Even she kicks and panics, surfacing for air, struggling upwards to the pale shaft of morning light.

Wind has been battering the city for four days solid. The air bites as if it's coming straight off the South Pole. Nina clutches her shoulder bag to her ribs with one arm and hooks the other round a lamp-post to stop herself from blowing across the road. This is the good part about the wind, the sense of fragility it gives her, the breathless idea that she's as delicate as a dandelion-clock, that a sudden gust could pick her up and carry her right over a hilltop. Everything else about this weather drives her insane. The constant unrelenting rattle, the whine of it, the way it turns umbrellas inside-out and flicks grit and hair into your eyes. It sends plastic bags skidding

around street corners to entangle your ankles and trip
you up. It shakes the roof and the walls of her house, it
slaps rains about like hard sprays of paint, it churns up
the harbour into a directionless mess of brown waves.
It's the worst thing about living in this city, worse even
than the stupid fault line the whole place is built on.
Compared to the wind, the earth barely makes its
presence known, only sending weekly tremors up
through the foundations of the house to rattle a glass on
the kitchen table, so slightly that you might not even
notice.

Nina ploughs, forehead first, over the road and into a
warm, orange-lit bar. Dolly's already there.
    'Hi, gorgeous.' Nina kisses the white powdered
cheek. 'I'm in a foul mood. Are you all right for a
drink?'
    Dolores nods at her vodka lime. 'Yeah.'
    Back from the bar, Nina sits down and takes a long
sip of her gin. She shuts her eyes and sighs. 'Thank
God.'
    The corners of Dolly's generous, maroon-coloured
mouth turn down and she looks at Nina with concerned
eyes. 'What is it?' she asks in her deep, busty voice.
'How's work?'
    'Boring.' Nina's hand moves from her throat to run
through the silky pale hair hanging down below her
shoulders. She exhales cigarette smoke. Her eyes, she
imagines, are glinting darkly. 'I used to love getting up
in the mornings. I'd just leap out of bed.' She laughs in
a jaded way. 'But now, I don't know, it's like where do
I go next?'
    'Mm,' says Dolores.
    'Anyway, this is the way of the world. I can't expect

to be thrilled by music videos for ever. I'll become old
and cynical.'

'No,' says Dolores.

'Well, that's enough about boring me. How are things
at the gallery?'

Nina likes to appear reluctant to talk about herself.
She listens with sympathetic interjections to some complicated story Dolores is telling her about the latest
touring show, involving lots of office politics and names
of people Nina can't remember. The bar begins to fill
up. Every now and then somebody looks over to their
table. Nina, facing out to the room, knows they're
looking at her, trying to place her. See that girl over
there, the blonde one, who is she? Is she off the butter
ads? Were we at school together? Maybe she's a friend
of Leon's? And then, perhaps, they'll get it right – or
maybe not until they're watching the light entertain-
ment bit of the ten o'clock news tonight. Then they'll
see the item she recorded this afternoon about the
benefit concert for the bird sanctuary and they'll say to
their companions, I saw that girl tonight. I noticed her.
And they'll feel gratified, as if they're part of the world
that makes news programmes, part of the glamour of
television. Even though they don't care about a bunch
of flightless birds two hours' drive away, and even
though Nina doesn't care either, they'll pay special
attention to her report, feeling fondly towards her, as if
she belongs to them. Knowing this cheers Nina up
enormously. Turning her head 180 degrees so the whole
bar has an opportunity to see her face, she can't even
remember what it was she was irritated about. Oh. Yes
she can. Kate.

★

Nina's thoughts sometimes take the form of answers to interview questions:

– I love this city, but the wind would drive anyone mad.

– My sister and I aren't close, but I don't think you have to be friends with a sibling, do you? Your family is what you've got in common. That's the point of connection, that's all.

– There's no one special man in my life right now. I know it's a cliché, but I'm married to my job.

– Yes, I do think it's sad when people of our generation refuse to realise their potential. Well, let's just say there are people close to me who I feel, quite simply, are wasting their lives.

Dolly's monologue has ended. 'Yes,' says Nina, nodding and hoping that this is the appropriate response. 'Mmn.'

'Are you all right?' Dolly's all concern again, her cleavage squishing together as she lights another cigarette.

'Yeah, I'm sorry to be so preoccupied. My sister's arriving tomorrow, with some bloke.'

'Oh, has she got a boyfriend?' The lighter is placed back on the table.

'God knows with Kate. I assume they're sleeping together. She's very good at short-lived flings.'

'Sounds like me,' says Dolores before Nina has time to think it. 'What goes wrong?'

'Who knows. They're always pretty useless. The last one I met was closet, I'm sure of it.'

'Mn.'

'Are you going to Stephen's party on Saturday night? Oh God,' Nina groans, draining her glass, 'I suppose Kate'll expect me to drag her along to it.'

'I don't know,' Dolly drawls as if she's not sure whether or not she can be bothered. This is the first she's heard of the party. Last time she saw Stephen she'd made an ill-judged pass at him – and she'd been certain it was a sure thing, Nina had said he was interested. 'Where are you going to put them?'

'Who, Kate and this guy? The sofa folds out into a bed. I mean, if they're not doing it, she'll at least be trying to get into his pants.' Nina laughs and stands to go to the bar again. 'So I'll be doing her a favour.'

Later, rubbing moisturiser into her neck before she goes to bed, Nina feels a twinge of guilt. It isn't really fair of her to bag Kate like that. In fact, it's mean. She studies her camera-friendly cheekbones, lit to perfection in the bathroom mirror, and lets some of the tension in her stomach soften and fall away. Who's going to be at Stephen's party? The same old same old. The people she's still friends with because they share a history together. She thinks she still spends time with them because of that and because there aren't many other options. This is true, but it's also true that it warms her to know she's doing better than most – any – of them. She does admit to feeling frustrated by the prospect of seeing them all there again and exchanging the usual gossip. It's her goal to move into a new social circle. Not just the work drinks parties she goes to as a matter of course. She want to go to dinner with the film people, she wants to be invited to cocktails in private homes where there is interesting and challenging conversation. She brushes her hair ten, twenty, thirty times, becoming more worked up with every successive stroke. The friends of her own age bore her. Apart from a couple of them, they just seem content to sift around,

moan about the lack of career opportunities and boy-
friends, trundle along to their meaningless jobs, muddle
through their lazy smalltown lives. She knows she's
being harsh, but really. Where are they going? What do
they want? And Kate — here she bangs the hairbrush
down on the bench and feels the knot harden again in
her stomach. Kate is the slackest, the laziest of the lot.
Why should she feel guilty for being irritated by her?
When does she ever hear from Kate unless she wants
something? God knows how long they expect to stay.
She'll put up with it for four nights, that's all. No.
Three.

Daniel asked Kate how long the trip took and she said,
Eight or nine hours — I've done it in six. Just like her
father. She can't stop herself from showing off in front
of him. But this time, she said, I think we should take it
slowly. Seeing as you're a tourist. And seeing as it's just
me driving. She had been surprised to learn that he
didn't have his licence. A man who couldn't drive was
like a virgin or a teetotaller. Rare, and slightly pathetic.
It was girly not to be able to drive. Kate loves driving
and thinks she's better at it than she really is. She got her
driver's licence the same year that she started having sex.
Both things were a revelation. She walked around open-
jawed at the thought that most people did them all the
time. The instinct and control, the responsibility for
others, the adjustments required by different terrain all
fascinated her. The way you had to be careful not to get
too drunk. And when it was all working, the effortless,
synchronized physicality that took over and let the mind
go, transported. Why don't you drive? she'd asked
Daniel. How can you not? He'd shrugged, unfazed, and

said you didn't really need to when you lived in London and besides he'd never been able to afford a car. These were valid reasons, but still she felt his lack of skill was unmanly in some way. She doesn't mind doing all the driving on this trip — as long, she said to him, as you don't think I'm your bloody chauffeur.

He's waiting outside when she pulls up, a dim blue figure alone in the early dark of the street. She leans over to unlock his door and the one behind it so he can swing his plastic suitcase and his camera into the back.

'You going away for a while?'

'What?' he asks, sliding into the passenger seat, rubbing the palms of his hands on his jeans to warm up. She shifts into gear and checks the rear-vision mirror, starts to turn the car around.

'That suitcase.'

'It's the only one I've got.'

The streets are empty. Kate drives in the middle of the road, giving red lights five seconds then cruising easily through. Daniel lets his eyes drift shut for a few moments. He can still feel the sensation of lying in bed. Inside the car the air is warm and soft. It's getting lighter. A milky blue glow covers the asphalt, the concrete pavement, the glass shopfronts and timber stripes of houses.

They fill up with gas before heading on to the motorway. There's more traffic on the road now. Kate stands by the sweet rack in the service station. She glances out to Daniel dozing in the front of the car and feels like a kidnapper. Like a kidnapper's girlfriend. When she slips back behind the wheel and turns left on to the motorway

ramp he shifts a little, sighs and makes a wet clicking
sound with his mouth. She wishes he would stay like
this forever.

It doesn't take long to pass the outer suburbs and the
Tip Top factory where Kate went on a school trip one
time. It reminds her of the monotonous clanking
machinery inside, workers in white coats and hair nets,
the sickly ice cream the class waited patiently for all day.
They'd been given visitor cards to wear safety-pinned to
their cardigans. She remembers turning hers over before
she put it on. On the back of the card was typed PLEASE
LEAVE BEFORE YOU GO. It took a few seconds for the
phrase to make sense to her, and when she understood
it she felt almost disappointed, as if some mystery,
something secret and potent, had evaporated. Now she
wonders if she really had lost that initial, paradoxical
meaning, or if leaving a place before she was gone was
the thing that she'd been doing ever since.

They pass mangrove swamps, scrubby fields, a sports
stadium with the floodlights still on. Daniel sleeps, his
breath slow and heavy. Green motorway signs thirty feet
above them name the upcoming turn-offs. Kate stretches
the muscles in her face like a zoo-girl. She flicks a
sideways glance at Daniel to make sure he didn't see.
Underneath the sign to Rama Rama someone has
painted, in enormous white letters, the words Ding
Dong. She bursts out laughing. Daniel starts awake with
a 'wha' sound.

'Did you have the Muppets in England?'

'The what?'

'Kermit the Frog.'

'Don't know.' He looks around him. 'How long have
I been asleep?'

'Not long.'

'Erh.' He shakes his head. He doesn't like sleeping in public. Being watched. Being vulnerable. 'Is there any water?'

'Coke in the back.'

The sun is stronger now, shafting ochre through the grey, damp-looking clouds. Ahead of them a quarter of rainbow bends down towards the road. It looks as if they're going to drive right through it. For some reason she finds this embarrassing.

Daniel lights a cigarette, unwinds his window and coughs. Kate wonders, if she were going out with him, whether she'd get him to cut down on smoking. She wouldn't want to be a nag. It seems like you either tell people what you won't put up with and you're a shrew, or let them do whatever they want and you're a doormat. It's this sort of thing that keeps her single, she thinks – it doesn't seem worth the hassle.

'What's your sister like?'

Kate blows air through the gap in her front teeth. 'Nina? Oh, she's fine.'

'Older or younger?'

'Younger, just. Mum banged us out pretty much one after the other.'

'Are you close?'

'We get on fine.'

Daniel laughs. 'Sounds like it.'

Kate laughs too. 'Do you have brothers or sisters?'

For a second he remembers the sister he invented to get into the country and his throat briefly contracts. He coughs. 'I'm an only.'

Maybe that explains his lone-wolf number. 'Well, you'll meet Nina.' Kate laughs again. 'She, uh, shut me in a fridge once.'

'When?'

'Ages ago, when we were kids. I don't think I'd fit now. I suppose I was pretty stupid.'

The road cuts narrowly through a hill and deep shadow falls across it. Kate's hands are cold on the steering wheel.

The kitchen was flooded with light. It reflected from every gleaming white surface. Kate, Nina and Ginny had spent the afternoon dusting and wiping and scouring and spraying all the yucky dirt away. Kate rubbed at the glasses carefully, trying to get every spot and smear off of them. Nina filled and refilled bowls of hot soapy water and carried them, wobbling, to their mother who was on her knees scrubbing the floor. The phone rang. Ginny groaned as she rose to answer it. Hello, she said in her special telephone voice. Then, Hang on a minute.

'Nina, I'm going to take it in the bedroom. Will you hang this up for me when I get there?'

Even then Nina was the one her mother asked to do important things. She nodded solemnly and took hold of the receiver. Ginny disappeared down the hallway. Kate heard her call, OK! Then she watched as Nina pressed the black buttons down carefully, slowly, and just as slowly lifted her finger off them, all the time keeping the receiver pressed to her ear. Kate knew that trick, the older kids did it in phone boxes to tap the phones so they didn't have to pay six cents. She stopped polishing the glass in her hand. 'Ninie,' she started, but couldn't finish. Nina's face looked strange, like she was concentrating really hard or watching something horrible happen. Kate didn't like it. She wanted to give her sister a hug. She jumped up and the glass fell onto the kitchen tiles with a smash. Nina slammed down the phone. Ginny came running into the kitchen.

'You two! Jesus – not for five minutes—' She was red-faced and wild looking. Nina stood grimly by the telephone. Their mother looked from one to the other and seemed to change, become more normal, too normal. 'Nina, help Kate clean up that mess. Don't cut yourselves.'

She walked back to her bedroom and her voice was quiet again in the distance. They picked up the pieces of glass in silence and wrapped them in handy-towels like they'd been taught. When Ginny came back into the kitchen she still looked funny, like when she was being nice to people she was rude about later.

'I've got to go out for a minute. Won't be long, promise.'

The front door closed after her.

'Let's play a game,' Nina said. She led Kate over to the unplugged fridge which their mother had pulled away from the wall. It looked like a different thing standing on its own in the room, not like the part of the kitchen that it usually was. 'Let's play *Doctor Who*.'

She opened the fridge door. It was empty, all the trays stacked up against its side. The sunlight that streamed through the window seemed to get sucked in to the fridge and disappear, as if it was a tunnel. 'You get in.'

Nina held her hand while Kate climbed into the empty fridge. Then she shut the door. For a moment Kate didn't know what was happening. She couldn't see anything. After the white glare of the kitchen it was completely black. Purple spots swam up in front of her eyes, knights on horseback. She lifted up a hand and it brushed her face. Her breath was fast and shallow.

Something was jumping up and down inside her. 'Nina!'
she called. 'Ninie!' Her voice went nowhere. Nothing
happened, then blackness took over.

'I don't know,' she says now. 'I mean I was fine.' She
hopes Daniel doesn't think she's told him this so he'll feel
sorry for her. Sometimes when people confide in you it's
like an intrusion, or a come-on. 'It's embarrassing more
than anything. Being persecuted by your younger sister.
You know, I was curious about the physical world,
always climbing up something or into something, always
breaking a collarbone or spraining my ankle. And Nina –
I suppose Nina specialized in the emotional world, that's
what she was curious about. So she had it all over me
really. Ah.' Kate shakes her head a little bit. 'I don't
know,' she says again. 'You'll meet her.'
      'Can we stop soon?' says Daniel. 'I'm starving.'

They drive past houses that stand alone on hillsides,
monuments to isolation. Past a caravan park and a series
of construction companies scrappy with wood piles and
rusted bulldozers and prefabricated sheds. The road runs
alongside train tracks, bumps over the railway crossing
and carries them into the blank main street of a hundred
rural towns. The first judder bar takes Kate by surprise
and they bang down on the other side of it, heads
jerking backwards.
      'Sorry.'
      She pulls over outside a 24-hour cafeteria. The ash-
grey curtains don't bode well. After a quick look up and
down the street – no, nothing – she pushes the glass
front door and holds it out behind her for Daniel. It's
the usual story, red-flecked Formica tables and a lino

floor so sticky it's as if, each time you take a step, it tries
to prevent you from going any further. There's fluorescent strip lighting and posters from the Ministry of
Health, held up with mismatched coloured drawing
pins. The Healthy Food Triangle. Eat New Zealand
Lamb. Faded studio shots of meat adorned with sprigs of
parsley.

Daniel slides back the plastic shelf doors on the
counter and piles a plate high with white bread sandwiches, a pie and two sausage rolls. It's beyond Kate
how he stays so skinny. She grabs a cheese sandwich that
doesn't look more than three days old and a greasy-
skinned apple.

'Two teas,' he says to the waitress. 'I'll get this.'

Kate's fishing in her jeans pocket for a note. 'Why?'

'Well, you're doing the driving and we're staying
with your sister even though – and—' He doesn't look
at her.

'Oh. Well, thanks.' Kate scratches the back of her
head.

'Two teas,' says the waitress. She holds out her hand
for Daniel's money, unmoved.

The only other person in the place is a man with a
heavily bandaged hand, his arm in a sling. Kate stares at
him in an absentminded way. He grinds his cigarette
out, bleary-eyed, scoots in behind the till and starts
counting the money out, one-handed, his gaze darting
up to the door every few seconds. All of a sudden Kate
remembers reading about a stabbing in this town last
week, a guy who'd had all the tendons in his hand
severed as he tried to fight off the knife. She hadn't paid
it much attention at the time. Most violent crime seems
to take place outside of the cities. Farmers with guns,

drunken pub landlords, loners who've let the solitude
get to them and warp everything out of perspective. She
wonders if this bloke's a local celebrity now, if it's true
that you don't feel pain until the knife's withdrawn, if
he'll ever have the use of his hand again. He's glaring at
her. She ducks her head.

'Shall we hit the road again? When you're finished?'

Daniel nods mid-mouthful. 'Uhn mnthe' – he swal-
lows – 'is there anything to see around here?'

'Doubt it. Do you want to do something touristy?'

'Yeah, if there's anything.'

'OK. We'll go to Waitomo.'

'What's Waitomo?'

'It's a place. With glow-worms and caves.'

'Worms and caves.'

'So it's hardly Eurodisney. But we should go. I haven't
been since I was about nine years old.'

On the way to Waitomo they get stuck behind a beige
van with right-to-life stickers all around its back windscreen: silhouettes of human foetuses and various sentences
naming the functions they have at twelve weeks, thirteen weeks, and on and on. At last the other side of the
road is clear and she swings out to pass it. Daniel's been
staring vacantly out the window. He senses the car
slowing down. They're directly alongside the van, on
the wrong side of the road. Kate toots the horn, twice,
and gestures across Daniel to the driver of the van. A
middle-aged woman in a headscarf looks over. Daniel
presses back into his seat as Kate honks again and gives
the woman the finger. She looks back to the road to see
another car coming towards them and just in time pulls
ahead of the van and on to her side of the road. There's

a light squealing noise between the cars as they pass in a
close rush of air.

'Shit.'

He looks at Kate. Her mouth and nostrils have gone
white and her eyes are lasers scorching the road.

'I know,' she says. 'I'm sorry.' There's a pause. 'Stupid
cunt. Pass me the Coke?'

The road is lined with poplars, sparsely covered in dull
bronze leaves. The sky, a high cornflower colour,
transparent at the horizon, is streaked with white clouds
like something out of Dali. Kate squints. Her sunglasses
are on the telephone table at home. She scams a cigarette
off of Daniel. Its buzz disconnects her head somehow
and she opens her window for the sharp air. Daniel puts
a tape on and they sing along loudly. La la, sings Kate,
instead of the words. After a bit she stops just to listen
to Daniel.

'You can really sing,' she says in a gap between songs.

'Oh, nah. Well, ah. So can you.'

She laughs. 'That's a lie. I just shout and hope I get
something right.'

'Yeah, but . . .' He really likes her voice. Its husky
edge that ends in a squeak when she's amused, her dirty
laugh. He doesn't tell her this.

'Hey, here we are.'

The strangeness of walking about after the intensity of
the car makes them weak and giggly.

'My idea of hell,' Kate says in the queue for tickets,
'is black-water rafting. Stuck under the ground, in
freezing cold water with only a flashlight to see with' —
she clutches her throat, eyes wide — 'squeezing through

tiny tunnels, up to your chin in water, wearing a tight
rubber wetsuit. What if you got stuck? Jammed into one
of those little crevices, the water rising and rising and
rising, you're pinned down by rocks, you can't escape,
it's so cold . . .'

Daniel has a light-headed sensation, an understanding
that this is the furthest south he's ever been in his life
and he's got further to go, a feeling like he's in a lift
dropping a long way down and the usual rules of gravity
do not apply. He and Kate join a handful of German
and Japanese tourists around the main cave's entrance.
An earnest young woman with a regulation sweatshirt
covering enormous breasts introduces herself as their
guide. While she's reciting the spiel about the history of
the caves Daniel studies Kate's back and legs. Her dark
goldy-coloured hair. The group shuffle forward into the
cave and he shuffles with them. Something about
stalactites and stalagmites, says the guide. Something
about limestone. They move down through a small
hallway in the rock. It's cool and damp and very black.
Daniel imagines the massive weight of stone above
them. His knee begins to shake. He looks at Kate again,
concentrates on her stubborn chin, the straightness of
her spine. They're standing on the edge of a large pool
of water. He thinks about going back, outside to the dry
air and the light. But everyone steps into the small row-
boat – the Japanese couple, the Germans, and calmly,
quietly, as if she's in another world, Kate. The guide
looks at him. Kate turns, slow motion, to look at him.
The whole boatload of tourists look at him. Without
smiling he puts one foot into the boat. He's like this for
a moment – one foot on the solid safe platform and the
other on the unsteady wood of the dinghy, moving

gently in the water. He takes a breath, shifts his weight and brings the other foot into the boat, sitting down in a quick and ungainly way. They rock slightly. The guide pushes off and begins to row out into the middle of the underground lake. Though no one has been talking, now a new kind of silence falls. The cave is domed, an enormous underground cathedral. As they move towards the lake's centre the ceiling rises above them, vaulted and vast. It's covered with clusters of tiny white gold lights. The air is moist and slow over Daniel's face and throat as he cranes his neck backwards, open-mouthed at the surprise of it, trying to discern a pattern in the constellation of sparkles.

The guide stops rowing and they sit balanced just inside the close surface water, protected from the depths by only the flimsy frame of the boat. In the dim light the Japanese couple are like a black and white photo-graph, dark hair and eyes shining. Their fingers are tightly intertwined, knuckles taut. The Germans' lumpy faces are Commedia masks, shadowed and lit in peculiar pockets. The guide starts to say something, the weary opening sentence of a rote monologue about the cave. 'Quiet,' says the German woman, her head dropped forward as if she's listening for something. It's like being under the Milky Way and under water at the same time. The glow-worms glitter like phosphorescent dust, like icy snow. The seven of them float suspended there, darkness above and below and all around them except for the scattered, random glimmers overhead.

One summer holiday when Daniel was small he went to stay with his mother's sister and her husband at their bungalow in Cornwall. They left him to play on his own during the day but he wasn't supposed to go as far

as the cliffs, and not down the path to the stony beach
either. This left him only the garden, where his uncle
sat on a kitchen chair reading fishing books, his head,
forearms and knees gradually becoming crimson. The
aunt was a nurse-aide to some old people in the nearby
town. She would disappear each morning, leaving a tray
of sticky honey sandwiches, and come back to cook
dinner and sit watching the flickering blue of the
television with her husband in their tiny living room.
Often at night Daniel would stand outside in the dark to
look at the bungalow. The windows were too small to
see anything except the erratic electric lightening and
darkening of the room. Then he would look up above
the roof of the house, above the cloud-shaped plane tree
behind it, to the spreading ink of country-dark sky and
the hard points of country-bright stars.

At school they'd learned about stars, and Daniel tried
to spot the different shapes. Mostly he didn't understand
how they could name a group of stars after something it
looked nothing like, not even if you tried really hard to
join the dots in your mind. He knew Orion, and the
Plough, and he looked and looked for the Pleiades but
couldn't find them. He'd liked the idea of the Pleiades,
a moving family of stars travelling together through
space. Daniel wanted to move through space too, but
thought he'd probably do it all alone. He wondered if
you could count all the stars in the Milky Way, or if
anyone ever had. The teacher had said that people used
to believe the Milky Way was a road and the dead souls
travelled along it on their way to heaven. He was
looking forward to that.

It was on the same holiday that he and his uncle had
watched an old film about Scott of the Antarctic, one
unusually cold afternoon. In black and white they

watched Scott and his brave team battle blizzards and
starvation, and attempt to cross the largest glacier in the
world. Captain Oates was the youngest one in the
movie, and the most good-looking. I'm going out, Daniel
heard for the first time in his life, And I may be some
time. That had been it. The words became a mantra to
him. He'd repeat them in the night until he fell asleep,
sometimes imagining himself stepping outside, frost-
bitten and starving, into the wide white promise of
oblivion. Other times he was falling into space, into the
infinite darkness, seeing all the stars from different angles,
moving with the Pleiades on their endless, questless
journey.

After another minute or two the subterranean quiet
becomes uncomfortable. The cavernous limbo oppresses
him. Hanging there in the in-between space the stalactites and stalagmites don't reach, Daniel nudges the
guide's leg with his foot. Come back to life, he thinks,
get us out of here. He wants to be on the shore, heading
away from this interior, this vacuum, blinking towards
the harsh southern light.

'You want to see some more stuff?' Kate shouts to
Daniel once she's back behind the wheel, music blasting
through the car and rushing out the open windows. She
feels weightless, elated, hungry.
   'OK,' he shouts back, his thoughts unknown to her.
   She smiles. 'There's a map in the glovebox. You can
navigate.'
   He's not bad either, apart from his pronunciation of
place names. They buy drive-in McDonald's for lunch
and don't stop. Kate balances a Coke between her knees
and steers with a cheeseburger in one hand. A sharp

bend surprises her and she brings the car back to the left
too fast. The Coke tips sideways with a rush of ice cubes
and starts to leak onto her leg. She brushes at her jeans
as Daniel retrieves the plastic cup. Their hands knock
against each other.

'Thanks,' she says.

He holds the cup out, straw pointing towards her
mouth. 'You want some?'

She bends her neck sideways and takes a sip, keeping
her eyes on the road, suppressing a smile. They rattle
over a bridge, low above its flat tan river. The hills
are rough and crumpled looking. Jagged valleys sit in
deep shadow. A strange animal is silhouetted on a hill
ridge.

'Is that a goat?'

Kate looks for it. 'Uh, a llama.'

'What are those trees?'

'Don't know. Some kind of palm?'

They drive past a sign saying Pigs Pigs, and another,
by a blackened tree stump, advertising Home Kills.

'Are we all right for petrol?' Daniel asks.

War memorials. Rotary and Lions Club signs. Flat lawns
with water tanks and bare hexagonal clothes lines. The
dark brightness of sun through rain clouds. And a stink,
a yellow, soft-edged, rotten-egg stink.

'What the fuck?'

'It's sulphur.'

'Jesus.' Daniel's face is elongated in disgust. 'People
live id this? All the tibe?'

'When I was a kid I used to wonder, if you lived
here, would normal air smell revolting to you the way
this does to us. But I knew someone from round here

once, in Indonesia. She said the smell made her feel sick every day of her life. But wait. It's worth it.'

They walk lightly, slowly, over wooden footbridges by the mud pools. Leaning on tiptoes over the chicken wire fencing, they gasp at the thick, boiling, elephant-grey mud. It gloops into ripples, heavy, lazy, surreal. Kate hangs on to the fence rail and curves her spine backwards in a languorous way, pulling herself slowly in again. She turns to Daniel and laughs from behind the cheap pink sunglasses she bought at the souvenir shop. He lifts his camera from around his neck and snaps a photograph. Does he have film in there? They walk on through the acrid steam.

A slight slope leads up to another platform. Brittle rock surrounds a large steam-shrouded pool edged with citrine yellow sulphur crystals. A gust of water sweeps the steam to one side and reveals opaque turquoise water, fizzing with millions of tiny bubbles. The day's gone Kodacolor vivid. Daniel's dizzied by the sharp blue sky, dark emerald leaves of the native trees, the endless varying khaki and beige in the tall grasses. Volcanic rock, cascading as if a fall of lava has been snap-frozen and fossilized, scored with sulphur. Kate's rose-pink sunglasses against the poisonously green water.

They race along a path up the side of a hill, between scraggled pines. From a viewing platform they stare down at the whole thermal valley, mud and whirlpools and steam gushing out of fissures in the chalky rock. It's like heaven and hell mixed together, thinks Daniel. Like the moon. At eye level, miles away past a distant lake, stands the dark bulk of a mountain.

'What's that?'

'Mount Tarawera. It blew up about a hundred years ago. There were these special rock formation terraces there, like the eighth wonder of the world.'

Daniel is leaning against a post with a fag in his hand, eyes hidden behind his fringe. She takes a step towards him. He shakes the hair out of his eyes to look at her and holds his cigarette hand up. 'Drag?'

She takes the ciggie from between his fingers, turning to look at the mountain again as she brings the cigarette to her lips. Kiss me now, she thinks, just step two feet closer and kiss me now. She exhales and watches the thin smoke disperse in the autumn air, the dense steam below. One. Two. Three. Four. Five. All right, she'll count to ten. Six. Seven. She swivels to face him − and he's not there, he's by the back of the platform, hands in his jeans pockets, shoulders raised to his ears.

'You cold?'

'A bit.'

She hands him back the ciggie as she passes him, like a relay runner. 'There's one more thing.' Stumbling and tripping, she leads them back down the path to the warm valley.

A large rock stands in front of some scrubby bush, surrounded by chicken wire. Kate skips a few feet away to read a wooden sign and comes back smiling. 'OK,' she says, jigging up and down. 'Couple of minutes.'

Daniel has adjusted to this seething, stinking, rumbling world. He raises his maybe empty camera and clicks it at each new sight, like he's getting to own the place by lying to it, making the gesture of capturing its image. He has a brief fantasy of himself as a comic-book adventurer, clambering over mountains, fording rivers, fighting off wild beasts with his bare hands, etcetera. Dangerous Dan, his comic strip would be called, or The Traveller. He rubs his eyes and cringes at himself, standing there spindly and pale in the flood of afternoon light from the low sun. The Pommie Git would be a more likely name. It's strange to think Europeans have only been here for a couple of hundred years, not even that. He wonders if Kate and the others feel as if they belong. There's a whack on his shoulder. Kate's jumping up and down on the spot. He's not sure where he should be looking, then a bush behind the rock releases a cloud-spray of steam. It's just disappearing and out of the rock surges a great blast of water. A fountain, jetting about thirty metres high in heaving pulses. It plumes and sprays above them, slowing and then bursting up again. Kate laughs, glad that Daniel is not the sort of person to shout out Whoo-hoo at the sight of this. He's looking up at the fine mist on the very top of the geyser, watching it catching the light, a small smile on his unreadable face.

Distant hills are scarred with bulldozer gouges, matchstick black tree trunks lying scattered against the orange clay. Large dark birds cruise overhead. Kate's tapping the steering wheel and humming along to a crackly country and western station she's found on the radio, singing softly every now and then as if Daniel isn't there. All my exes live in Texas . . . And on the other hand . . . there is a wedding band . . . She's cross with him for not kissing her and cross with herself for wanting him to. They get held up by some roadworks.

'There's some waterfalls down there, you want to see them?'

'I don't know. Do I?'

'They're pretty. But just waterfalls. A guy was killed there a few years ago as part of an S&M routine. Trussed up and chucked in the river. Like one of your politicians.'

'Do you want to see them?'

'Not really.' She gets out of the car to ask one of the roadwork men how long they're going to be. Minute or two, he says, and she wanders over to the verge, looks up at a huge eucalyptus, stretches her arms out above her head. Wellington. Nina. Shit. She walks back to the car. 'What time is it?'

'Five. Just after.'

'Oh.'

'Is that OK?'

'Well.'

They can make it there tonight, easily, if she drives in the dark. The light is softening already. If they find a place round here to stay, will he think it's a set-up? Is it a set-up? She doesn't trust herself much. The road guy waves them forward.

The lake is as massive and serene as ever. Kate cringes, as usual, passing the turn-off to the holiday camp of her childhood. She pulls over by a fruit and vege stand at the lakeside, just past the town.

'You coming?'

Daniel lights another cigarette and listens to a scrawny woman haggle with the fruit-seller over the price of some apples, as Kate sprints across the road and down to the water's edge. He cranes to see what she's doing then, oh fuck it, jogs after her. Her shoes and socks lie in a grubby-looking heap on the pebbles. She's ankle-deep in the water, her arms held out horizontally, waving slightly up and down. 'Oh my God, oh my God, oh my God.'

'Cold?'

'Fucking freezing. You've got to do it.'

'No way.'

'You've got to.' She stands breathless in the bone-chilling water, the pure clear water, and shoots him a look of contempt that isn't all mockery. 'Pussy.'

A windsurfer drifts past behind her.

'Just come and feel it with your hand.'

He walks up to the edge. Closer. Closer. And – he knew she'd do this – is hit in the face with a wet splash of ice. It drips from his hair and Kate cackles, staggering to regain her balance. He yanks his trainers and his socks off. She looks unashamedly at his long bony feet, then up to his darkening eyes. He wades in, the bottom of his jeans soaking up water, cups his hands and hurls as much as he can right at her. She shrieks and he does it again, not even noticing how cold it is. They kick water at each other, Kate shouting in her hoarse way, Daniel panting and silent, until Kate stumbles out of the water, feet aching on the bumpy stones. Daniel collapses on the bank beside her and rubs hard at his feet. Forcing them wet and cold back into his trainers is extremely unpleasant.

'I can't move my toes.' Kate laughs. She makes a half-hearted attempt to pull her socks on and gives up. 'It's no good. I'm going to die of hypothermia.'

'Come on.' Daniel grabs her shoes with one hand and pulls her up with the other. He lets go as soon as she's on her feet. Cheers, thinks Kate, he might as well wipe the girl germs off on his jeans. He runs across the road

without looking behind him. As he slams into the side
of the car there's a sharp squeal of brakes. He turns. A
scarlet car swerves and speeds off, horn blasting. Kate's
standing in the middle of the road. It must have just
missed her. Her face, white, mouth open, stares across
the black asphalt at him. A bird lands in a tall tree. He
makes a gesture and she puts one foot in front of the
other, like a sleepwalker, until she is standing with him
beside the car. He reopens the driver's door and she sits
down, still looking straight ahead, eyes full with water.
A tear edges over and she shakes her head, crinkles up
her face, controls it.

'Are you OK?'

She nods. 'Yeah, I'm fine.'

'Hang on a sec.' He comes back with a chocolate bar
from the fruit and vege man. 'Eat this.'

She grins.

'What?'

'You'll be offering me a nice cup of tea next.'

'Fuck that. Sure you're OK?'

She nods again, mouth full of chocolate bar, holds it
out to him and mumbles, 'Want some?'

'No. Uh, here are your shoes.' He places them on the
gravel below her dangling brown feet. 'I could drive.'

'You can't drive.' She sniffs and laughs. 'I feel so
stupid.'

'Just take it easy.'

So she does, past the glass-topped lake, its far side
blanketed in mist. They take it easy driving by red hot
pokers, toe toe, agapanthus skeletons. In and out of
shadows through the bends carved in layers of volcanic
soil. Pylons line the road either side of them. A road
sign warns of wild horses.

'That's the volcano.'

It lies black and white, immense, to the west.

'It's not doing anything.'

'Comes and goes.'

They fall silent. Light zigzags in the leaves of cabbage trees, reflects off the trunks of poplars, the sheeted bark of gums. The shadows lengthen and lengthen until, on the long straight of road, everything flashes into negative, back again, and the last of the sun drops behind the horizon. It's still and cold. They follow a khaki tarpaulin-covered army truck into a town and stop for petrol.

'Are you OK?' Daniel asks, stamping softly on the concrete forecourt, hugging himself under the fluorescent light.

'Yeah. But listen. Have you got much money on you?'

'A bit.' He's got what Josh gave him as a loan. It's more than a bit but he needs to be careful with it.

'It's just— I might see if there's anywhere we can stay near here. Uh. I don't really want to do another four and a half hours in the dark.'

'Oh. OK'

Kate studies the petrol meter intently. 'Do you mind?'

'No. Whatever.'

But when she asks the red-nosed, almost albino attendant he tells her there was a murder in the nearest town last night, at the pub, and the hotel owner's been taken in for questioning.

'Small-town bloody Gothic.' Kate helps herself to a freeze-dried cappuccino. 'Shooting or stabbing?'

'Shooting. There was a knife too, I think. Did unholy damage to the upholstery what I can hear. Bit of a brawl.'

'Yeah, right.'
'You could head west. Other side of the mountain.'

Kate's first holiday away from her family was at the ski
village he's talking about. Her then boyfriend had
organized a skiing trip with his mates and she'd tagged
along. The mountain was snowed in so they sat around
the pub all weekend, drinking rum and Cokes and
playing pool. Her first proper boyfriend, the first one
she'd slept with. He was the one who said to her 'You're
my ideal woman', except the way he talked it sounded
like My Ordeal Woman. She was probably his perfect
girl because she looked like a boy. She'd loved that
holiday – being treated like an honorary bloke, losing
at pool and drinking games, wearing her boyfriend's
flannel shirt and rolling cigarettes for him. He was thick.
She knew it at the time and it didn't seem to matter,
given everything else he had going for him. But she
changed.

A bright moon rises and bounces white off the moun-
tainside, shiny on the cold road in front of them. Stars
appear, frosty in the thick blackness of the sky. Daniel
chainsmokes. Kate concentrates on the blinking cat's
eyes lining the road, on the rough asphalt being swallowed underneath them, framed in the unmoving beam
from the headlights. She's not going to try anything
embarrassing on him. He won't come on to her, that's
clear, even if he is interested.

'Look at that,' he says, pointing to steam seeping out
of the limestone hills like smoke in the moonlight.

They push on past one small town, hotels closed for
the off-season.

'Is South Island like this too?'

'The South Island. I haven't been there much. It's mostly empty. Beautiful and empty.'
'That's what I hear.'

The pub is neither where Kate remembers it being or how she remembers it looking. It's a 1940s stucco building, lounge bar and public bar either side of the reception desk, rooms in the upstairs extension and at the back. An oldish woman with grey chin whiskers and a floaty floral smock answers the cracked ding of the bell. Her horn-rimmed glasses are so scratched it's impossible to see her eyes. Any more of that beard, thinks Daniel, and she'd be ready for a Diane Arbus snapshot.

'Double, twin or singles?'
'How much are the singles?'
'Thirty. Twins are fifty.'
'Two singles, please.' Kate smiles at Daniel in a cheery way as if to say, isn't this all quite normal. He wanders off to the cigarette machine while the woman takes their names and Kate ducks out to the car park to check the registration number. The eerie landscape has left a free-falling feeling in him. He'd like to get smashed.

The rooms are identical, small rectangles with pale yellow candlewick bedspreads and matching watercolours of a brown mountain river edged with reeds above the handbasins. A smell of dust and soap. Kate wanders into the left-hand room. There's a window looking back out to the car park and, beyond that, over a field to dark tree shapes hedged against the lighter horizon of sky. She presses her forehead against the cold pane and stares. She feels homesick for something but it's not her home.

Daniel dumps his suitcase on the bed and just about

sprints down the stairs to the bar. There's a couple of large geezers leaning against pool cues in the public bar. One of them gives Daniel a level stare. His mate checks him up and down, then looks back to the bottom of his pint glass. Kate'd probably rather be in the lounge bar, Daniel decides. He sets himself up there with a pint, a chaser and a copy of the local newspaper. He skim-reads the lead feature about wild horses and the damage they're doing to native plants, then a piece about a new type of carrot that might be ideally suited to the region's soil. Letters to the Editor pleading people to spare a thought for dog owners, or wild-horse lovers, or turnip growers. Several women are in competition for the local home-spun knitting market. A crèche is going to close down if they can't raise enough money. Plans for a casino are being brought before the regional council. Local man arrested for sex offences – no details and no name.

'Hey.' Kate hops on to the barstool next to him. Has she done something to her hair? There's an undefinable difference in her appearance, like when someone switches from specs to contact lenses, or when his dad shaved off his moustache and neither Daniel nor his mother noticed for two days. He squints at the empty pint glass on the bar. He's losing tolerance if it's beer goggles time already.

'Gin and tonic, please,' she says to the suddenly atten-tive barman. She shakes a cigarette out of Daniel's pack and lights it in an urgent way. 'I just called my sister.'

'Is that why you're smoking?'

'Yeah. Usually out my ears.'

★

'Where are you?' Nina had said.

'Just over halfway.'

'Oh.'

'We'll be arriving tomorrow now. If that's still OK.'

'Well, of course, you can arrive whenever you'd like.' Nina was giving her vowel sounds a phony BBC edge that she always laid on when she was pissed off. 'It's just that I was expecting you this evening. That's all.'

A brief pause. Don't say sorry, don't say sorry, Kate told herself. 'Oh, well. We'll see you tomorrow.'

'Do you have any idea what sort of time?' asked the Queen of England.

'Not really. Could you leave a key in the letter box?'

'All right.'

'Well take care then, see you tomorrow.'

'Goodbye.'

'Nina?'

'Mm?'

'Sorry if this is a hassle, eh.' Damn.

'No, it's fine. See you.'

And Ice Queen had hung up. Kate clunked down the receiver and looked at her reflection in the glass door. You're pathetic, she said.

Kate and Daniel spent the next day's petrol money on lager for him and gin for her. One thing they're both pretty good at is getting drunk. Daniel loosens up, he chills out. He laughs at himself when he tries to pronounce Maori place names, when beer dribbles out the side of his mouth, when his elbow slips off the table. That one really cracks him up. And Kate, Kate smokes like a demon, she can't work the cigarette machine, she thumps it, she sings into her tonic bottle, she eats the flesh out of her lemon segment and sucks on the rind, she laughs when Daniel laughs and sometimes when he doesn't. She says, Fuck Nina. And thinks, You probably will.

After the bar stools become too precarious they migrate to a couple of squishy armchairs in a corner by the non-operational fake fire. Further drinks are ordered.

'Do you have a boyfriend then, Kate?' Daniel asks. He pulls his chair right up close to hers.

'No,' she says, with a flick of her head, as if people ask this question every day of the week and she doesn't mind in the slightest. 'Do you? Back in London?'

'Nah. Don't have a girlfriend either.'

'Ha ha.' Kate coughs and wonders what to say next. 'I came here with a boyfriend once.' Now he's going to think it's a special romantic place she brings prospective shags to. 'Ah, yeah,' she covers for time. 'The first guy I slept with actually.'

'Really? What, here?'

'No, we, ah, I mean I slept with him here – God – but we, we had done it before that.'

'Oh.'

Actually, that's not true. They'd fooled around a lot before, done everything but. It was here – in this pub – when his mates were comatose in the next room, that they'd pushed their beds together and had quick, drunken, painful, lights-out sex. Oh Christ. Now if Daniel asks her the virginity question she's going to have to make something up, and if she does that it'll be a lie between them and when they're old and married with grandchildren she'll always have to remember the fabricated version – oh, stop it, she tells herself, stop it stop it.

'What was he like?'

'He was a cunt. Well, when I say cunt—'

'He binned you?'

She laughs. 'No, actually. But he did start fucking someone else. And I found out about it, so.'

'What a cunt.'

'Exactly. Another one?'

Up at the bar she wonders if she's got him in the bag. And if she has, is she really interested? What about her new pledge of no sex without love? Oh, of course she's interested. She imagines what Lucy would say: Get conscious, Kate, why do you think you manoeuvred this little overnight stay in a bed and breakfast? You wanted him secured before you arrive at your sister's. I know, I know, she'd say, I'm a hopeless, deluded fool. But the thing is this – as she watches the barman open another bottle of gin – she doesn't trust her reasons for wanting to sleep with him. At this stage of the evening, the quality of the potential shag is highly questionable. He's a distraction, she realizes with sudden clarity. A distraction from the uselessness of her life. A fucking Band-Aid.

Back at the armchairs, the distraction's nodding off. He rubs his eyes at the millionth pint glass placed in front of him. Takes a mouthful. Makes a face. Wonders if Kate expects him to take her to bed. Wonders if he wants to.

'What did you want to be,' she's asking him, 'when you grew up?'

He shrugs.

'Sorry. Bad question.' She exhales. The conversation's run dry fast.

'What about you?'

She thinks. 'Well, when I was at school I wanted to be a keyboard player. Specifically, I wanted to be the

girl on keyboards in that band that Joy Division turned
into after that guy killed himself.'

'New Order.'

'Yeah, New Order. I wanted to play keyboards in a
band like that and have no facial expression.'

'And how long was this your ambition?'

'Oh – three, four years.'

'What have you found to replace it?' He smiles.

She smiles back. 'I don't know. Sometimes I think
what I'm looking for is a life, not a lifestyle. Does that
sound dumb? No,' she laughs, 'don't say.' There's a
pause. 'What's my ambition? Nothing really.' She looks
off to the side.

'You look off to the side when you're self-conscious,'
he says.

She looks off to the side again, still laughing. 'Oh
great. Now I'm self-conscious about being self-
conscious.'

When the barman starts putting the stools away and
turning off the lights and they stand up to go to bed, she
plays that game where you act as if you're not expecting
anything to happen with the other person and then
you'll act surprised when it does. Daniel stretches in a
fake way. Businesslike, Kate climbs the stairs, slowing
down a little when she senses Daniel falling behind. She
stands outside the door to her room with a platonic
smile. 'Night then.'

'Night,' he says, scratching his head with one hand
and opening his door with the other.

'Ah,' she says, 'what time do you want to get up?'

'Whenever,' he says, 'does it need to be early?'

She yawns, hand over her mouth. 'Oh no. Not too
early.'

'Hmn.' He grunts and falls into his room.

She cleans her teeth and washes her face and lies on the bed, thinking alternately, Damn. Thank God. Damn. Thank God. Damn.

NINE   Five glasses of water. Two Panadols. Three pots of tea. Egg, bacon, tomato, sausage and toast. A Coca-Cola. More toast. Kate scarfs this lot while Daniel nibbles at a dry biscuit.

'You need to stock up.'

'No, thanks, I don't feel so good.'

The slow hangover calm hangs over them. Kate moves at half speed. They do not say much, as if oxygen's a precious commodity that needs to be conserved. Kate studies the map and decides which route to follow, a process that takes several minutes. It's a cloudy day and the air is damp. Slowly, calmly, they get into the car. Kate stretches out lightly shaking fingers to pick up the tacky pink sunglasses from the dashboard and hooks them over her ears. She rubs the back of her hand across her mouth and revs the car. A quick look to Daniel's pale green skin and closed eyes. 'You going to be all right?'

'Mnph.'

It's on the tip of her tongue to say, Lucky we didn't have sex, eh, but she bites it back. The vice tightens around her temples like Buddha's disapproval. 'Daniel?' Her voice is hoarse and her throat burns.

'Mn.'

'Did you have that TV programme called *Monkey*?'

'Mn.'

She negotiates a tricky corner. 'If Monkey was called Monkey and Pigsy was called Pigsy, why do you think Sandy wasn't called Fishy?'

He opens one eye about a millimetre. 'Kate. These thoughts are meaningless. They do not need to be vocalized.'

'Of course. Thank you.'

They cruise through the hills back to the state highway, past spikes of flax and creamy toe toe. If someone sends you a white feather, thinks Kate, it means you're a coward. Or is it a yellow one? 'Daniel?'

'Mn?'

'Never mind.'

Fat drops of rain explode onto the windscreen, thicker and faster with every telegraph pole they pass. Hills and railway tracks and tussock. A corrugated iron barn dripping, rusting in a paddock. The rain drums down, sluicing off the windscreen, on to the black road, on to scrumpled gorse roadsides, on cows and wooden houses and a long orange truck pulled over in a layby. Grey rain in the fallen oak trees, in the dark native bush, in a grey river they cross on a one-way bridge. In the shelter belts of pine and macrocarpas, rain. It stops just as they come down the coast road into Wellington, revealing Kapiti island looming dark and silent out on the purple sea.

She tries three wrong, lookalike winding streets before finding Nina's. Crazy city, all jammed up in the hills. The harder it is to drive around a suburb, the more exclusive it seems to be. If this is true, Nina's not doing too badly for herself. It's early evening and the sky is pink. Kate turns off the engine, undoes her seatbelt and sits looking for a minute at the gold light on the wall of Nina's one-storey wooden house. She turns to Daniel and smiles. 'Well. This is it.'

It's an odd feeling, getting the keys from the letter
box and letting themselves in through the stained-glass
front door, walking through the silent house. Large
mirrors in the hallway, the living room and the kitchen
send the rooms angling off into disconcerting extensions.
The place is spotless, as though it's been professionally
cleaned. Kate's only been once before, with Ginny, for
a disastrous Christmas a couple of years ago. Nina had
spent a fortune on elaborate food and was deeply
offended when Kate got an inexplicable stomach cramp
and couldn't eat it. There had been one nice moment –
when was it? – they'd sat outside in the little garden at
the back and fallen asleep together, their heads in the
shade of a large apple tree and their legs warmed by the
sun. Kate checks through the kitchen window that the
tree is still there. It's shivering in the wind, only half
covered with leaves. There's a note on the sink bench:
Back 6.30.

Daniel's in the middle of the living room, an uncertain
expression on his face. Every fashionable novel of the
last decade and several impressively dog-eared classics lie
about on shelves and on the floor in an extremely casual
way. The sofa is covered with a worn but once beautiful
throw rug thing. Two mismatched armchairs are draped
in the same way and one of them is piled high with
magazines, the expensive kind. There are various lumps
of stone and shell and curious little objects thrown
around the place. On one wall is a large abstract painting,
all brooding oils; on another is a black and white
photograph, unframed and curling at the edges, of a
woman and young girl.

'Is this her?' he asks.

'Yeah,' says Kate. 'And Mum.'

'There's no telly.'

'It's in the bedroom.'

'Is it OK to leave the bags here?'

'Yeah, I'm sure.'

Oh God. The fold-out couch. Last time Kate and Nina had shared it while Ginny slept in the bedroom. Somehow Kate can't see Nina giving up her double bed for Daniel. Which means . . . Oh well it'll just have to be done. 'I'm fucked. Do you want to go out soon, hair of the dog?'

'Yeah, all right.'

'I, uh, might just have a shower.'

And it was, of course, while she was in there, slowly rotating her body under the warm water, that she heard the front door slam. Either Daniel had made a run for it or her sister was back early. The distant rise and fall of voices confirmed Nina's return. Kate quickly shut down the shower, leaving unrinsed-off soap under her arms, and tried to dry and dress herself and call out Hello at the same time. With the result that she now stands in the doorway to the living room, her T-shirt back to front and knickers twisted, hair dripping down her neck and onto the intentionally kitsch linoleum floor.

'Kate, hi.'

They step towards each other in an A-line hug. Kate's hair drips. Daniel is standing behind Nina, hands in his pockets and shoulders high, studying some fascinating detail on the floor.

'Uh, Nina this is Daniel.'

They nod at each other and Nina smiles. 'Yes, we've just done all that. Are you exhausted? You're dripping wet. I'll get you a—'

She disappears into the steamed-up bathroom before Kate can say anything and comes back with a fluffy

white towel. She holds this out to Kate, faintly wrinkling
her perfect nose. 'Good, you found that shampoo. It's
lovely isn't it. Unbelievably expensive. Shall we all have
a glass of wine?'

'Hey,' says Kate, 'I saw that interview you did. It was
great.'
  'Oh, it was OK.'
  'The photo was nice.'
  'What's this?' asks Daniel.
  'Oh, nothing—'
  'Nina's been in this magazine, being famous.'
  'Have you got it here?'
  'I doubt it.' Nina stands up and goes straight to a pile
of magazines on a table in the corner. She flicks through
them in an off-hand way. 'Oh, yeah, here it is.'
  'Thanks.'
  I'm hoping people see the longevity of me, Daniel reads,
*and not just see me as the girl of the summer. — It's a privilege
to be able to promote home-grown musical talent. — What
people don't understand is, reading an autocue is a real skill.
It's hard not to let your eyes move from side to side. — There's
no one special man in my life right now. I know it's a cliché,
but I'm married to my job.*
  'I was in a couple of bands,' he lies, 'in London.'
  'Oh, really? Who?'
  'Was that after art school?' asks Kate.
  'Mm,' he says to her, and to Nina, 'You wouldn't
have heard of us. Do you know a band called Bill?'
  A flicker of excitement crosses Nina's face. 'Yes,' she
says, 'were you with them?'
  'Well, no,' he says, 'but a mate of mine was, he was
their drummer for a bit, then he left to form this band
with me.'

'Oh. I see.'

'We used to hang out with the guys from Bill a bit, you know. But ah, we didn't really have any success ourselves.' The lying makes him laugh, and the sisters laugh too. Nina has a new way of laughing that Kate hasn't seen before, throwing her head back and arching her throat. 'We were more in it for the lifestyle.'

'Did you get that?' Nina asks.

'Nah, not really.' He blushes. 'Never had that much luck with girls.'

Nina seems to know all the staff at the Indian restaurant she takes them to. She exchanges greetings with the manager, a middle-aged woman wearing a pom-pom jumper. 'This is my sister Kate,' she says, 'and this is her boyfriend Daniel. They've—'

'Oh, uh—' says Kate.

'Just come down from Auckland.'

'We're just friends,' Kate smiles to the manager, 'uh—' She looks at Daniel who is staring at the menu. She sort of shrugs and laughs once, through her teeth, and picks up her own menu to hide behind. Oh well, she mouths to herself. Oh, well.

Nina's doing a superb job of appearing not to have been present during the last seven seconds. She touches the manager's arm lightly, gracefully, and without looking at the menu orders for them all. 'Is this all right?' she smiles at Daniel, who nods hard and says, 'Brilliant.'

'Brilliant, oh that's so *English*,' she says in the sort of voice she might use while squeezing his biceps. If he had any. 'I love all your British expressions.'

Kate cringes but he doesn't seem to mind.

'So,' Nina dimples, 'does everyone ask you what you think of New Zealand? We're supposed to be famous

for that. You know, Oh great European please pass
judgement on our little country.'

'Oh. No, not really. I haven't been asked. But I like
it, it's freaky looking. Slow. Kind of like England in the
nineteen sixties.'

Kate grits her teeth. As if he would know. He was
barely born then.

'Oh I know what you *mean*,' says Nina. 'It is a little
sleepy here. Still, we do our best to have a good
time.'

'Daniel's staying at Frank's place while he's away,'
offers Kate, but Nina doesn't say, Oh Frank, he's
gorgeous, didn't you used to go out with him? like she's
supposed to. It's hard to tell if she's even heard because
at that moment a young girl comes up to the table,
blushing furiously, and says, 'Excuse me, are you Nina
from the music programme?'

Nina looks at Kate and Daniel with wide, bemused
eyes. 'Yes I am. What's your name?'

'Tracy.'

'How are you, Tracy?'

'Um. Could I have your autograph?' The kid holds
out a dirtyish scrap of paper. Nina laughs and goes a bit
pink. 'Oh, how embarrassing. Who's it for, Tracy?'

'It's for my dad. He's outside. We saw you in the
window.'

Nina's favourite table faces out onto one of the busiest
streets in the city. 'Shall I put For Tracy's Dad, then?'
Nina signs away and gives the girl a reassuring smile as
she hands the paper back. 'And what do you want to do
when you grow up, Tracy?'

'I want to be on the television like you.'

'Well, good luck!' She waves her away with a little

flutter of her fingers. 'God I'm sorry about that,' she says
to the others.

'You're pretty famous here,' says Daniel, grinning.

'She's their golden girl, aren't you? You might be
moving to Auckland?'

'Oh, did Mum tell you that? Don't say anything to
anyone, nothing's finalized. So. Daniel. What exactly
are you doing here? Just tripping around?'

'Yeah,' he smiles. 'You could say that.'

Over dinner Nina uses a combination of flattery and
journalism-school interrogation technique to extract as
much information from Daniel as she can. She asks him
about himself, about his childhood, about art school,
why he left, what he's done since, why he chose to visit
New Zealand. Kate listens intently, hoping for a revelation, for a clue, a tit-bit she can take back to Lucy and
Josh. But Daniel is a master of evasion. He tells them
stories about the other kids at his school. 'Was it like
Grange Hill,' Kate asks, and he says, Yeah, exactly.
There are stories about art college and a guy he knew
there who had something like a sex addiction and it got
so bad he'd shagged every tutor and the dean and the
dean's mother so they chucked him out. He tells them
about the music scene in London, about the bands he
was in and the struggles, getting ripped off by gig
organizers and the drugs problem his mate Richard
caved in to. How he worked for a major recording
studio there but kept falling asleep on the job because
he lived the other side of London and worked such long
hours he'd miss the last tube home and have to sleep on
the studio floor, how because of the long hours he never
had time to look for a new gaff so he was always

knackered and then he got the push. He tells them that he saved enough money to buy a ticket somewhere and just walked into this dodgy little travel agent one day and booked the cheapest ticket to New Zealand – which meant travelling for forty hours to get there and stopping off in Abu Dhabi, Manila – the airport transit lounges he's seen. Nina touches his arm the way she touched the manager's and when his cigarette smoke drifts across her face she does not fan it away.

Kate watches Nina disappear, reappear, disappear as she shakes a double sheet over the folded-out couch. 'Now. You two don't mind sharing a bed do you? Or I can always share with you and Daniel can have my bed—'

'Oh, well . . .' Kate starts, and doesn't know how to finish.

'No, don't worry about it,' Daniel says, 'don't go giving up your bed. We'll be fine.'

'Night then,' says Nina, leaning over and kissing him – kissing him! – on the cheek. 'See you in the morning,' she nods at Kate, who grabs her bag and runs for the bathroom.

When she comes out, Daniel is in bed, flicking through a paperback. 'Shall I turn the light out?'

'No, I'll get it in a minute. If that's cool.'

'Fine.' She climbs in between the sheets, elbows and knees pointing in on themselves in a tentative way. 'Uh, night.'

'Night.'

She has to lie on her wrong side to face away from him. She needs to go to the loo again. Her arm gets pins and needles from being squashed underneath her body.

There's the light sound of Daniel breathing and of pages turning. She can feel a very faint warmth coming from his direction. The lamplight makes her eyelids flutter. It's impossible to relax. Then – ah – the disembodied, floating, slightly nauseous feeling comes. For a minute – for ten? she drifts, then a falling jolt wakes her. Did she twitch? kick out? She sighs, pulse calming, and sinks again.

Daniel's sleep is disturbed, light, sensitive to every lorry that passes in the street and every blast of wind that shakes the windows in their frames. He has one moment of nearly full consciousness, where he wakes without knowing where he is or with whom and thinks, I want to live in a building that doesn't move. Images loom inside his head, ghosts and spectres that rise and fall in his dreams. These are mostly flashcards of views from the car window, with a subconscious spin: a truck that he and Kate drove past inching its way up a steep hill, a one-storey wooden house strapped to its back. The house, lifted out of its home, exposed to the world, windows dark against the stares. A line of electricity pylons, stalking each other across a stretch of tussock and scrub. A girl with blonde dreadlocks, hitch-hiking south. Given the coolness of the room and the thin layer of blankets, Daniel's body is unusually hot.

Kate sleeps on her stomach, clutching the cushion under her face, pressing close into the mattress. Her sleep is heavy, constant, almost drugged. She sleeps the sleep of the grieving, of the jilted, the deep denying sleep of someone who needs sensory deprivation, of someone who doesn't want to be themselves.

When weak sunlight angles in through the Roman

blinds on to the living room floor, Kate and Daniel are lying, deceptively peaceful-looking, side by side, bodies almost touching – but not quite.

They're in another fishbowl café with Nina, who seems more eager to spend time with Kate than she's ever been before. She waves at various people at other tables and every now and then pops up out of her chair to go and have a chat. Kate and Daniel read the newspaper.

'It's pretty thin here, isn't it,' he says, and Nina rolls her eyes and goes, 'Oh please, the print media in this country is just awful, I so envy you those brilliant English papers. I try to keep up with the *Observer* but of course by the time it's shipped out here it's weeks out of date and I'm not on the internet yet—'

Why, wonders Kate, would you want to read old news from across the other side of the world? She goes to the bathroom and when she gets back some lipsticked cadaver is sitting in her seat. Oh yes, she's met her before, she works at the art gallery, how's it going, she asks, still standing beside her chair, oh really, yeah, I'm still ushering, mm, well it pays the rent. The cadaver finally stands up, kisses Nina, touches Daniel on the arm – what is it about his arms? – moves her fingers in Kate's direction in a gesture that might be interpreted as a wave, and minces off. Before she goes she mumbles something to Nina, who throws her head back, exposing her throat, an expression of amused surprise painted on her lovely face, and laughs her new throaty laugh ah ha ha ha.

At Nina's before they go to the party. She says, looking at Daniel, 'So, Kate, when are you going back?'

'I've got to work on Monday. Tomorrow morning I guess.'

Now Nina's looking down at her own cleavage. 'Do you have to go to work as well, Daniel?'

'Well, I might be doing this show at Josh's radio station, but it's not until next Monday. I mean, it's a pretty casual arrangement.' He knows this is what she wants him to say. Nina's agenda's been obvious from the start. What he isn't certain of is how Kate feels. And how much it matters to him.

'It seems a pity that you have to race away. Couldn't you stay on and then take the train back? Get to know Wellington a bit more.'

Daniel looks at Kate. A smile seems to be expected, so she gives him one. And shrugs. 'Yeah, you should. I don't mind driving back on my own.'

'It's – I'd have to call Josh—'

'Give him a call now. Find out about the show. The code's 09.'

Nina's virtually shoving the receiver in his hand and pressing the buttons for him.

'I don't think they're – oh, hello? Lucy? Hi, it's Daniel. Um, how are things? Is Josh about?' There's a pause in which Kate realizes she is chewing the ends of her fingers. She moves her hand away from her mouth. 'Hi. Yeah, all right.' Daniel's voice is different when he's talking to Josh, more relaxed, less self-conscious. 'Yeah. Nah.' He laughs. 'Shut it. How's everything going? Oh shit. Really.' He fumbles in his pocket for a cigarette, brings it to his lips. Nina clears her throat and he remembers her house is non-smoking. 'Oh, yeah, for sure. Some kids larking about. Can you go ex-directory or something? Right. Well, the reason I'm calling is, I

might stay here for a bit if you don't need me to do that
show straight away—'

As soon as the phone call is over he's outside the front
door firing up that cigarette. Kate appears at his side.
    'Are they OK?'
    'Yeah, he says it's cool, whenever.' Daniel takes a
long drag and watches the smoke drift up into the
dimming sky. It's clear and cold.
    'But are they all right? Josh and Lu?'
    'Yeah, fine. Been having some crank phone calls,
hang-ups, he said it's weirding Lucy out a bit. She
sounded pretty tense.'
    'Oh. I guess she has to be careful because of her job.
If some nutter husband knew where she lived.'
    Crank calls, he thinks. Shit. All it would take is for
Sticksy or Richard or whoever the fuck it was to ask for
him, and he'd be screwed. He stands smoking, facing
the street, in a way that makes Kate shut up. She can't
imagine what it's like, being him, alone here. Though
she can't think of anything to say, she wants to keep him
company. Shivering, she huddles back into the wall of
the house for shelter. Nina's inside somewhere, the *Jaws*
theme pounding through her body, a smile on her face,
mission accomplished.

So-and-so's party is the usual affair: groups of people
who know each other standing around in impenetrable
clumps; girls dressed to draw attention to legs, midriffs,
breasts, dancing in pairs; girls dressed demurely talking
to out-of-it blokes in the kitchen; a couple of people
who clearly just heard the noise from down the road
and wandered in, trying to look as though they belong.
Kate and Daniel stand by a wall and watch as Nina darts

around the room in a flurry of kisses and hair-tossing
and new laughter. She looks to be having a Very Good
Time. It's hard to explain the significance of someone
like Nina at a party – what you think is very different
depending on whether you're a boy or a girl, or one of
her friends. She twirls, she strikes a pose, she's caught
in the flash of a camera bulb – one arm around her
girlfriend, one stuck out at right angles to her body,
tonsils displayed and eyes a-sparkle. If you're a boy she
likes she might grab both your hands in hers and lead
you on to the dance floor, wiggling her hips to the
music. If you're a girl talking to a boy she likes another
one of the things she might do is come and stand very
close to him and start a conversation, her eyelashes going
at double speed, about a mutual friend of theirs that you
don't know. Or she might walk past arm in arm with
one of her best girls, stroking her hair in a sexual way,
laughing a low laugh. These are just some examples.
Whatever she does and whoever you are, you'll notice
her. That's a guarantee.

'How long do you think you'll stay here?' Kate yells up
into Daniel's ear. She's been panic drinking for the last
hour and wobbles slightly as she leans towards him,
almost falling into his nearness.
    'What, in Wellington?'
    She nods.
    'Dunno,' he shrugs, 'not too long.'
    'You think it's too windy to go outside?'
    He shrugs again. 'No, come on.'
    Why can't I just say, Let's go outside, she thinks. Why
can't I say what I mean? They push through to the
relative quiet of the balcony, where another couple – *a*
couple, she tells herself, she and Daniel are not a couple

they're just two people who know each other – are
standing in the corner. The wind has died down a bit.
They light cigarettes. Down the hill are the warm lights
of houses and the shining city buildings. The harbour
water is so black it's invisible, a great hole of nothing
ringed by the chain of lamps along the harbour front.
Looking into the void. They smoke in silence. Kate
gradually tunes into the conversation coming from the
dark corner.

'I thought she'd be here tonight,' says the girl.

'She might turn up later. With Tony or something.'

'I hate that guy. It pisses me off that she hangs out
with him, he's such a turkey.'

'Well. You know why she does.'

'Winds me up. As soon as there's any shit in town
he's round to our place like a shot, flashing his coat
open, luring her away for days on end.'

Daniel lights a cigarette off the one he's just smoked.
Kate holds her hand out for another and he passes it to
her in a mechanical way. The guy is talking now but
he's lowered his voice and it's difficult to hear. Kate
feels a peculiar thrill from trying to listen. He's saying
something about, 'Don't want to have to tell you this –
saw him last week – something in town as well—' What
did he say? *Eight* in town? *Page* in town? The girl says
something Kate can't hear. Then the guy talks again, a
little louder, 'He was all tensed up, it was supposed to
be sooner but I don't know the details, don't want to
know, it's bad enough at the restaurant as soon as they
get a hold of it—'

'Fucking social users,' says the girl. 'If Lisa gets into
that shit I will fucking kill Tony.'

'She's a grown-up, babe. She knows what she's
doing.'

Babe sighs. 'I know. I know I'm not her mother. I
just don't want it in the flat. I don't want anything to go
wrong.'

There's the sound of a match being struck, then the
soothing smell of cannabis and sulphur wafts over to
them. Kate hopes to be offered some, but she isn't. The
couple's mutterings get quieter. She turns to Daniel to
ask if he wants another drink. But he's gone.

Later, the place is even more filled up. Nina and Daniel
are nowhere to be seen. For once, Kate doesn't care
about having no one to talk to. Maybe it's because this
is not her home town. There's no need to worry about
anyone she might know spotting her tragic and abandoned in the corner. She's even considering dancing
when two hands grip her waist from behind, and
squeeze. There's time to think, Surely not Daniel, as she
turns round to face a total stranger. He's tall, with dark
hair, and – well, that's it.

'Sorry,' the stranger says in an unapologetic way. 'I
thought you were someone else.'

'Well, I'm not,' says Kate, 'I don't think. Today I'm
pretty sure I'm me.'

'Lucky you. Why so certain?'

'I don't know anybody here.'

'So you're not anyone else's idea of yourself?'

'Exactly. I can make myself up. And there's nobody
around to tell me any different.'

'What's your name then? Esmerelda? Tatiana?'

'Anastasia,' says Kate. 'I'm of Russian descent.'

The stranger, almost touching her elbow, steers her
towards the drinks table. 'Do you think this is a good
conversation, Anastasia, or do we just think it is because
we're drunk?'

'I think it's as good or as bad as we want it to be.'

He fills her glass with white wine. It mingles with the red already in it. 'Rosé. My favourite.'

'Russian princesses are renowned for their drinking abilities.'

'But it depends on their companions, doesn't it?'

'Allow me to introduce myself.' He bows at the waist. 'Vladimir,' and bends to kiss her hand. Kate gives the room a swift check for any sign of Daniel.

'Vladimir. That reminds me of a book I once read.'

'I'm afraid I don't read.'

'Are you illiterate?'

'Quite.'

'How awful for you.'

'Oh, I don't mind. It keeps my mind free for other things.' He's leaning towards her. Kate realizes fatally too late, My God he's pissed, and steps back just as he lurches in for the kiss. He totters and regains his balance, smirking at her as he shakes his head.

'Vladimir,' she smiles, 'I hardly know you.'

'But the Cossacks are coming for us. We must make the most of our brief time—' He lunges again, landing an open-mouthed kiss on her cheek as she twists her head to the side. One hand finds her waist as he tries to nuzzle her neck. It dismays her how pleasant it feels to be touched in that way. With an effort she disengages herself, patting at his hands lightly to keep them from getting too near. One of his eyes is wandering in the wrong direction. This is not as flattering as it might be. 'Vladimir, Vladimir.' It's like a tongue twister. If she gets it wrong someone'll shove a shot of tequila in her hand chanting, Skull, skull. 'I have to go. The Cossacks are waiting to shoot me in the basement. I really have to go.'

'I'll come with you.'

'No no, I—' She looks wildly around for Daniel. If he's run off with Nina she'll kill him. The stranger is swaying from side to side, shifting his weight from one foot to the other, wine sloshing out of his cup and over his hand. 'I know you,' he says, grinning like a loon. 'Nina—'

There's Daniel, in the corner next to the balcony, watching with an irritating smile. She marches over to him, pushing past dancing people, moving faster and more nimbly than the stranger, who staggers after her for a couple of paces, is defeated by the crowd and turns away, bewildered.

'Who's your friend?' Daniel asks when Kate reaches him.

'You cunt. Give me a cigarette.' She pulls the fag out of his hand and leans over a candle to light it.

'Hello?'

'You could've come over.'

'What for? You didn't need rescuing.'

I did, I did, she wants to say. She glares at him. 'No, of course I didn't. Where's Nina?'

'Don't know. I was just looking for her.'

'Oh.'

'Thing is, I wouldn't mind getting out of here.'

'Me neither. I'd love to.'

They trawl the room for Nina. When they squeeze past the drunk stranger Daniel nudges Kate in the ribs but she ignores him. Finally they sight her emerging from the bathroom, wiping a delicate thumb under her nostrils. She won't be leaving the party in a hurry.

'Daniel, *hi*.' She opens her mouth extra wide and smiles. 'How *are* you? Are you having a good time? Come and dance. No, the music's shit, isn't it. Fucking

cock rock. Have you ever watched my programme?
Come and dance.'

'Well, me and Kate thought we might head off. She's
got that long drive tomorrow, and—'

'Oh, Kate, yes, you head off, early start. Come on.'
She grabs Daniel's wrist and starts for the living room.
He grabs the doorframe for support. 'No, Nina, I'm
going too. We'll get a taxi.'

'Oh stay, stay, don't be such a *loser*— '

Vladimir's wall-eyed face appears over Nina's
shoulder. The hands reach forward and encircle her
stomach. She squeals and spins and squeals again. They're
swallowed into the living room crowd.

Reasons not to make a pass at Daniel:

1. Men like to make the first move. If she tries it on
first, he will feel like the hunted rather than the hunter.
She will appear a predatory, desperate monster.

2. Humiliation. She's not equipped to deal gracefully
with a rebuff.

2a. Humiliation. What if he told Josh?

2b. Humiliation. He actually wants to screw Nina
but won't be able to say so.

3 (the big one). Ambivalence. Is she really interested
in him?

4. She hasn't shaved her legs in over a week.

With these thoughts in Kate's mind, it's unsurprising
that when Daniel comes into the kitchen and puts his
hand on her shoulder her heart starts going crazy inside
her chest and she pours hot water into the pot without
thinking to add the tea.

'Can I have a word with you about something?'

'Sure.'

They sit at the kitchen table. Daniel stands straight up

again and glances around the room. 'D'you think she'll
have a fit if I smoke in here?'

'No. Open that window maybe.'

She dips a teabag in and out of her cup of milky
water, crossing her legs in a nonchalant way. 'What's
up?' she says, trying to sound cool and American, but it
comes out Wossar and she clears her throat and hopes
he didn't notice. 'Are you all right?'

'Oh, yeah.' He rolls the lit end of his cigarette around
on a saucer and taps it though there's no ash to flick off.
'Did you – did you hear those people talking on the
balcony tonight?'

'A bit. They were talking about some girl with a –
drug problem.' Kate says the last part of the sentence
slowly. Did she sound like a girl in a horror movie
realizing that the killer is the boyfriend who she trusted
all along? She flicks her eyes to the dripping tap at the
sink. He wants her to score some drugs for him. 'Listen,
I don't know anyone – Josh might, or Nina even—'

'No, it's not that, I'm not after anything.'

Kate takes a sip of her tea and waits.

'Oh, it's stupid, it doesn't matter.'

He's a junkie. He's an ex-junkie. His sister died of an
overdose. No, his girlfriend. He's HIV, that's why he
hasn't made a pass at her. That's why he's so skinny.

'No, what? I mean, you don't have to say.' Say, say,
she's thinking. She's dying to know.

'No, I was just – is it hard to get hold of round here?'

'Pretty much. Depends what you're after. Smack
comes and goes, depends what dealers are in town I
think.' She holds her fingers out for the cigarette and
takes a drag. 'I hate it, I used to know this guy' – she
remembers the banker's sallow face, the way even when
he was smiling he was like a dark shadow in the room –

'he thought he was in control of it, it's shit. It's a waste of fucking time.' She smiles. 'Though you could say I don't exactly use my own time to best advantage.'

Daniel touches his dry lips with the tips of his fingers. He's not going to say anything. Oh, but he wants to.

'There was this guy in a police cell down south,' she's saying, 'did you hear about him? They were holding him on suspicion of possession or something and he wouldn't, ah you know, take a crap and so they were convinced that he'd swallowed some condoms, whatever—'

'Yeah?' He'd love to have another drink now. Why did they leave the party?

'And he refused to eat anything and the whole country waited, and they got an injunction to keep him there longer, and then finally – he did.'

'And?'

'He got busted. I mean, he was lucky the condom didn't disintegrate right in his stomach. He could've died. I'm sorry,' she says, 'is this incredibly bad taste?'

'No, no.' He looks preoccupied. 'Doesn't matter. Anyway—'

And at that moment they hear the metal fumble of Nina jabbing at the front door with her key.

'Hey,' she calls out, 'did you guys feels the earthquake? Oh God, I'm so *caned*.'

When Kate leaves in the morning, Nina isn't yet up. Daniel stands outside by the car, hugging his jacket around him. He wrinkles his nose, wipes some sleep out of his eye, and smiles. Kate frowns. Daniel frowns too. They hold their palms out towards each other in motionless waves. Then he turns, runs up the steps to Nina's front door, taking them two at a time – and disappears into the dark hallway without looking back.

TEN   There were four people in the waiting room. Three of them, women in
varying stages of middle age, looked up every now and
then from their magazines and cast their eyes about the
room, just taking it in, making sure it was still there.
The blonde girl didn't. She turned the pages of her text-
book slowly, marking paragraphs with a random pencil
tick. I'm never going to remember this, was what she
was thinking. I don't even know what it is I'm marking
up. The book was about Roman architecture. On an
ordinary day she could transport herself, imagine the
gleaming mosaics, the smells in the bath buildings,
sounds and colours in the forum. She'd never been to
Rome but she'd seen photographs. This day the words
meant nothing to her. They sat on the page, flat and
incomprehensible. Still, she ticked away, following some
unknown logic that she would later have to decipher.
Outside, traffic whined up and down the busy road.

'Mary?'

The blonde girl looked up from her book. 'Yes.'

'Come through, please.'

It should come as a warning to Josh that there's something different about his and Lucy's house. He isn't sure
what exactly, but as he rounds the corner and walks up
to the front door he notices the place. Usually he's
completely unaware of it, it's just the background setting
for his life, just wallpaper. But today he looks at it, the

funny shack-like shape, the stack of corrugated iron down the side between the house and the fence, the chipped blue paint on the front door. Four years they've lived here and he's never thought about doing anything to the outside except put some tomatoes in the back garden. Maybe he should give it all a new coat of paint. As he turns his key in the lock he realizes what's different. Lucy's playing music. He opens the door and walks into a new planet of sound. Those speakers are holding up pretty well, considering. And the new stylus he bought last week is cool. He feels the satisfaction given by high-quality equipment obtained on the cheap. But it is strange, he thinks, dumping his work-jacket in the living room. Lucy never plays music when she's on her own.

Every bowl, dish and cooking utensil is piled on the kitchen table. Two chairs are covered with spice packets, pasta boxes, tins of tomatoes and beans.

'Hey. What's up? Autumn cleaning?'

Lucy stands on the sink bench, scrubbing at the shelves above it with a soapy cloth. She can't have heard him.

'Hey. Lu. Hi.'

Still doesn't turn round. He taps the back of her calf. With a small shriek of surprise she kicks back at him, her heel glancing off his collarbone. He clutches it, mock-hurt.

'Ow. Easy.'

She's turned back to the shelves again.

'Hey, Lu.' If she's in a mood he should probably leave her alone, but he can't help himself trying to get her attention. 'Lu.' He squeezes her calf again and again she kicks out, hitting him in the shoulder this time. He slaps her leg, not hard. 'What?'

She climbs down from the sink top with a thud, grabs

her cigarettes off the table and marches out the back
door to the garden. She doesn't slam the door. She must
want him to follow her.

She's sitting on an upside-down apple crate, putting her
lighter back in her pocket. When she sees him come
out she stands up. He knows better than to try and
touch her. 'What's the matter?'

She takes a quick, hard puff on the cigarette and looks
him straight in the eye. 'Who's Mary?'

'Sorry?'

'Who's Mary.'

Keep her gaze, he's thinking, hold her gaze. 'Mary
who?'

She laughs in an unamused way, and begins to pace
back and forwards in front of the apple crate. He can't
feel his head. This is the thing he has feared for seven
months, feared so much he has refused to even think
about it. This situation has occupied hardly a moment
of his conscious thoughts. It only comes to him, blurry
and nauseous-making, in the Vaseline-smeared grey of
guilty dreams.

'A funny thing happened to me today,' Lucy is saying,
the cigarette held no further than a half-inch away from
her lips. 'I was working, as usual, Saturday morning, the
Saturday morning job I do so we can have extra money
for petrol and wine and dinners out, and anyway, there
I was in that ridiculous uptight wank of a place and it
was full of ridiculous uptight girls forcing themselves
into undersized clothes – '

Christ, Josh is thinking, I'm really going to have to go
through this. Did Mary bloody turn up at Lu's work?
Did she figure it out for herself? He's desperate for a
cigarette but his are in the pocket of his coat lying on

the living-room armchair. It wouldn't be worth breaking this flow to get them.

' – but I'm getting on with it, it's hardly demanding,
and I'm standing by the desk mostly making sure none
of the rich little girls pinch anything when two of them
come up and start looking at the earrings and sunglasses
and shit under the glass counter. Right?'

Lucy takes another drag. The smoke burns her throat.
It smells sharp in the clear autumn air.

'No, they don't want any help, just looking, but can
one of them try on a particular watch strap – so I stand
close by them in case she tries to pocket it, and they're
talking about some friend of theirs who's shagging some
bloke and is it working out or isn't it and then' – she
stops pacing and folds her arms around her middle, not
looking at him, looking at the branch of the tree where
she saw that baby bird fall from last year – 'and then, this
is quite funny, I've got some dumb CD on, right, and
they start talking about how they really like this song
and always hear it on your radio station, and then one of
them says, oh, you know' – Lucy takes a short breath,
say it, say it – 'Mary's been having an affair with the guy
that runs that station.' She briefly presses her lips together
and continues. 'And the other one says, Really, who is
he? And the first one says, I don't know, he's a bit older
than us, he's got a girlfriend though and the other one
says, No, and the first one says, Yeah, but Mary's really
hooked on him and the other one says, What's his name
and the first one says' – she's running out of air – 'I
think his name is Josh.'

She takes another breath. The garden, the street, the
neighbourhood is unbearably silent. She looks at him.
'Shut up,' she says. 'Don't say anything. And then the
first one says, Oh, but it's a really big secret, don't tell

anyone, and then she says, But it probably won't be a secret for very long.' Lucy laughs, once. 'And that's the funny thing. Because it's not a secret now at all. So.' She lights another cigarette. Josh watches, helpless, hands and forehead slick with sweat. 'So, of course, I was completely surprised to hear about this, but I didn't say anything to the girls. Not even when one of them tried on every pair of sunglasses in the shop and then left without buying a thing.'

Her voice cracks on the last sentence. Her arms have fallen to her sides, hanging there loose like a rag doll. All the hardness has gone out of her eyes. Josh takes a step towards her tiny limp figure. 'Lucy—'

But in a split second she seems to grow in size right before him and next thing he knows her hands and feet and knees are aiming blow after blow at him, accurate and precise inflictions of pain. He doesn't strike back. His stillness makes it worse. All the time, though, she's not hurting him as much as she could, and they both know it. After a full minute of this she backs away as quickly as she went for him, her body soft again. She sits back down on the apple crate, wipes her nose with the palm of her hand and lights a third cigarette.

'There's something else those girls said about Mary.' She won't look him in the eye. Her voice is thick with uncried tears. 'She's pregnant.'

Then she asks him to leave and not come back tonight. He goes along with this, mostly because it seems like a good idea. It's impossible for them to talk right now. And he needs to find Mary. Once he's outside the house though, the door slammed shut behind him and the scrappy street in front, he doesn't know what to do. How stupid he was to lend Kate his car. For a moment he stands there, feeling small in his stomach, feeling weak. Then he starts to walk. A yellow bus crawls up the hill just ahead and Josh runs for it. He pays the money and swings into a seat without checking where the bus is going. They drive round the bays and back through the quiet slow-motion of the suburbs. When he'd dared think of it at all, he'd assumed that he could lie to Lucy about this, that the most she'd confront him with would be a suspicion, that he could gauge the danger of being discovered and fold up the operation accordingly. Mary couldn't be pregnant. It couldn't be his. She'd told him that she slept with other men. It can't be his. Five years with Lucy, four in that house. He doesn't even know what had drawn him to Mary. It wasn't like she offered him something that Lucy did not. It had been insane, an appalling situation, something to keep him from being bored. Something to reassure him that the boat could be rocked. Even now, stuck on a bus in the slow stream of Saturday afternoon traffic, he feels a guilty, moronic smile crawl over his face. At least he knows he's not firing blanks.

It had become real only two days before. On the way home from the doctor, Mary wondered why this had happened to her. It didn't really surprise her that it had even though they were careful. She couldn't think about what to do. It was impossible to think about because every potential outcome was bad. Except one, there was one thing that would be good. She knew it wouldn't happen. Josh would never leave his girlfriend. Her life didn't include that kind of solution. Mary's life, as she abstractly visualized it, had a grey, linty, amorphous shape. Nothing worked out tidily. It had the shape of half-promises and abrupt endings. Other people had three-part narratives.

Other people found a new lover as soon as the old one had broken up with them. Other people won money on the lottery. Other people got the haircut they wanted every time. Other people managed to sculpt the stories of their days before presenting them to the world, so everything has a reason, a purpose, a useful or beautiful form. Other people didn't get pregnant when they were halfway through a degree and broke to a man who lives with his girlfriend. Other people had luck.

The slowness of the bus is getting to Josh. It would be all right if he could drive, could be in control. But there's an unpleasant sensation of things falling away and he's passive, there's nothing he could do. At last the streets become familiar, near where he needs to be. He gets off to find a phone box. It's a couple of days since he's spoken to Mary. He wonders why she hasn't told him. Pregnant. Such a round, horrible word, like fecund. Those clay earth mother goddesses with grotesque hips. He leaves a message at Mary's place and goes to Frank's flat to wait. It had seemed such a good idea, this secret, this place. A place he only ever visited for one reason. Just walking up the stairs inside used to give him a kick. Now the thought of coming here specifically for sex seems embarrassing and teenage.

It's not easy to tell if Daniel's even been here. Funny, thinks Josh, the guy hasn't got enough stuff to make a dent on a room, and my life's managed to overflow into two houses. Out the window the shadow of a tree falls on the wall of the house opposite. Clouds pass rapidly in front of the sun. The shadow appears, melts, appears again. She arrives.

★

'It's yours,' she says, her chin jutting out. 'I haven't slept
with anyone else since we started.'
   'But you said—'
   'I know. I wanted— I didn't want you to think I was
more into it than you. Are you angry?'
   There's a pause.
   'I'm sorry. I'm not angry.'
   There's another pause.
   '*Are* you?'
   'My God, no. No. I'm just − I don't − shit. Why
didn't you tell me?'
   'I was waiting to decide what I wanted to do.'
   'Have you?'
   'No. What do *you* want to do?'
   'Well—' He'd kill for a drink. 'I mean, whatever you
want.'
   'Do you mean that?'
   No, no he doesn't. That's the last thing he means. He
can't have a baby. Lucy. 'I love Lucy.'
   'That's a television show.'
   'Do you want it?'
   'I don't know.' No, is the truth, there's no way she
wants it, but she doesn't want it all to be decided straight
away like there's no big deal.
   'How far—?'
   'Five weeks.'
   'Oh, Mary.'
   'Look. I'll think about it. OK?'
   There's no reason to put off the decision, but it's her
little way of making him hurt a bit too. She's no
hysteric, she won't call his house or demand to see him
or tell his girlfriend. Some part of her wishes she was
that kind of girl, the kind to make screaming midnight
phone calls and slash his tyres and doorstep the radio

station. Preferred method of revenge: the anchovies under the car's sun visor? the alfalfa seeds scattered and watered in the living-room carpet? the truckload of horseshit delivered to the front lawn? These are the suggestions offered by women's magazines and they divert her briefly but only in the same way that junk food does. She's not even sure if it's a matter for revenge, or blame. It's just a thing that has happened.

'Can I stay?' she asks him, and he is horrified.

'No. I don't think it's a good idea.'

'I don't want to be on my own.'

I do, he thinks, I want that more than anything else in the world. 'Aren't any of your flatmates at home?'

'I don't mean alone in that way.' She looks as if she might cry. He thinks of Lucy on the apple crate. How can he feel so blank towards this girl who's pregnant with his baby? He feels nothing, nothing at all. He just wants her gone.

'Mary.'

'It's horrible being pregnant. I've been vomiting and I nearly fainted yesterday in a lecture.'

He's never noticed before how little-girly her voice is. Her face looks peaky and sharp. 'Mary, I need a minute to think about all this.'

She glances up at him. 'You need a minute? *You* need a minute? Jesus, Josh. Don't push it.'

After he'd closed the door Lucy went into the kitchen and put the kettle on. She put the teabag in a cup. She lifted a stack of dinner plates out of the cupboard. Standing just outside the back door, she hurled a plate on to the concrete square at the bottom of the steps down to the garden. It smashed and she jerked her head away. She threw another one, and another one, and

then she stopped. She put the remaining plates back in
the cupboard, drank the cup of tea and smoked a
cigarette, staring at the blank wall opposite until her eyes
watered. When the phone rang she ignored it. She was
busy out the back, sweeping up broken bits of china and
wrapping them up in yesterday's paper.

Mary lights a cigarette. Josh glances at her, equal parts
repugnance and relief. If she's smoking—
   'Can't we just spend the night together here? Just
think about what we're going to do?' Something slowly
occurs to her, and her face changes. 'Does Lucy know?
Have you told her? Did she throw you out?'
   If she keeps talking about Lucy he might — what? slap
her? oh, that's nice. 'I'm sorry,' he says. 'It's a shock. I
don't think I can be very, ah, supportive tonight. I need
to be on my own.'
   'She's thrown you out.'
   'Yes,' says Josh, 'she has.' And it dawns on him that
this means he has nothing to fear from Mary any more.
There has, he now realizes, always been an unspoken
power she's held over him: that she could tell. He never
imagined that she would, but unconsciously he adapted
his behaviour anyway. He'd go along with her wishes
just in case. If she wanted to meet up and he wasn't
really in the mood, he'd find a way out of the house and
over to hers or, once Frank had gone away, to this flat.
She got to choose what takeaways they ordered, what
music they listened to, what they drank and when they
had sex. His acquiescence was partly to compensate her
for the fact that they couldn't go out in public together
and partly because once it had gone too far, she could
ruin everything for him if she told. She knew enough
about him by now to convince Lucy of the truth.

What he didn't realize was that she would never have told because that would have been the end of it. She wasn't stupid, she knew that her only power lay in keeping silent, in never exercising the threat of telling, of never even saying it out loud. She's wanted Josh, and she's wanted more than an affair. She's in it for the long haul. Of course she hadn't intended to get pregnant but it's funny how it means that now Lucy knows. It's the ultimate thing she's got over her. Mary operates on the level of blind cunning and to her, the pregnancy is a trump card. It doesn't occur to her that it might mean nothing to Josh, that it might reshuffle his priorities so he finds that all he is concerned about is Lucy, and how to get her back.

The phone rings. Mary walks away from it.

'Hello?' says Josh.

There's a pause. Then, 'It's me. I thought you'd be there. I can't believe I didn't figure it out before. Is that where – you used to go?'

'Lucy—'

Over by the television, Mary doesn't flicker.

'I mean, tell me. You may as well tell me everything now, anything I want to know.'

'Can't we meet up?' He doesn't care if Mary hears, he doesn't care if he hurts her.

'No, not now. I suppose you'll tell me you're confused. And sorry that you've fucked up and all that.'

Her voice is clear in pitch but bewildered in tone. He feels a burning in the pit of his stomach.

'Um, so, what else. How long's it been going on for? How old is she? Is she a student? Did you meet her at the radio station? I could always send you a list of these so you've got time to—'

'Lu, we can't do this over the—'

'I'm not going to ask you any questions about sex because I don't want to know. Maybe that's a relief to you.'

He can't speak.

'Are you still there? Oh that's right, that's the other question I wanted to ask. Who have you told? I guess Frank knows because you're using his apartment, and the guys at work, do they know, when I call up for you do they think, oh poor cow she doesn't know her boyfriend's shagging that young student, do they do you think? Is it only her? My God is there anyone else as well?'

Mary lights another cigarette, gasps and coughs.

'What's that noise?' There's a pause. 'Josh? Is she there?'

'No, I—'

The phone goes dead. Josh puts his hand over his mouth. Mary stops coughing.

Lucy runs a bath but when it's full she lets it out again. She doesn't want to take her clothes off. She puts another jumper on, and shoes so that her feet don't feel soft and vulnerable on the floor. The heater's turned up as far as it will go. It would be nice to have some music but there isn't anything that will take her mind away. The television helps for about ten minutes. She should call Kate, or her mother, but somehow she can't. She feels ashamed, and stupid. Despite what the girls in the shop were saying, she had hoped Josh would just laugh and reassure her it was nothing to do with him. It still seems hard to believe. Thinking about it gives her a headache. She lies on the couch in all of her clothes and falls asleep.

When she wakes up it is only just light outside. She

thinks, There's something I should have dreamed about, but I didn't. Then she remembers what has happened and for the first time she starts to cry.

Ginny pauses, spade in hand, to admire the evenness of the steps she's cutting into a sloping section of her garden. A friend's been telling her about some wonderful slate from Nelson that weathers beautifully. That will be perfect. And the bougainvillaea's winding over that trellis nicely. It's maybe not damp enough for those hostas though. The thing about gardening, she thinks, looking up as an aeroplane floats overhead, is that it's therapeutic. So good for the soul. She's almost forgotten about the disagreement she and Andrew had last night. The telephone rings and she drops the spade, runs lightly up to the back door and into the kitchen.

'Hello-o?' she trills.

'Ginny? It's me.'

'Ninie! This is a treat. How are you?'

'I'm fine, how are you?'

'Just on top of the world. I'm in my wonderful garden amid all the fruits of nature.'

'How lovely. I wish I could be there too.'

'So do I, darling, so do I.'

'Have you, ah, seen Kate since she got back?'

'She left a message last night. I haven't spoken to her though.'

'Oh. I hope she was all right. She left without saying goodbye.'

'Really? That's a bit rude.'

'Well, it doesn't matter. It was nice to be able to give her a bed. And her friend.'

'Who was that?'

'Some stray bloke she'd picked up, I don't know.'

'Oh. I hope she's careful.'

'She did seem a bit — distracted. You know how she is.'

'Yes, well how's everything else? Work going well?'

'Oh, I'm being paged. Oh dear. Sorry, Mum, I'm going to have to go.'

'That's all right, darling. It's just lovely to hear your voice. Any news about coming up here?'

'Not yet. I'd better go. Love you.'

'Love you.'

It was a funny thing, Ginny thought, how before you become a parent nobody ever tells you you're going to have favourites. Not that she's ever neglected Kate, or made her feel less loved — it's simply that she and Nina are on a similar wavelength, they understand each other. They're both *doers*. If she's honest with herself, she doesn't understand Kate and all her waffling. Not at all. Why can't she just find herself? she wonders, as she heads back outside to tackle the convulvulus.

The bus is stuck in traffic. Kate reads the advertising billboards until she almost knows them off by heart. The one selling jeans looks as though it's pushing class-A drugs. There's an exciting new make of family car available. A department store downtown is having a sale on all cosmetics. It took a while for what Lucy was saying on the phone this morning to sink in and until it did Kate was just making stupid Oh no noises and Oh, I'm so sorry. It seemed as if she was acting. She had to stop herself from asking Lucy if it was really true. I'll be straight over, she said, and then thought, What shall I do with Josh's car? Well, she tells herself as she gets off the bus and starts half-walking, half-running, to Lucy's place, it's not the car that is important here.

'Can we go for a walk? I don't want to sit around this place.'

'Sure,' says Kate, and they're closing the front door behind them when the phone rings. Lucy turns towards the door, key ready, then turns away again. She looks at Kate. 'I don't know what to do.'

Nor do I, thinks Kate, but 'Come on,' she says, linking her arm through Lucy's and steering them away from the phone, away from the house, away from the street and towards the botanical gardens.

The usual rule – never mouth off about your best friend's ex, no matter what he's done, because when they get back together you'll be the doom merchant who confessed that you thought he was a complete turkey and in fact you're wrong, he's lovely, they just had a misunderstanding and you're only bitter because you're single – goes out the window as Lucy tells Kate the full story. They sit beside a huge bird-of-paradise plant, on a bench overlooking the downtown office buildings. Lucy looks vacant, hollow.

'I can't believe it. I just can't believe I had no idea.'

'Have you eaten anything?'

'No fucking idea. How stupid is that?'

'Lu?'

'No.' She lights another cigarette. 'It's like – like I've been waiting for the thing that would happen to remind me that I'm no different to anybody else, you know? That the world's not divided into two groups of people – people who get sort of knocked about by life, like the women in the refuge, and people who maintain control, who don't let things get out of hand, like me.'

It feels to her as if somebody else is talking, as if somebody else, a character from a book or a movie maybe, is sitting on the sloping bench with their friend, having just found out that their boyfriend's having an affair. She continues quietly, almost to herself. 'Even while I'd slipped into that way of thinking I knew it was untrue. And now this thing, this thing, has happened and it's – definite, irrevocable proof. I don't have control. Not of anything.' She's got to stop talking. Everything she says is nonsense, as soon as the thoughts come out of her mouth in words they are inadequate and wrong.

'What are you going to do?'

Lucy closes her eyes against the glare from a mirror-glassed building. 'There's nothing *to* do. I keep changing my mind about whether or not I want to see him. I know this bit will pass. I know it'll seem crazy – the second day of knowing, thinking I could figure a way out—'

'Can you think of what you might want?'

'Now?' A breeze sweeps up over the hill, ruffling the grass. Isn't it strange, Lucy thinks, how that can feel nice. 'The only thing I want now is for yesterday never to have happened.'

Meanwhile, Daniel and Nina are having their own shit to deal with, on a slightly different scale. It was obvious to them both that they were going to go to bed together. Nina knew this because she was compelled to go one better than Kate in terms of getting close to the stranger. Daniel thought he was quite prepared to go along with being a trophy lay. Then things got a little complicated.

ELEVEN The moment of contact was extremely romantic, Nina thought. Yesterday, the day of Kate's departure, she'd had a scented bath and dressed in a soft silky shirt and trousers, Oriental style. She'd twisted her hair up and admired the long whiteness of her neck. They decided to see a movie as part of the hangover recovery programme. It was a costume drama about manners and politics in the French court and it did not break Nina's delicate mood. Afterwards they went to dinner in a restaurant she reserved for first dates. All the time she talked, and asked him questions, and made sure not to say anything mean about Kate. Daniel smoked, told lies, and enjoyed the show. They decided to have coffee back at her house.

Pouring it out, she kept her movements small and light and careful. Daniel stood in the back doorway. Three freckles made a kind of path from her collar bone down to the undone top buttons of her shirt. Without warning, a coffee cup fell from the table to the slate stone floor, as if some new energy in the room, a poltergeist, had knocked it. It lay there in two clean pieces, the white china on the inside exposed in a vaguely sexual way. Daniel chucked his cigarette out the door behind him and bent to pick it up at the precise moment Nina knelt to do the same. At chair level on the floor, they looked up at each other. She waited for the kiss, the delicate silk brushing lightly over her skin with every shallow breath. He did not disappoint her.

The next morning he woke up to the sound of—
   'Oh my God. Oh my *God*.'
   — from the bathroom. He pulled his trousers on and stood outside the door. 'Nina?'
   'Don't come in,' she shouted, 'don't come in. Oh my God.'
   'What's happening?'
   'It's my eye. Oh Christ. Elephant Man.'
   The door opened a tiny bit and she ducked past him, hands either side of her eyes like a carthorse's blinkers, into the bedroom then, clutching something white in her hand, back to the bathroom.
   'Cup of tea?' he called.
   There was much clattering of product jars and the sound of running water. 'Oh, I'm going to be sick.'
   After a bit she wandered into the kitchen, white fluffy dressing gown loose around her shoulders, black sunglasses masking her face.
   'I'm disfigured. I'm never going to work in TV again.'
   'Let's have a look.'
   'No.' Her hand flew up to the glasses. 'It's like a golfball. It's almost touching the lens.'
   'Just one?'
   'I can't even open it. What am I going to do? How did this happen? God's punishing me.'
   'What for?'
   Going to bed with you, they both thought. 'Anything, anything. Vindictive bastard. *Oh*.'

★

That evening, Nina lay on her bed with antiseptic cream over her swollen eye and a scarf tied around her head, feeling sorry for herself and watching rubbish television. That presenter was useless. Even with elephantiasis of the eye she, Nina, was much better looking. The phone beside her bed started to ring.

'Oh, fuck off.' She counted to four rings. 'Hello?'

'Nina?'

'Who is this?'

'Uh, Josh, a friend of Kate's, I think I met you last—'

'Right, hi. Did Kate get back all right? She left without saying goodbye.'

'Yeah, I think so. I haven't actually seen her. I was just wondering, is Daniel there?'

'He's gone for a drive. He might be an hour or so. You can try again tomorrow.'

'A drive?'

'All right, then? Bye.'

'Bye, Princess,' Josh says as he hangs up the phone. Probably got him chained up in the basement. A drive? That can't be right.

But it is. Well, a drive is not what he's gone for – he has driven Nina's car, true, but that is not the purpose of his mission. What he has gone for is a drink, what he has gone for is the prospect of an anonymous encounter, and more specifically what he is going for is that bird with the jaggy haircut and skinny white T-shirt. Anyone wearing a T-shirt like that is asking to be gone for.

He's in a bar, Guinness in front of him, Josh's loan in his pocket, a smoke between his lips and guilt in his heart. Mild-flavoured, low-tar guilt only, hurting his conscience just enough to make this more enjoyable. What is he guilty about? One – lying to Kate about the fact that he can't drive. Two – having sex with Nina when he thinks she's a horrible person and he is quite possibly interested in her sister. But then, that's exactly why he did it. And three, the third thing he currently feels guilty about – he hasn't done it yet.

What it is, is he's going to buy that girl a drink. He's going to get chatting with her, ask her about herself, allude to his life in London, explain that he's visiting friends. He's going to find whatever she's interested in extremely interesting. He'll ask her if she's a dancer. She's not? Oh, but she must have been. Well, it's also that she looks a bit like this girl he knows in London, she's a dancer and a model, so that's what made him think— He's going to buy her another drink. He's going to sympathize about her missing cat or noisy neighbour or pestering ex. He's just broken up with someone himself. Yes, back in London. He still loves her but as a friend, you know what I mean, and she was starting to want children, so. He'll laugh at her jokes. He'll buy her another drink. He'll ask if she knows anywhere around here that's still serving food. Is she hungry? Of course she is.

It's good travelling around, he'll mention over dinner, but staying in hotels is so impersonal. Like this city – it's great but unless you get to meet people who actually live in a place it can be hard to have a proper idea of it. Has she travelled much? No? He thinks she'd like London. No, he doesn't know how long he'll be in town. Christ, he's going to say, it's so great to talk to some-one on your own wavelength. He'll ask her where she lives and she's going to accept his offer of a lift home. He's going to accept her offer of a whisky. Then, when

she's looking at him with blunt expectant eyes, her
mouth slightly open, he's going to ask if he can kiss her.

A slippery slope. One casual fuck like this, one major
deception – letting himself silently into Nina's house at
five a.m., collapsing on the sofa and saying, Yes, thanks,
he had an interesting drive up some hill and sat looking
at the night view, lost track of time – one reminder of
that blissful combination of physical intimacy and
emotional detachment— He bites his fingers, listening
to the sound of Nina's shower, remembering last night's
girl and the look on her face at that moment when she'd
wanted it, she'd wanted him and nothing else, nothing
else would do. It's an appealing idea, tapping on the
bathroom door, slipping into the steamed-up air, drawing the shower curtain back inch by inch. But no. Nina's
over. Friends and family need not apply. *Stranger.* Even
the word does it for him. Stranger and stranger, in this
upside-down world. There's a rush of warm, rose-
scented air and Nina wanders through to the kitchen,
towel precarious around her. He regrets his rule but
it's got to be kept. There have to be limits. Otherwise,
what?

'Bathroom's free.'

His liar's face stares back at him appraisingly as he
brushes his teeth and studies his neck for bitemarks.
There it is again, the old look about the eyes. Not a
flinty, metallic glint as you might expect of a liar, but a
flat impenetrable blankness in the hazel of his irises. A
little lie in itself, that dull unreflective green, because
underneath it behind the eyes, back in his mind, colours
spark and leap like fireworks.

★

'Your eye's better.'

'Thank God. I hardly slept for worrying about it. And the bloody phone.'

'Yeah?'

She touches lightly around her eye and wonders whether or not to tell him that Josh called. It's a bit bloody much, him getting messages here, and he hasn't even asked how long he can stay on for. It was pretty rude that he was out so late last night, considering. She slips a hand between her dressing gown and the warm silky skin of her ribcage. Considering what happened between them, and everything.

'That guy Josh called for you. He didn't say what it was about.'

'Oh.'

'And then there were those anonymous phone calls, Christ that was really late.'

'Uh?'

'Did you hear them? It must have been after you got in.'

'How many calls?'

'Two. The first one was just a hang-up and the second one I thought I could hear something, but it might've just been static. Didn't you hear them?'

'No,' he says slowly. 'I must have been out of it. I was pretty tired.'

'Oh my God.' Her eyes widen and her fingers leap to her throat. 'I just thought of something.'

Already he's working out how long it will take him to shove his stuff together and get out of here. 'Yeah?'

'It might be someone who's seen my programme, some crazed fan.' Her gaze twitches around the room,

as if to find a window through which to escape. 'A
stalker. Oh my God, oh my God.'

'No. Really?'

She thrusts her chin towards him, neck extended like
a turtle's, and exhales a disbelieving puff of air. '*Yes*,
really,' she nods, 'I am on local television every week-
night, my ratings are pretty high this quarter, I mean
that's the greater lower North Island we're talking about,
we cover a lot of towns, there could be anyone out
there who's become' – her mouth trembles – 'fixated.'
Abruptly she shoots up out of her chair. He follows her
through to the bedroom where she's flinging on clothes.

'What are you doing?'

'I've got to get to work. I've got to talk to security,
call the police. I might need protection.'

'Nina, just a second—'

'You can drive me there, I don't want to go on my
own. What if they're watching the house? Quickly,
you'd better get dressed.'

And so it happened that he dropped Nina off at work,
with promises to pick her up later and take her out for
dinner, in fact not to leave her side, to be a bodyguard
slash escort for the rest of her life. He drove the car back
to her flat at a leisurely pace, had a shower, made himself
a sandwich, pocketed a pair of her knickers for safe
keeping. For the hell of it, he called the phone number
that girl from the night before had given him. A man's
voice answered, saying, 'Outpatients'. That's weird. He
must've written the number down wrong. He banged
the door shut, chucked his bag in the back seat of the
car and got behind the wheel. Then stopped.

He was at the end of an island. Where could he go?

Back north, through the same scrubby roads he drove
with Kate? Or further, down, over the strait, over those
swaying grey waves to the south? South. He felt the
word like an urgent breath out. He wanted to travel
south, to take a straight line down as far from everything
as he could go. He imagined acres of ice and snow,
deserts of white southern sky and wide, vast cold. Kate
had told him about mountain parrots, red and emerald
thieves that'd take the wing mirror off your car if they
could. Lakes of milky turquoise and glassy green.
Strangely stacked rocks, glaciers moving as slowly and
certainly as the rising sea, large things, seabirds, alba-
trosses and whales. An upside-down fantasy world is
what he imagined, with himself in the role of Gulliver
or maybe Alice, though he'd never read either of those
books and only had a shady idea of what might be
involved. He remembers the Scott film he watched with
his uncle all those years ago. I may be some time, he says
to himself now. Some time.

*Nina, it's Daniel. Don't worry about your car, it's at the ferry
terminal. Keys are in the ticket office. Sorry to take off like
this, but— You'll be fine, I'm sure there's no need to worry
about a stalker, you know? Yeah, so. Bye.*

He's halfway across the sea when Nina, already furious
that he hasn't come to pick her up, bangs her front door
shut and stalks straight to the answer machine. She plays
his message once and lets out a small scream of rage,
followed by another one. This is so humiliating. She can
never tell Kate about this, or even their mother. If
anyone found out that she'd slept with that creep and
then he'd done this – this! She's damned if she's going
to let him get off lightly. He'll regret thinking he could
insult her, Nina from the television. He didn't know

how lucky he was. Dozens – hundreds – of men would kill to have had what he had. It was as much a slap in the face to them as it was to her. Lips tight, she presses erase and watches the black tape rewind to the beginning of the cassette. A light film appears over her eyes. She picks up the receiver and presses 111.

'Police, please.'

During the pause another wave of white, hot anger swells up in her and spit comes into her mouth. She licks her lips and rubs them together. Her spine seems to lengthen. 'I'd like to report a stolen car, please. Today. Yes I know who it probably was.'

TWELVE   Daniel stands on the freezing deck and looks at the receding harbour, at the dull-green hills against the white sky. The air, wet and salty, clings to his face and hair. He tries to smoke but in the wind his cigarette paper burns too fast down one side. He chucks the butt overboard and watches it rise slowly on a current behind the boat then disappear. He hopes Nina won't be too upset about him leaving without saying goodbye. He hopes that wherever he stays next, the phone calls won't follow.

He leans against the rail, out over the rushing wake, and stares into the yellow-blue froth until it isn't water any more, it's a mass charging from underneath, churned in constant movement and never going anywhere. Gazing into this, he thinks about lying and he thinks about telling the truth. About stealing things and about earning them. About the deal with Sticksy, what he'd colluded in and what he was a carrier for. The verandah conversation at the party, Kate's darkening eyes when she'd mentioned her friend. He isn't sure where his responsibility begins and ends. The boat pushes away from the long arms of harbour and out into the strait. Daniel's eyes sting in the wind. He'd like to make a new start.

Nobody ever gets the full story on Daniel's journey south. In the end he was away for just over two weeks. As he imagined it, his goal had been to reach the South

Pole. Unsurprisingly this didn't happen. Instead, on that
ferry crossing, he made a promise to himself. He wasn't
going to lie any more. It would stop. He would find the
white space of honesty, his mental South Pole. He'd
plant a flag, experience an epiphany, discover that from
here the only way was up. He'd forgotten that under
the clean clear miles of ice lies uncharted land, mountains and valleys and crevices ancient and unchangeable.

He got a lift with a family on the first car leaving the
ferry. Just as they drove off the ramp and through the
terminal park he saw police cars pulling in behind them.
It looked as though everyone was going to be searched.
From the back of the family's station wagon, jammed in
with rucksacks and tent poles and his suitcase, Daniel
watched, sweating. The father, driving, said, 'Bugger
this for a game of soldiers,' and put his foot down. The
cops didn't call them back.
    'They're only doing their job, Dave,' said his wife.
    'Go, Dad,' said the kids.
    Yeah, thought Daniel. Go.
    So when the family dropped him at a turn-off just
past the town, he didn't mind too much. Until he'd
been waiting there for three hours twenty minutes and
the sky began to get dark. The wind was picking up and
the air was almost moist with cold. Finally, a small truck
pulled over and Daniel hopped in.
    'Where you headed?' said the driver, a sinewy man
with crinkled hair. In the light from the dashboard
Daniel could see his forearms were covered in tattoos.
    'Don't know,' Daniel answered. 'Wherever.'
    'Righto,' the man said, and tapped the glovebox.
'Roll us one, would you?'
    They drove in silence along the coast road. Waves

crashed on to the asphalt beside them. Everything was covered in mist, sea spray, a strange half-light. All of a sudden Tattoo Man pulled over to the side of the road, just above the sea.

'Get out of the truck,' he said.

'Sorry?'

'Come on.' The man opened his door and started to step down, then said, 'I'm not getting out until you do.'

Daniel pushed his door open, gave one nervous look to his suitcase, and stepped out into the sea fog. Fine rain spotted his cigarette. It was as if he was alone in the half-liquid air. Then the hazard lights on the truck's cab started flashing. The driver was standing by his side. This is it, Daniel thought. I'm going to get bum-rushed, I'm going to die here, thrown down on to those slimy black rocks, washed out to sea, my eyes picked out by gulls. And the rocks shone through the mist at him, basalt black, bladed with sharp scalloped frills.

'Yous got a camera?' the truckie said, following Daniel's gaze down to the rocks.

'Yeah.'

'Film?'

'Yeah,' he lied. It's the first untruth since his decision on the ferry. It's only five hours later.

'Get them.'

'Now?'

'Quickly, now.'

Either, thought Daniel, I'm being robbed and abandoned by the side of the road, or the guy is a serial killer who likes to photograph his victims. I hope he doesn't want me to suck his dick.

'Righto,' Tattoo Man said when Daniel emerged again from the truck, camera slung around his neck. 'Follow me.'

He could have made a run for it. Why didn't he? It
was cold, it was near dark, he didn't know where in the
world he was. He followed the man, over the white
wooden barrier, carefully down a worn path in the shelly
rock, towards the turmoil of grey water below. Daniel
brushed at his face as if to remove a cobweb, but the
mist wouldn't clear. The driver stopped a few feet from
the bottom. He turned back towards Daniel. 'Get your
camera ready.'

'It's too dark, it won't work.'

'Try it,' said the man. 'You'll want a picture.'

Then he pointed out to sea. At first there was nothing,
only the gloomy mist, salty from the waves so that
Daniel could taste it. Then it cleared and out there in
the water he saw a massive black shape. It heaved,
enormous, into the air then it vanished and all he could
see was the surface of the water, rippled and dark. The
thing appeared again, closer.

'Get a picture, take a photograph now,' said the
trucker.

Daniel lifted the camera to his face but it was
impossible to see through the viewfinder. 'Not enough
light,' he said. 'Won't come out.'

'Take it anyway. You never know.'

So he had to go through the pretence of taking a
photo though there was no film in his camera. While he
was doing this he lost sight of the whale. It disappeared
from view, back down into the depths, leaving only a
dark blur printed on Daniel's mind, a memory that he
would never be sure was real, an image he would always
doubt.

'How did you know that was going to happen?'

The trucker pushed past him and started the clamber
back to the truck. 'She's been coming here this time

every day for the last couple of months. Won't last much longer. You're lucky.'

Back in the truck the guy said, 'Where are you sleeping tonight?'

'Wherever,' said Daniel. 'I don't know, I'm just heading.'

The driver raised a fuzzy eyebrow. 'Well, there's nowhere round here for you to stay. Come and kip down at ours if you like. Vic won't mind.'

Vic was the tattooed guy's brother, had to be. They looked identical apart from the different designs crawling over each of their necks and arms, out of their clothes. What a way to make sure you could tell them apart.

'Hi,' said Vic. 'You got any tattoos?'

'Uh, no,' said Daniel.

'You want one? Cheap.'

'Thanks,' said Daniel, 'but I haven't got any money.'

'That camera's nice.'

'There's no film in it,' said the trucker. Daniel looked at him. He shrugged. 'I'm not an idiot. Still a nice camera but—'

'Have a look at these. Some people like to make up their own designs but I prefer the traditionals myself.'

What he'd thought was a shed at the front of Vic and the trucker brother's shack-like house was in fact Vic's place of work: a tattoo parlour. The inside looked as though it hadn't been altered since the early nineteen fifties. On one wall there was a series of photographs of Vic and his brother as younger men, the passing of time marked by the new markings on their bodies. In the middle of the room was something like a dentist's chair, with what must have been the tattoo gun attached to the ceiling above it. A few ominous looking silver cords hung around the gun. The room was tidy, empty apart from the chair and a trestle table covered in tubes of ink and other things Daniel did not examine closely. Another wall was covered by a huge chart of tattoo designs – love hearts, bluebirds, a sprawling eagle. The place smelled of disinfectant. Vic switched on a bright overhead light and drew a patterned curtain over the small leadlight window. Really, thought Daniel, it was just like being at the dentist. As long as Vic didn't turn out to be an ex-Nazi, he might be all right.

'The autumn's a good time for this,' said Vic, fussing around the trestle table while Daniel flicked through a book of photographs of tattooed men and women. They all looked straight into the camera, through the lens and out of the pictures at him. Each facial expression seemed similar. What was it about them? – a certain pride in the way they stared down the viewer, a squareness, the impression of self-knowledge. It was this that convinced Daniel to go through with the tattoo. Maybe if he chose his symbol, if he wore it on his skin the way these people did, he could also achieve their look of certainty, of permanence.

'I'll have this,' he told Vic, pointing to an anchor.

'Right,' said Vic. 'Very nice. Very traditional. Sailor, eh?'

'No,' said Daniel. 'Not really.'

'Where do you want it? Upper arm?'

'Ah, sure.'

Vic rolled up Daniel's T-shirt sleeve. 'No need to shave you. Some of the blokes round here are pretty hairy. I've done most of this coastline. It's an ancient art. The Polynesians do a beautiful job of it. Every now and then I get some tourists, some American kids or

whatever, wanting one of the old Maori designs.' He
wheezed, laughing. 'I send them to Pita's down the
road. That usually sorts them out, ha ha. Or I show
them pictures of the Samoan leg designs, tell them
they've got to have those first, part of the tattoo
initiation, they can't get out of here fast enough after
that.'

While he talked he had rubbed Daniel's arm with
Vaseline and pressed a piece of tracing paper with the
anchor design onto it. He peeled the paper away and
Daniel looked down to see the picture there, like the
temporary tattoos his cousins had been given one
Christmas.

'You can keep looking if you want,' said Vic, 'but
some people can't hack it. Just so you know.'

He wiped over the anchor and the skin around it with
something that felt cold like alcohol, pulled the gun
down from the ceiling and said, 'Right. Don't jump.'

Jumping was out of the question. So was looking at
it. If he was going to do anything, it might have been
vomit. His skin was being cut into with a burning hot
knife. Vic drew the anchor in short deep lines. As soon
as the needle was taken away the burning stopped, only
to start again in the new place Vic touched on. Every so
often Vic wiped blood off the arm with a paper towel.
He filled the lines in with a rubbing motion that hurt,
but not as much.

'Now there'll be a scab, all right? Come off in a
couple of weeks. Don't pick at it.'

Daniel's upper arm was on fire. He sat there for a
minute as Vic packed up, feeling good, feeling somehow
clean.

That night, he and Vic and the trucker watched a
television programme about Antarctica. Even through

the scratchy reception on the screen the illuminated
blue icebergs, the steely sea and overcast skies streaked
with golden light pulled at Daniel like a magnet. From
a helicopter the camera panned over a fraction of a sheet
of ice the size of India. The narrator talked about how
the sea ice expanded by double in the winter and melted
again in the warmer months. Like breathing in and
breathing out, Daniel thought, like the slowest breath in
the world. Humpback whales rose and dived slowly in
the waters off a shingled peninsula shore.

Daniel's arm throbbed in his dreams, filling them with
a heat to counter the mountainous, torqued anvils of
rock and ice, swathed in cloud, that loomed through the
mist of his sleep like secrets. In the morning he ate toast
and eggs with Vic and the trucker. Then he left his
camera with them and set out for the main road.

'Wait a second,' the trucker had called as Daniel
jumped down from their sagging verandah on to the
stony path. 'Vic! Come here for a bit.'

And Vic had stood next to Daniel, both of them
squinting up to the trucker beside a peeling verandah
post, Daniel's suitcase on the ground between them.
'Righto,' said the trucker, 'smile!' as he held the filmless
camera up to his eye and clicked the shutter. 'One for
the scrapbook,' he called after Daniel's retreating figure,
and Daniel waved goodbye to the breathless wheezing
sound of Vic the tattooist's laugh.

Without his camera, with nothing but his battered plastic
case, Daniel hitched across to the West Coast. He stared
out of the windows of cars, trucks and vans at volcanic
rock formations, teetering against the sky. From the
back of a ute, shingle roads bouncing underneath him,
he saw lakes of teal and green. He got a ride further

south over steep mountain passes, black with earth and white with early snow. He saw rainbow trout in a river, and apricot orchards full of golden light, and leaned against a wood and barbed-wire fence under a vast, deep sky. For days he was conscious of breathing clean, soil-smelling air, of falling asleep with the taste in his mouth of rainwater and tobacco smoke. He slept in barns, in sheds, in an abandoned caravan in a field. He woke with sore limbs and the smell of mouldy tarpaulin on his clothes. Two or three times he stayed over in a ride's house. It was nice to sleep in sheets and to wash in warm water, but the thing he didn't like was having to talk. To every driver he rode with, he lied. What are you doing here? they asked him, Why did you come? How could he answer these questions with the truth? Where else have you been on your travels then. What did you say you were doing here again? He had to lie. He had to.

After ten days it occurred to him that he was behaving as if he was running away. All that time he thought he'd been running to something, moving forward with a sense of the future, of adventure. But his life had become like that of a fugitive. Guilty of what, he wasn't sure. He found another place to sleep under another pale pink sky. Grey swirls of cloud slid over the sinking sun. He was cold, and hungry, and he'd run out of fags. It surprised him how easy the slip was from being a person with means of support to a person without food and shelter.

He spent the night in an abandoned shed standing lonely in a fallow paddock. His tattooed arm and his fear of rats made it hard to get comfortable but eventually he curled right up into himself and fell asleep. In the middle of the night he woke up, not knowing where he was. Light from the moon came in through holes in the shed's timber roof. The place looked much bigger than when he'd gone to sleep. He sat up, seeing his breath mist out in front of him. With a terrible sense that something was wrong, he opened his suitcase. There in the white stripes of moonlight were the bags of heroin he'd brought with him from Thailand, just as they lay in the case when he'd handed it over in that car. He had never got rid of them, he would never be able to get rid of them. They sat there, poison that had passed through his body, that was part of him now. As he picked up a bag, thinking he could dig a hole and bury them all, its plastic coating disintegrated under his touch and brown powder covered his fingers, stuck under his nails, fell all over the suitcase and through his clothes. He woke up to the sound of his fast breathing, his pulse thundering in his throat.

That was it. He had to get back. Back to what, he had no idea. But he was out on the road again before sunrise, standing there with the real, innocent suitcase at his feet, the demon night-time case locked back inside his heart.

THIRTEEN   Kate has moved in with Lucy to keep her company. It's been a week. Josh has phoned every day and every day Lucy has refused to speak to him. Kate saw him once, when she dropped the car at the radio station.

'Here are the keys.' She chucked them on his desk.

'Kate.'

'You look like shit.'

'How is she?'

Kate shook her head. 'She's all right.'

'Really?'

'Yeah, really.'

'I've got to talk to her.'

'Well. I suppose that's up to her.'

It's odd, she thought, standing over him while he sat cowed behind his desk, this is like a scene from a movie. Only this was Josh, and this was her. And at home there was Lucy who talked in her sleep and sat in the bath crying and said to Kate, first thing in the morning, I just don't understand. 'Josh,' Kate said, 'you're such a fool.'

He looked down at his desk, then up at her again. 'I know. I really fucked up. I don't – I just want to see her.'

'I'm not going to be a messenger for you. You know, she doesn't even want to hear your name.'

'So she's not all right?'

Jesus Christ. You want me to bring her used tissues over? A tear-stained handkerchief? Is that what you're

after, proof? This is what Kate thought when she was
running down the stairs fast to get out of there, to get
back through the rain to the bus shelter. But standing
there in the station office with teenage boys coming and
going and giving each other special handshakes, she
didn't think like that. Even if she had, it's doubtful she'd
have said those things. They're words somebody else
would say, someone maybe in that same movie she felt
like she was in for a minute back there. In real life, she
was sorry for him. In real life, she said, 'What are you
going to do?'

The wall behind Josh's eyes looked for a second as if
it might crumble. 'I don't know,' he shrugged.

'Does – uh, Mary? Know?' She felt disloyal just saying
the name.

A skinny teenager came up and stood beside Kate.
'Hey, Josh, man, you've got to hear the new Demolition
single.' He laughed a cartoon character laugh, oblivious
to Kate's stony stare. 'It's the shit man, it's the shit.'

'OK,' said Kate, 'the car's out the front. On a one
hour park. See you, maybe.'

It's still raining. It's been coming down for days. The
grass they used to lie on in the back garden is a wide
pool of dark orange mud. A few plants cling around its
edges, roots exposed, their grip on the soil weakening.
Most of the leaves have broken off under the pressure
of the rain. The cabbage tree and the banana plant alone
are unaffected, broad spikes slick and slimy with wet,
bark black against the dripping green hedge and grey
sky.

Lucy turns away from the window. She shoves
another biscuit in her mouth and slurps her tea. 'God,'
she says, 'this weather makes me want to eat non-stop.'

'Good,' says Kate, looking up from her crossword. 'You were developing anorexic tendencies. You could just about fit the clothes in that stupid shop you work in.'

'I suppose I should be worrying about all that shit now I'm single.'

'You've got to be on a constant diet and obsess about your clothes else you'll never get a boyfriend,' Kate recites. 'It's a desert out there.'

'Then what? When I do get one?'

'If.'

'If I get one.'

'Then you can get lardy and gross again like you used to be. What's a five letter word meaning purgatory?'

'My life. We are such a couple of old women. What about the wild youth I was missing out on all those years with Fuckhead?'

'This is it. Wild and crazy, isn't it.'

'Listen, Kate.'

She looks up from the newspaper. 'Mm?'

'Men suck.'

'I know.'

'No, I mean it. They suck. I know it's a cliché. But we have to face facts. Men are emotional cripples.'

'Yes,' says Kate, 'but then look at me. I'm hardly an emotional decathlete myself.'

'Your tiny intimacy problems are nothing compared to the vast deserts of emotional wasteland your average bloke has inside his heart.'

Kate puts her hands over her eyes. 'I don't want to hear this.'

'They smell.'

'True.'

'They're selfish.'

'Mm–hm.'

'Vain.'

'Yes.'

'Self-important, uncurious, dithery—'

'This is all true.'

'Oh God!' Lucy sits on the armchair and rocks, her hands clasped behind her bowed head, elbows pointing inwards. 'I can't believe my mother had to sit through all those ludicrous consciousness-raising sessions and talk to other women about masturbation just so I could sit here with you – no offence – and blah on about exactly the same things she blahed on about when my father left her. You know? Fuck. After resisting it for so long at that bloody Women's Refuge, trying so hard not to become full of that men are scum shit.' She peers up at Kate. 'That's what I hate Fuckhead for the most. For turning me into my mother.'

'You were always your mother, Lu. You're just looking for someone to pin it on.'

'You think?'

'More tea?'

Lucy follows Kate into the kitchen and leans in the doorway. 'I've gotten used to you being here.'

'Me too.'

'You're not going to stay though, are you.'

'No. Eventually I'll go back to my stunning palatial home. Whenever you're ready. Where's the sugar?'

'On the shelf. Like me.'

'Ha ha.'

Lucy knocks her head lightly against the door frame, twice. 'It is the same though, it is a pattern.'

'What is?'

'Dad left Mum for a younger woman. It must be the way we are. Josh must have been stifled or something.'

Kate shakes old tea leaves out of the pot. This is the first time she's called Fuckhead by his name in six days. 'Lucy. Josh is a freak. He screwed up, and I don't think he knew he was going to. This is not a pattern.' She leans against the sink bench and looks at Lucy. 'If there's one thing men do suck at it's taking responsibility. Don't do that for him, OK? Enough second-guessing. This is his mess.'

'Yeah. Maybe. I don't know.'

'Look, at least your mother's a good person to be. What about me? If only I could turn into my mother. I'd be able to cook Sri Lankan food for fifty while levitating in the lotus position.'

'And then I'd have to kill you.'

'I know. Two of Ginny, can you imagine. This island's not big enough.'

'Do you think we should leave the house,' Kate calls out later from the bathtub.

'Possibly. I've been checking out the cupboards. They're getting pretty bare.' Lucy comes in and sits on the edge of the bath, facing away from Kate. She locks her gaze on the tiled wall opposite. Now is not a time she even wants to consider her latent lesbianism, if it exists. 'We could go and get food and then come back. A video maybe.'

'Mn.' Kate keeps her voice light. 'Andre's having a party.'

'Andre? That bald guy?'

'I think he shaves his head.'

'Because he's going bald.'

'OK, yeah. That guy.'

Lucy chews a fingernail. The idea of having to dress properly, having to worry about looking good – what if

he was there? What if they both were? Anything's
possible in this place. 'Uh, nah. I'm not really experien-
cing full party capability just yet.'
  'Fair enough.'
  'But you go. If you want.'
  'Oh no. I won't go.'
  They sit for a minute in the warm damp air.
  'Thanks,' says Lucy.
  'Well, you know. I probably would have had to get
drunk and make a pass at the host. And I don't think I
can face being rejected by a man who disguises the fact
that he's losing his hair with the modern equivalent of a
comb-over.'
  'Kate.'
  'What?'
  'I think Andre's gay.'
  She sinks her head under the soapy water and comes
up spluttering. 'Oh my God. Oh my God, you're right.'

Just as well they're not going, thinks Kate as she's getting
dressed. Josh could easily be there. It's one of the rules
of living in a small place that the person you least want
to see is the person you're most likely to bump into.
Any activity short of bolting yourself inside your home
with the windows barred and the telephone off the
hook is probably going to result in an encounter with
your current nemesis, or, failing this, one of their
envoys. A few months ago she'd called in sick to work
and was then spotted by her boss's daughter's boyfriend,
the one she insulted at last year's Christmas party,
flagging down a taxi with an armful of shopping bags.
No, you had to stay indoors and keep your mouth shut.
If you didn't think much of someone's new book or
play or movie or single, you'd better think twice before

being honest. She remembers a dreadful silence falling
in a university tutorial as one of the students proceeded
to criticize, in scathing undergraduate terms, a theatrical
production that had, unbeknownst to the student, been
directed by the lecturer's wife. She pours out too much
moisturizer and wipes it over her neck, her hands and,
in desperation, off onto the sleeves of her jumper.
Another hazard of a small population, she thinks, is that
if your appearance was blighted by an unsightly sore, it
goes without saying that you will run into, under harsh
fluorescent lighting or the broad midday sun, whoever
it is that you have been desperately keen on for the last
six months. These conditions are part and parcel of
living in a city inhabited by less than a million people.
Unfortunately, what Kate forgets to do is remind Lucy.

So, when Lucy puts on her figure-hugging tracksuit that
doesn't have a trace of ironic cool about it, and doesn't
notice that her hair is greasy and her nose is red and
swollen from crying, and when she walks up the road to
the deli and the video store with Kate, it's because she's
got no idea that it's an absolute certainty she is going to
be seen by Josh.

Meanwhile, Josh and Mary are in Frank's a.k.a. Daniel's
apartment, having the same scene they've been having
for the past week. And . . . Action!
    'Why can't I move in with you here? Why not?'
    That's it. He's going to change the phone number
and the locks. 'Because it's not my place. It's Frank's.'
    'That didn't matter when you wanted to fuck me in
it.'
    'Jesus, Mary.' She's right but he's going to ignore it.
'And Daniel's staying here.'

'Where is he then?'

'He's coming back any day. You can't stay here.'

'But my flat's awful, it's cold, my flatmate keeps asking why I'm throwing up all the time—' Her flatmate has actually been extremely sympathetic, having gone through a similar thing herself, and keeps offering gin and tonics, but Josh doesn't need to know this.

'Look, I'm sorry. It's just not a good idea.'

'Why not, why not?'

Because, he wants to say. Because I don't want you to. And I don't understand how you can want to stay here when you know I don't want you to. Is it possible to let this truth escape out into the room? No, he decides, it is not. With the effort of suppressing it Josh goes red in the face. 'Mary, please. I've got a lot to think about.'

'OK.' She's backing down. A miracle. 'I'll just stay tonight then.'

They both know what this means. She'll stay tonight, and tomorrow night, and the next and the next. Josh feels a band tighten around his throat. She's winning. She's going to win everything.

'I've got to go out,' he says, in a voice choked of air.

'OK. We need something to eat.' She laughs and pats her tummy and in her baby voice says, 'I want gherkins and ice cream.'

The grossness of this is so intense that, as he's virtually reeling down the stairs, he doesn't have the strength to raise any objection when she calls out behind him, 'Wait a minute! I want to come too.'

Without giving it any thought Josh drives them to the shops that are nearest to his and Lucy's place, the same shops he's been going to for the past four years. It's only when he parks that it seems strange to him. Mary's never

been here before. He supposes it's too much to hope
that she'll want to stay in the car.

The girl behind the late-night deli counter is bored.
Two and a half hours to go. Closing time isn't anything
to look forward to though, what with wiping down the
surfaces and cleaning the meat slicer and sweeping and
mopping the floor. The smell of garlic and artichoke
hearts really pisses her off these days. She sticks her little
finger in the asparagus dip and sucks it, not caring if
anyone comes in. Maybe she'll sneak out the back for a
cigarette and ring her girlfriend. She's about to carve a
slice of honey-roasted ham to take with her when the
electronic doorbell chimes. Two girls about her own
age walk in arm in arm. The boyish, blondey-haired
one's all right. The other one looks like hell. Maybe
they're making up after a fight. She hopes they don't
giggle and simper and buy sex food. It's so cringey when
customers do that.

'Shall we cook something?' asks Kate. 'Or just have
treats?'

'Treats,' says Lucy. 'Lots of treats. I need an oral
fixative.'

'Oh my God,' it occurs to Kate. 'You haven't been
smoking. Why not?'

Lucy sighs, her face up to the display glass, studying
the cheeses. 'I don't know. It's a stupid time to give up,
God knows I could do with an emotional suppressant.
But I just – don't feel immortal any more.' She looks up
at the girl behind the counter. 'Do you have any
artichoke hearts?'

A few minutes later they've accumulated quite a little
pile of goodies but Lucy's not satisfied. There's another
taste sensation she's craving and she can't think what.

Something vinegary? sour? some chocolate maybe? She envisages the map of a tongue they had on the wall at primary school, with all the different taste areas charted out. Something gives her the jitters. They've been in here too long. It's not a taste she needs at all, she realizes. It's touch. Something to satisfy her skin hunger.

The girl gets the adding up wrong on the cash register. She curses mentally and starts again. That one with the tawny hair's got a cute gap in her front teeth. Maybe she'll write a cheque for this, put her phone number on the back. The girl smiles to herself. As if she'd ever cheat on Liz. Still, it doesn't hurt to look. The doorbell rings again. The deli girl watches as the guy stops just inside the door. The woman coming after nearly crashes into him. She slips in under his arm, hugging his side. Then the tawny-haired girl looks at them, something happens, she twitches, a current in the room trembles. She reaches her hand back towards the other girl, the hungry one who's still reading the back of the almond nougat box. As if she feels a touch on her shoulder, the hungry girl's head jerks up. She looks straight at the guy who's just walked in, like on a clear night if somebody says Look at the moon and without thinking you look straight to it, you know exactly where it is. The girl under the guy's arm looks up at him too, in a curious way. They're all looking at the guy. Then the tawny-haired girl looks back to her friend.

'Hi, Josh,' she says. 'We're just going.'

The deli girl hasn't finished adding up their food. Kate heaves the plastic bags off the counter and shoves a couple of notes at her. She yanks Lucy by the arm. 'Are you ready to go?'

'Hang on,' says the deli girl, 'I'll just get your change.'

Nobody listens to her. Kate stands beside Lucy,

waiting to see what she wants to do. She's looking at the girl now, the girl that's with Josh.

He clears his throat. 'Um,' he says. 'Hi.'

'Hi,' says Lucy. She breathes in, and seems to grow taller, like she did in the back yard before she hit him. He prepares himself.

'Hi,' she says to the girl. 'You must be Mary.'

'Hi,' says Mary.

Lucy's hand moves a little bit, as if she's going to stick it out to be shaken, but she puts it back in her pocket. 'Well, we're going.'

'OK,' says Josh.

Kate follows Lucy like a bodyguard as they move past Josh and Mary to the door. Josh takes an unnecessarily large step backwards and bumps against a stand of corn chips. The rustle of the shifting packets is the only sound in the room, apart from maybe the buzz of the fluorescent light.

'Bye,' says Lucy, half-turning her head back towards them, not far enough to see.

'Bye,' says Mary.

The deli girl holds out their change. She says to Josh, 'They forgot this. You going to be seeing them?'

'No,' says Josh. 'Uh. I don't know. Here.'

He takes the money and puts it in his shirt pocket. The coins are cold. They feel like burning against his chest.

When Kate's at the cinema the next night Lucy turns the music up loud again – this break-up's going to give her tinnitus – puts kitchen gloves on and wades into their bedroom with bin liners, to sort out his things. The gloves aren't simply a dramatic touch, they're there to protect her from feeling the texture of his jumpers,

his T-shirts, his trousers, his socks. If she could do this
job with a blindfold on, she would. Jamming his one
suit jacket, the one Ben had given him for what? – his
brother's wedding, into a rubbish bag, she has to sing
along extra loud to prevent herself from stopping.
Stopping and holding the jacket to her. She remembers
one day after they'd first moved in together, coming
home to the empty house and finding his raincoat on
the floor. She'd picked it up and placed it gently over a
chair, so it took on some of his shape, so it looked more
like him. She digs her fingernails into her palms. Ties
the top of the bag closed. A gulp of a sob escapes and
she stamps her foot, thumps her leg with her fist. Runs
back to the living room, leaving clothes strewn over the
floor. She can't stand to be in the same house as that
stuff. Holding her breath, she walks back to the bedroom
and without looking inside it, she slams shut the door.

Daniel's on his own as usual, making his slow way back
north, back to the closest thing he's got to a home.
Money's really tight. He's just glad to have the return
ferry ticket. A return ticket. He can't believe he was
dumb enough to leave England without one. Now he
wonders if he really wants to go back. Course he does.
It's where he's from. What sort of a life is there for him
here? Sure it's beautiful, but— Maybe if he confessed to
Josh about the DJing, explained that he'd need to learn
it from scratch, he could do other work there to pay
back the loan, he'd do anything at all. He's got to do
something while he's saving for a ticket back.

He's got his thumb out in a small town near the ferry
port, can hopefully make it there today. Shame it's not
the right season to kick around here doing some fruit-

picking. Nothing except a tractor comes down the road
for an hour and a half. Then an old green car speeds
past. Wankers, thinks Daniel, then, Christ. There'd been
a shape in the back seat that might have been a large
black dog. Was that a flash of peroxide blonde hair he'd
seen in the front? Is that who it was, Tony's friends? His
stomach seizes up and he has to sit on the ground. This
stuff is haunting him. He had to have imagined it. He
looks up from between his knees, around him at the
shiny afternoon, the autumn trees. It's all real, everything
here. It isn't going away.

FOURTEEN Indonesia. It's hot, almost unbearable. She's walking along a beach except it's the beach from the camping ground they visited when she was small. Though nobody else is visible there is the sense that the place is full with people. Daniel's there, only he looks like Frank, and Nina's there too. Kate is hoping Daniel will notice her. They're all at a tennis court. She's kissing Lucy. A man with no legs is doing handstands. He's there with the travelling freak show, but he's beautiful.

'Kate. Kate.'

Her flatmate's in the bedroom doorway. Kate croaks. 'What time is it?'

'Eight. You've got a visitor.' His voice is dripping with innuendo. 'I'm off to work.'

'Who is it?'

But he's gone. I've got to get my own place, she thinks for the millionth time, pulling a jumper over her pyjamas and checking the mirror. Gorgeous. She pulls back the curtain to see a slice of grey sky, the clothesline bare except for a pair of jeans that have hung there for days. Her toes curl on the cold floor. A voice calls out Hello. She turns from the window, letting the curtain drop, flooding the room with darkness again. Oh. Him.

In the four seconds it takes her to walk to the living room, images snap and pop in her mind with the speed of a music video. Those jeans on the line – his denim jacket – uncut brown hair – the empty movie theatre, a pink streak in the sky on their drive south, Lucy's bedroom without Josh. Then there he is, his back to her, not looking towards the door but pretending to read the newspaper lying sports-page up on the dinner table. There's a split second when she can grin at the efforts he goes to, before he turns towards her, leaner, more starved-looking, than ever.

'Well,' she says, smiling because she can't help it. 'Hi.'

He just looks at her. 'Kate—'

She holds up a hand. 'Hang on a minute. I'm going to clean my teeth. Then I'll make us some breakfast.'

'So. Have you seen Josh?'

Daniel stirs sugar into his coffee. 'He's in a pretty bad way.' He shakes two cigarettes out of his pack and passes one to Kate. Sorry, Lucy, she thinks, and leans forward into the flame from his lighter.

'That girl's had a miscarriage.'

'Oh, Jesus.' Kate rubs her forehead and exhales. 'Poor her.'

'He really wants to see Lucy.'

'Yeah, well. Did you know he was – you know?'

Daniel bites his thumb and squints at her. 'Yeah, he said something.'

'And Frank knew too.'

He shrugs. 'I suppose.'

Kate shakes her head. 'Prick.' She looks up at Daniel again and he feels her gaze sharp as razors. 'Why are you guys so lame?' she asks him. 'Don't you know anything?'

For a second he wonders if she has heard about Nina, but no. She'd have said. He smiles and shrugs and says, 'No. I don't know if I do.' He grinds his cigarette out, carefully. 'What about you?' he says.

Suddenly she wishes she'd got dressed properly, instead of just sitting here in her pyjamas and old torn jersey with no bra on or anything. 'What about me?' He doesn't look at her. 'What is it that you're looking for? Why do you look so hard?' There's a small pause. 'Why do you feel so guilty? Why not just be?'

She laughs, about to brush him off with a Don't be so stupid. Then she hears the question. 'I— It's not—' There isn't anything to say.

He lights another cigarette.

It's when she gets up to take the plates back to the sink that he reaches out, hooks her waist with one of his arms, draws her into him, puts his face into the warmth of her jersey. She looks at the wall, her mouth opened in surprise, then leans over his back and puts the coffee cups and toast plates down on the table. Placing her hands on his shoulders, she tries to push him away. If I don't say something I'm going to make a mistake, she thinks, and I don't even know who you are. Her mind races, trying to find a disclaimer, at the same time as his hands grab at her body, pulling her face down towards his. 'You're a stranger to me,' is all she says, so quiet that she doesn't know if he'll hear. She's pushing at him but she's not and she almost laughs, this is so hopeless, so hopeless.

There are two choices, she realizes afterwards. Either enter right into this, as far as it's possible for strangers to go. Or ignore the fact that her life's been rocked, ever so slightly, that it's set at a different tilt and a crack has appeared to show a thin sliver of blue, blue that could be open sky or blue that could be deep dark sea. For half an hour after he's gone she sits with her fingers to her mouth, on the brink of these possibilities, knowing that if she wanted, everything in the room could appear changed. She looks at the table and sees it in multiple focus. She sees the table beyond the table: the imagined table that she sits at every day and never notices; the real table she's studying now; the table as it might be through somebody else's eyes – millions of humming molecules. Everything, everybody could be viewed in these infinite indefinite ways. She could decide to not know who she is, to not know anything. Instead, she concentrates on the table until it's nothing more than clean wooden planes and edges again, reaches over and picks up the phone.

She tells Lucy what Daniel told her about his trip. 'So the next day he went out in the tattoo guy's boat and actually swam with the whale. With a wetsuit on and everything, but he could still touch it.'

She doesn't realise that Daniel was lying. She has no reason to suspect him. She has no idea that the more he lies, the worse he feels about himself. And the more he lies.

'It was incredible,' he had said to Kate, self-conscious between sex, searching for something to say. 'You could tell that the whale was really ancient, really wise. When it bumped up against me, it was like being touched by something so connected with the planet – that sounds crappy doesn't it?'

'No,' said Kate, 'it sounds fantastic.'

And, 'Fantastic,' says Lucy, as Kate relays Daniel's words verbatim.

'I know. I've always wanted to do that. It's weird, we were talking about it in the car on the way down, and then the lucky bastard goes and does it. And you know, I think it's really changed him.'

'You would think that.'

'Yeah, all right. But something has.'

'So what else did he get up to?'

'Nothing much, from what he said.'

'Did you take many photographs?' she'd asked, aware of his anchored arm's weight across her naked back.

'No. I gave my camera away to a ride.'

'Won't you miss it?'

'No,' he said, and this at least was the truth. 'It's like, I just wanted to see things for the way they were, not for what sort of picture I might make out of them.'

'Why'd you come back?'

'I don't know,' he said. 'I just had to.'

Kate had nodded. I won't read anything into that, she thought. He means nothing by it.

'It was your classic no no yes yes,' she sighs that evening, sprawled on Lucy's living-room floor.

'Was it good?'

'It was pretty fucking good.' She smiles. 'Kitchen table, bedroom, shower.'

'Stop it.'

'I know.'

'Then what?'

'I kicked him out. I didn't want anything to be said.' She groans. 'I feel as if I made a huge mistake.'

Later, she says, 'I mean who is he? Sorry, not to bang on, but do we even know? Some waif and stray that Josh picked up in the street, practically.'

'He did live here for a bit. As far as I know he never nicked anything.'

'You've got nothing to nick.'

'And you have?'

There's a pause.

'Did you use a condom?'

'Yes,' Kate says in a small voice.

'Kate?'

'What?'

'Kitchen table? Shower? Condom?'

'Well.' She clenches her teeth and looks pained. 'We were careful. Mostly. I mean, we were.'

'He pulled out.'

'Nn. And a condom, another time.'

'Oh, Kate. For fuck's sake.'

'Well. Yes.'

Kate smokes, sitting by the window, the outside air cold against her neck. She pulls her legs into the lotus position. Feels the soreness in her thighs.

'Josh called me at work today,' says Lucy, 'while you were giving Daniel a guided tour of your house.'

'Did you talk to him?'

'Yeah.'

'Was it all right?'

'Nah, not really. He said that girl's had a miscarriage.'

'I heard.'

'I was glad. I didn't tell him that, but I was.' Lucy grabs Kate's pack of cigarettes. 'Fuck it,' she says, and sparks one up. She laughs a little bit. 'Glad that some other woman's gone through a miscarriage. I've really maintained the moral high ground over this one. Anyway, he's going to look after her for a bit obviously but he's told her he wants to break up. That's what he says.'

'Do you believe him?'

'I don't know. I don't think it makes any difference.'

'Really?'

'You know, he wants us to try again, he said he was really sorry, he knew he couldn't expect anything. Then he cried, and that's when I really got fucked off. So. I told him to come round and collect all his shit.'

'When?'

'Tonight.'

'I'd better scarper then.'

'No, stay. No. I don't know.'

'I think you should see him on your own.'

Lucy takes a long drag on her cigarette. 'What if it's awful?' she says. What she doesn't say is the thing she's really thinking: What if I end up sleeping with him?

For two weeks, Nina has been seething with anger about Daniel. The police didn't pursue the case because her car was found in the ferry terminal car park. She didn't know how he managed to avoid them at the other end, but suspected they didn't try very hard to search the boat. Overall she's been disappointed by the calibre of police attention. In the movies all you have to do is lose your handbag and you get some gorgeous young officer at your beck and call. She had hoped she might win a broad-shouldered detective as a consolation prize for being mistreated by Daniel, but no. She wondered if he was back in Auckland yet. Thief. Liar. Seducer. He virtually raped her. For a second she considered – but no, even she wouldn't go as far as a false allegation. She didn't need the publicity a court case would bring. And secretly she didn't regret the sex at all. It was pretty fantastic. What she did regret though, was calling Dolores and telling her all about it before he disappeared. She had to go and meet her for a drink now, and she just knew Dolly would be laughing to herself about

Nina's misfortunes. Her hand shook as she applied another coat of lipstick. The idea that Kate might be getting her claws into him enraged her. There had to be a way she could exact revenge.

'Dolly, let me buy you dinner. There's something I need to ask you.'

The bovine eyes widened and the cleavage heaved in anticipation.

'So that's the problem. I really feel that Kate may be in some danger. From her so-called friend.'

Dolores stroked a finger down between her own breasts. 'You're right. Do you know – has anything happened between them?'

Nina shrugged. 'Well, obviously not before they stayed with me, otherwise I would never have let him seduce me—'

'Of course not.'

' – like that. But if he's back there now . . .' She turned a graceful hand palm upwards, pouting. 'Who knows?'

'You've got to warn her.'

The table rattled slightly, a mini-tremor from the earth. Dolores and Nina didn't take any notice.

'I know. But. The problem is, Kate can be a little bit – oh, we're not terribly close, as you know.'

'She resents your success.'

'Well, I'd never say that. But it does mean that she tends not to listen to me. I just need a way of getting through to her that won't make her feel alienated, that will be the best for her.'

'Yes.' Dolly licked her lips. 'I see.'

'Because also,' Nina said as though it had just occurred

to her, 'she may be very jealous. That Daniel was unable
to – control himself. With me.'

A girl walked into the restaurant wearing a tight little
T-shirt that said *I'm with Stupid*. Nina watched her
slink over to a table full of men. It'd be good to get
something like that for the show. Maybe you can get
them custom-made. She lights a cigarette and the match
flame flares a yellow reflection into her eyes. 'Do you
know,' she said to Dolores, smiling, 'I've just thought of
something.'

Lucy's been in a panic since Kate left. Josh could be
here any minute. Her pulse is right up in her throat. She
despises herself for going to the mirror every few seconds
to check the way she looks. The way she looks is terror-
struck. She alternates between smoking and biting her
nails. She's too scared to go to the loo in case she's in
there when he turns up. Finally, there is a knock on the
door.

'Uh, your stuff's there.' She points to a row of rubbish
sacks by the door. 'I think that's all there is. Oh, and
there's a box with your CDs in, I'll just get it.'

'Lucy,' he says, 'can I come in?'

'Oh, sure, yeah, ah . . .' He follows her into the living
room. She picks up the CD box and goes to hand it to
him. He doesn't put his arms out to take it.

'Can I – can we talk about this?'

'I don't know. Maybe it's not such a good idea. I
don't want to cry in front of you and I'm sick of
being—' She sits down on the couch, hands on her
knees, eyes focused on the skirting board of the opposite
wall. There's a long silence. In the middle of it she
glances up to see if he's watching her but he's watching

the floor. Even for a brief second, it's hard to look at his face. She never much cared about people's bodies, it was Josh's face she'd fallen for, it contained so much life and mischief. In a small voice she asks, 'Why did you do it?'

There's another pause and he sighs. Then he says, 'I think – I felt trapped.'

She exhales. 'My God. I didn't expect a cliché.'

'Well, you wouldn't would you? Because you expect things. You're hard to live up to.'

Even though she'd asked him, she hadn't anticipated any criticism. 'Well why? I'm not that difficult. Why didn't you say something, instead of—'

'Because you're the talker. I'm not, I can't—'

'But I had no idea, I didn't know anything was wrong, I would have said, we could have discussed it.'

'You see? We couldn't. There'd have been – endless conversations, analysis, you would have always been right.'

She wipes her nose and says softly, 'Jesus Christ.'

They fall into another silence. She can't believe this is the way things are happening.

'So,' she finally says, 'why do you want to get back with me? Is it because – what you did – made you scared?'

'I don't know,' he says after a bit. 'Maybe. It's been a – difficult time.'

Hugging her knees to her chest, she realizes that what she'd imagined was, they'd talk about it, maybe shout at each other, and he'd be apologizing and saying how wrong he was and how much he loved her. And though she hadn't admitted it, she'd hoped passion would take over and they'd lie in bed and he'd tell her that all the time he was thinking of her, that she just had to give him another chance, couldn't she see they were meant to be together? And, she thinks now, in the room which seems whiter and emptier than it did while he was gone, she probably would have agreed.

'So what do you really want? Maybe you need to be on your own for a while.'

'I—' His tongue forms a 'l' sound but he doesn't say it.

'You know, Josh, I'd like you to leave.'

He doesn't move. She says it again, and pinches the skin on her hand. 'Please.'

'I'll call you,' he says, taking a step towards her.

She shakes her head. 'No. Don't call. Don't do anything.'

Kate? It's Ginny. Now I've just had a call from Ninie and she says be sure and tell you to watch the programme tonight because there's something special on it. Maybe one of your old friends is in a band. Wouldn't that be exciting! So I've left you the message now, I've done my duty. Have you heard from the polytech about your course? Call me later. Oh no, I'm out later. Call me tomorrow. No. Where's my— Don't worry! I'll call you. Bye! Sorry to take up so much of your tape. Hope it isn't a problem. Bye!

Kate's flatmates fall about laughing when she plays the message back. Mike says, 'That's what my mother's like. And I hold her fully responsible for how I turned out.'

'I should be nicer to her then,' says Toby.

'Guys, do you mind.'

'Oh my God,' says Mike. 'It's nearly time. I'll get the drinks.'

G&Ts in hand, they sit on the floor in front of the television while the epilepsy-inducing titles for Nina's video show flash and splatter out of the screen.

'There she is, there she is!'

And there she was, in all her edge-of-fashion, now-ironic now-enthusiastic glory. 'Wow,' says Kate, 'she looks great.'

Light bounces from Nina's cheekbones, it glitters in her hair and flares off her un-gappy white teeth. She imparts music industry gossip as if knowledge of it is crucial for the survival of the species.

'She's good,' says Kate, 'she's really good.'

'Do you think she's a nascent gay icon?' Toby asks.

'Don't push it.' Mike nudges him with his foot. 'What's on that T-shirt she's wearing?'

At that moment Nina looks down to her T-shirt and points at the lettering. The camera zooms in.

'Turn it up, turn it up!' Toby cries.

'And this T-shirt,' she's saying, 'has been sent to me by a fan living in Auckland who comes *all* the way from London.' She rolls her eyes and smiles. 'Viewers so far afield! It's caused *quite* a fuss in the production office.'

'What does that say?'

'Belt up.'

'So *thank* you, Daniel from London,' she twinkles, 'I'm glad you're enjoying the sounds. And, as for the personal sentiment, well – are we out of family viewing hours?' Her eyes give a come-on to the camera. 'You know where to find me.'

And the programme's logo and post-office box number spring up in wacky bright handwriting on the screen. They go to a commercial break.

'What did it say, could you read it? I've taken my contacts out.'

'It said,' says Kate, hand tight around her frosty gin glass, 'GIRL OF MY DREAMS.'

★

Daniel is thinking how odd it is that he's used to Auckland now, though he's hardly spent any time here. His first few days in the city seem increasingly dreamlike. Losing the money, that mad girl at the casino, his rapid slide into near-destitution. How can that have been only a matter of weeks ago? Even the landscape, the red gravel footpaths and immense pale sky, has become familiar, almost comfortable. He likes staying at Frank's apartment too, even if Josh is there and in a right state over Lucy and that other girl. Daniel feels sorry for Josh, who seems a bit of an amateur at deception. He has to admit, though, that the romantic crisis has distracted Josh from the fact that Daniel can't do half the things he said he could at the radio station. He's been in twice since he got back, surreptitiously learning the ropes from that scrawny boy, who in return pesters him non-stop for information about the music scene in London. Daniel is coming off a lot more knowledgeable than he really is. He explains his ignorance of the studio equipment by pointing out how ancient it is compared to the hi-tech stuff he's used to. Soon he'll have the hang of it, and then he can start earning money properly. In the meantime, Josh has lent him some more cash, and stuck him on the station payroll so it looks above board. As a thank you, Daniel takes him out to drown his sorrows.

At the carefully chosen, un-faggy bar, he can't stop himself from spinning shit about his time down south.

'You tinny bastard,' Josh says. 'A blonde in a sportscar and she asked you to stay at hers?'

'She was gagging for it. I mean, she wasn't that hot-looking, but she was pretty fit.'

'Tinny bastard.'

'It was a shame to leave her, but you know. I wanted to keep moving.'

Josh nods. 'Sure mate. I know how it is.'

'I got another lift pretty fast.'

'No more sportscars?'

'Nah, I think that was my lifetime's quota. Hey, ah, don't say anything about that to Kate, will you?'

'Course not.' There's a pause. 'Why not?' There's another pause. 'She finally get you into the sack?'

'Just best not to say anything.'

Damn, thinks Josh, he's kind of curious to know what she's like.

'I know things are crap for you just now, mate,' Daniel is saying. 'But I really appreciate what you've done for me, you know? Helping me get sorted here.'

'No problem, man.' Josh scratches his chin. He's been forgetting to shave. 'We can probably find you an on-air slot next week, week after.'

'Excellent.'

'So, ah, if you don't mind me asking, why'd you come here with no money in the first place?'

'It got nicked,' Daniel says, 'from my room at the hostel.'

'Oh right. Hey, listen, I'm sorry to bring this up, but you do have a work permit, right?'

Daniel nods his head, hard. 'Yeah, yeah,' he says, and takes a long pull on his beer. 'But my, ah, passport was stolen as well. But I can just go to the embassy and get it fixed up.'

'No, no worries.' Josh makes a face. 'Just in case, you know, I thought I'd better check. For the station accounts and shit, tax and that.'

'Yeah, whatever.'

There's an uncomfortable pause during which they both wonder if they have anything more to say to one

another. Then Daniel spots a familiar figure over the
other side of the room. She sees him at the same time,
and drunkenly – it's five o'clock in the afternoon –
makes her way over.

'I know you,' she says to him.

'Yeah, you do.'

Josh is checking her out. Tight black trousers, pale
green fally-offy top. A good – great – body, if a little on
the anorexic side. Big lips, dulled eyes.

'I know you,' she's saying to Daniel, 'but I don't
know your name.'

He shoots a look to Josh. Can't let him see an obvious
lie. 'Daniel,' he says. 'This is Josh. Josh, this is Tara.
Who'd like another drink?'

Later, after Josh has swerved off in the direction of
home, Tara drives Daniel dangerously to her flat. It's
strange, he thinks, it's only been a few weeks but she
looks about five years older. 'I hate this town,' she's
been saying all night. 'I have to get out of here.'

Her living room is a mess, magazines and clothes flung
everywhere. Three ashtrays balance on one arm of the
couch, all full. A poster of some American rock idol
hangs dog-eared off a wall. He notices cups tucked
alongside the couch and armchair and makes a mental
note not to look inside them. Tara slaloms in and out of
the kitchen, carrying vodka, glasses, another ashtray. So
far, she hasn't made any attempts to stick her hand down
Daniel's trousers. This doesn't bother him. He sits on
the couch and she slumps down next to him, her shirt
all but coming off her as she leans forward to pour them
both a drink. They clink glasses.

'So,' she says, reaching for a cigarette. 'What are you still doing here? I thought you were just passing through.'

'I am,' he says, wondering what sort of conversation they might have had with each other on that bender evening. 'It's just taking longer than it was going to.'

'Got a ticket back?'

'No.' He draws back to the far end of the couch and looks at her. Something occurs to him. 'Where did you get to that night?'

She raises her eyebrows and pouts, as if trying to remember. 'The casino?'

'Yeah,' he says, 'we were there together and then you vanished.'

'No, we were in that bar. Up the top. With the view.' She smiles. 'And it was raining.'

She'd come to find him there. She was in the bar. 'And then what?'

'Then— D'you want some more?' She refills her vodka glass and hugs the bottle to her chest. She laughs. 'Don't you remember?'

'I just want to hear it from you.' There's a nasty smell like old socks. Daniel pulls the cushion he's been leaning on away from the couch and sees – what is that? – underwear? crumpled down there. Not a good idea to investigate. When he looks back to Tara her eyes are closed and her mouth half open. 'Hey.' He prods her with his foot. She twitches her head and groans. 'Tara.'

'Wha.'

'Tell me about that night.' He nudges her again.

'Mm.'

'Tara.'

She mumbles something that might be, 'Can't remember.' This pisses him off.

'OK. You know what I think happened?' He stands up. 'I think you took the casino chips I bought you and you went and squandered the lot and then you came and found me in that bar and thought, here's an easy ride, here's a fucking patsy, and you dragged me outside and fucking screwed me for all the money I had in the world, the only money I've ever had in the world—' He's more angry than he'd thought about losing that money and Tara's non-response makes him angrier. 'Hey! I'm talking to you.'

Her eyes snap abruptly open, dazed. 'What?' She laughs. 'Sorry, did you say something?'

He looks around the room. She slowly moves the vodka bottle towards her lips but he leans in and snatches it off her. 'Hey,' she says, 'that's mine.'

'And ten thousand fucking dollars was mine,' he says, his voice rising. 'Where the fuck is it?'

She looks at him as if for the first time. 'Ten thousand dollars?'

'Ten, twenty, I was loaded, you fucking know that.'

Cat-like, Tara leans forward with her forearms on her knees. 'Twenty thousand dollars,' she whispers.

It's raining, heavy. Lights gleam yellow off wet glass-walled buildings and shine out from puddles. In the marina, boats rock and jangle, and salt waves splat up against the barnacled wooden jetty posts. A street of office blocks forms a wind tunnel, scattering papers and battering placards with a metallic whupping noise. Telegraph wires whip up and down. Rain sweeps along gutters in small floods, swirling at the mouths of drains. Clubbers straggling out of a large metal doorway into the night find themselves pelted by the rain. Some of them shrink back beneath shop awnings while others shriek and splash in the oily kerbside pools. There's the sound of drumming water and the wet rubbery hiss of cars. Sheets of rain break against the Skytower. Its red lights glint through the curtains of charcoal drops. Two people emerge from the ground floor, the casino floor, moving as slowly as if it's the middle of a sunny afternoon. They inch down the hill towards the main street, into the wind. One of them stops to lean against a wall. The other one says something but it's drowned out by the swish of a passing car. They totter on further, towards the rectangular orange lamps of taxis lined up along the road. Halfway there, one of the figures grabs the other by the elbow and drags them across the street to a car-park building. In the first-floor darkness they embrace, and pull at each other's wet clothes. Now they're kissing. They're taking all their clothes off, up against a concrete pillar, they're closing their eyes and touching one another's rained-on skin.

Tara's eyes shine hard. 'But you couldn't do it, remember?' She takes a swig at the vodka. 'No wonder you couldn't if you were in blackout the whole time.'

'Then what,' says Daniel. If he'd taken his clothes off, fuck knows what—

'I don't know, then we went and got our taxis.'

'Really.'

'Jesus,' she says. 'Do you think if I had twenty grand I'd still be here? Do you think I'd have come up to you in that bar?'

'I don't know,' Daniel answers. 'I don't know anything about you.'

There's the sound of a key in the front door. It surprises Daniel that Tara lives with anyone, that anyone could

handle sharing with her. The flatmate's a short girl with
black hair. She stands in the living-room doorway a
second too long, taking in the scene.

'Hi, Liz,' says Tara.

'Hi.'

'This is – uh.'

'Daniel,' says Daniel.

'Hi.'

Nobody says anything. Tara lights a fresh cigarette off
the end of the one she's been smoking.

'Where you from?' asks Liz.

'London,' he says.

'Oh.'

'Why? Could you tell?'

'No. Just wondering.'

'Drink?' says Tara to Liz, and with bemusing agility
hops up out of the couch and through to the kitchen.

'No, thanks,' Liz calls after her. 'I'm going to pick up
Annie from work. You want any deli food?'

'Nah,' says Tara without looking at Daniel, 'we don't
need food.'

When Liz has gone she laughs and says, 'Don't mind
her. Doesn't like your sort.'

'There must be something else. That you remember.
Did you come back with me?'

'To the hostel? No.'

'How'd you know I was—'

'You told me,' she says, giggling. 'For fuck's sake.
That's half the reason I didn't come back.'

'That's a nice stereo.'

'It's Liz's. And it's hardly worth twenty grand.'

Either she's sobered up or she was never that drunk.
He can't tell which. He can't tell anything. Perhaps he's
only suspicious because he's a liar himself. Or perhaps

she's just better than him. She could have done anything with that money. Stuck it in the bank. Bought drugs.

'Listen,' she says, 'if you really want to get out of here, and if you really are skint, I know someone who might need something taken to Sydney.'

'No,' says Daniel. 'No way.'

'Why not? It's all totally legal.' She laughs. 'I'm not suggesting you become a drug smuggler in order to get out of here. My God.' She rifles through some papers on the mantelpiece and hands him a card. 'It's a courier flight company. Free flights to Sydney if you take their packages. Short notice, one way.'

He looks at the card and is filled again with the prickly heat of Pattaya. The man with his high-pitched voice, saying, Memorize this.

'Can I keep it?'

Tara shrugs. 'Sure.'

She drapes herself in the doorway. 'I'm going to bed,' is all she says.

'Tara.'

'Mn?'

'I'm going to go.'

'Oh.' She sashays back into the living room and sits on a chair, facing him. 'Really.'

'Yeah,' he says, standing, patting his pocket for his cigarettes. 'Really.'

Kate can't get that T-shirt thing out of her head. Why would Nina do something like that? She must be warning her. She must suspect. Every time the phone had rung in the last three days Kate hoped it would be Daniel. She'd done the maths – they have sex on the Monday, it's acceptable for him to call Tuesday, Wednesday or Thursday. Friday is embarrassingly late

and if he hadn't called by Saturday he probably wasn't
going to. By last night, Wednesday, Kate was telling
herself, Don't call him, whatever you do don't call him.

Nina's doing her a favour, she thinks, staring at the
finger-marked telephone. She's just letting her know
that something happened when Daniel stayed on in
Wellington. She figured Daniel wouldn't tell. Kate
wiggles a fingernail between the gap in her front teeth.
But. This reminds her of something. That time when
she'd come home from school exams – School C
History, she'd guessed all the multi-choice about dates –
and her first boyfriend had been waiting in the living
room. He was sitting on the couch looking at Nina,
who stood in a shaft of dust motes in the middle of the
room. Kate had sensed something, an almost aggressive
energy that had confused her. She'd plonked her bag
down and flopped onto the couch next to her boyfriend,
expecting the slightly embarrassed play-fighting that was
his usual greeting. But he shrank away from her,
adjusting his grey flannel shorts, and Nina walked out of
the room without saying anything. None of them had
said anything, not since Kate's first hello.

Thinking about it now while also thinking she should
really go and get dressed for work, Kate wonders what
had gone on. The boyfriend moved to Australia with
his parents for a year and then came back, tanned and
sporting a self-conscious feesh and cheeps accent. They
picked up where they left off and after another year, on
the skiing holiday, started sleeping together. It was a few
months after that when Nina had come into the bedroom she and Kate shared, stood with her neck bent to
the side in that way of hers, and suggested that she ask
the boyfriend what he'd been doing the night before
because she, Nina, had seen him in town with Kate's

so-called best friend. 'I don't want to be a doom merchant,' she'd said, looking concerned, 'but I think you should know.'

'They were probably just hanging out together,' Kate had said, thinking about how the boyfriend had told her he was going to a mate's place to watch the footie. And her best friend was having dinner at her grandparents', Kate remembered her moaning about it. 'No,' Nina had said, her eyes full of pity. 'I saw them – kissing. And stuff.' Kate hadn't asked what 'and stuff' meant. She guessed. It was a hard few months, losing a boyfriend and a best friend at the same time. But she was grateful to Nina, for having said.

The telephone bleats into life and Kate flinches. She puts her hand out to pick it up, then draws it back. Her flatmate Mike walks into the room and stops when he sees her frozen there.

'What?' he says.

She turns her head towards him, eyes locked, the phone still shrilling.

'Oh, for heaven's sake.' He marches over and picks up the receiver.

'It's for you,' he stage whispers. 'It's that Anglo bloke.'

Kate thinks about it for a second. She shakes her head.

Mike raises his eyebrows and says into the telephone, 'Sorry, no.' He hangs up. 'Well, that was satisfying for me. But are you all right? What's going on?'

'Nothing,' says Kate, drawing her sleeves down over her hands. 'It's too humiliating.'

Lucy visits Kate at the cinema. 'You got time for a fag?'

'Janice,' beckons Kate, whispering, 'can you cover for me a minute?'

The hefty girl gives one affirmative upwards jerk of her head.

'I owe you,' Kate tells her as she and Lucy sneak past into the staff changing room. Once they're in there she closes the door, giving Lucy a look. 'I really owe her. I break a million more rules than she does and I'm supposed to be her supervisor.'

'You been promoted?'

'Don't. It's so depressing.'

'Won't it get Ginny off your back?'

Kate lights two cigarettes and passes one to Lucy. 'I told her I'd been promoted ages ago.' She grins. 'It's just not fashionable any more to be this useless. Is it?'

Lucy blows out a thick stream of smoke. 'Listen. I'm going to a fortune teller tomorrow. Want to come?'

'I thought you didn't believe in that shit.'

'I didn't believe in infidelity either. Look, it's cheaper than a shrink. What do you think?'

Kate pulls at her earlobe. 'I don't know. What if they tell me there is no foreseeable change ever in my life and this is it? Doomed to a round of meaningless tasks and inconclusive relationships? I mean, our oven *is* gas.'

Lucy isn't sure if she should ask, but, 'Have you heard from Daniel?'

'What do you mean he fucked Nina?'

Kate tells Lucy about the T-shirt. 'So obviously they got it on. He's a – I don't know what he is.'

'Do you believe her?' Lucy squints.

'Yeah. I mean, she's my sister, she wouldn't lie about that.'

'Kate, I hate to say it but Nina's fairly ruthless. She could just be in a sabotaging mood.'

'No. You reckon? No. I mean, how would she know? That anything had happened? She must be in touch with him. Ugh.' She shudders, and rubs her arms. 'It makes me feel sick.'

'Might be worth asking her.'

'That makes me feel sicker.'

There's a short rap on the door and Janice pokes her peroxided hair through. 'Kate. They're coming out.'

Good, thinks Kate. Maybe I should as well. Men are too weird.

But instead she goes with Lucy to the fortune teller.

'Are you nervous?' she asked her as they waited for the bus. 'I mean it's not like tarot or anything is it? Where you can put things down to some dodgy cards or bad tea leaves. It's your actual future.'

Lucy peered up the road. 'I'm only doing this for a laugh. Start looking forward, you know, not rehashing the stupid past.' She flashed Kate a forced-looking smile. 'Get on with getting over this,' she said, almost to herself.

She lost her preoccupied air once they were on the bus, and by the time they were walking up the path to the one-storey brick house with a swirly-painted letter box, they were giggling like schoolgirls. Kate imagined the fortune teller to be an old gypsy type with fucked teeth and whiskers. 'She'll smell,' said Lucy, 'of cat piss and old food.' 'And she'll stroke your face all the time,' said Kate, 'with her hairy fingers.' 'Six on each hand.' But the woman who comes to the door as they stand there elbowing each other is not old, only middle-aged, with a wardrobe not dissimilar to Ginny's. A tie-dyed scarf flows from her neck and she wears a floaty tie-dyed blouse over a floaty tie-dyed skirt. She has ginger hair

knotted back in a plait and bright blue staring eyes. The
fortune-telling room is really the sunroom, with smoked
glass windows, an orangey ragrug and a pretend electric
fire beating out warmth. There's a couch, an armchair
and two office chairs either side of a fake-wood desk.
Nothing on the walls. Kate clocks a box of tissues on
the floor. Uh-oh.

The fortune teller doesn't speak until they're standing
in the middle of the room, then: 'Hell-o,' she says, with
a gesture of her thin tanned arm. Hers is one of those
modulated voices that you can tell only gets slower
and quieter in a crisis. 'You're here,' she breathes.
'Welcome.'

Lucy is first. Kate waits on a chair in the hallway, flicking
through a cheapo women's magazine. There's a strange
glow against the cream walls from a pink light bulb, and
the faint smell of air freshener. She's not altogether sure
about this. Twenty-five dollars seems a lot to spend to
be told a bunch of stuff you want to hear. And if it
wasn't an ego massage it was a risk. The future. She's
never been good at imagining it, and certainly not at
planning for it. *Que sera sera* only gets you so far. She
can hear the fortune teller's low voice murmuring
through the door. After she's checked the women's
magazines for the horoscopes of everyone she knows –
a week old, funny that, so you couldn't accuse the
woman of cheating – and read a heart-rending account
of one family's fight against obesity, the noise of voices
stops. Kate looks up as the door from the fortune-telling
room opens.

'That was quick.'

Lucy's eyes are red round the edges and her voice
comes out choky. 'I asked her to stop.'

'What? What was she saying?' Kate stands and puts a hand on Lucy's arm.

'Nothing specially.' She shakes her head and smiles a faint smile. 'It was dumb of me to think of this. I'm not in the right—' She bites her bottom lip as tears well in her eyes.

'Come on. We'll go.'

'No, you go and do yours.'

'Don't be stupid. We know she'd have nothing to say anyway.' Kate laughs, 'I've got no future, ha ha. Anyway, whatever it is, I'd rather not know.'

'Are you sure?'

'Yep. Sure.'

The fortune teller appears in the doorway, her eyes anxious.

'Sorry,' says Kate. 'We have to go.' She shepherds Lucy out through the narrow pink hall, calling out Bye without looking back. Arm in arm they walk down the pebbled garden path. The sun is pale and almost wintry but it's a clear day. Trees and houses are outlined sharply against the washy sky. It's five minutes of pure suburb to the bus stop. Lucy's face is streaked with wet, tears clinging to her lashes and dripping off her jaw. Kate pulls out her cigarettes.

Legs up on the desk, Josh sprawls back in his swively chair at the radio station, rattling a biro between his teeth and looking at the door. 'Skinny!' he calls out as he sees the stick figure passing. The boy comes in. 'Hey, Josh.'

'Listen, ah, sorry for losing my temper before, eh. There's a lot of shit going on right now.'

Skinny nods. 'No worries, man, no worries.'

'OK. Cool.'

Skinny, still nodding, backs towards the door. 'OK, man, take it easy.' He makes a gripping gesture with his fist as he disappears. Josh sighs and swivels around in his chair to face the window. For a minute he has a feeling of déjà vu. Then he realizes that he's just recently seen a movie where somebody's in their office having a similar moment, only the view out the window is the sky-scrapers of New York. He tries to remember the soundtrack.

He'd left Mary's place this morning wishing it could be for the last time. She was on the couch, a hot water bottle between her legs, reading about Rome.

'I wonder,' she'd said out loud, eyes still on the book in front of her, 'how people like us felt when they lived then. It would have been rough for girls. But how did they *feel*? They didn't have Freud, or Jung. I wonder if they ever felt guilty. If they ever wanted to live in a different culture, in a different time. I wonder what they were like, when they were happy.'

'Can I get you anything from the shops? I'll cook dinner tonight.'

'Thanks.' She glanced up at him. 'Could you get me some eyedrops?'

'Sure.' He bent down and kissed her on the cheek. 'Sorry,' he'd whispered, and made for the door without looking back.

But now, as he gazes out at the swaying palm tree in a vacant way, he's thinking about how long he might have to look after her for. Initially he'd thought she would really string it out, want him to hang around for as long as possible. Since the miscarriage, though, she's become more self-contained. He doesn't know what she's thinking. She's distant with him, as if he's a glorified slave boy. But he doesn't feel enslaved. More than anything, knowing that soon Mary will have had enough of him, and knowing that Lucy doesn't expect to get back together, he feels free. He likes the idea of being on his own. Yeah, he says to himself as the sky begins to darken. It's about time.

With a coat on it's mild enough to lie on the roof of Frank's apartment building, looking at the stars. There's no Pole Star in this hemisphere. No constancy. Daniel tries to imagine the distances between the four points of the Southern Cross. A cinematic idea of space is all he has: the underbellies of motherships, 3-D asteroid showers and slowly spinning planets. What other images could he have, other than those which have been projected before him on a giant screen? He wonders if ordinary people will travel to the moon in his lifetime. This morning he called the air courier company and gave them his name and number. They run daily flights to Sydney and give anything from two to twenty-four hours notice when they want you to go. Once he's there, thinks Daniel, he can start over. Get a job for certain. Maybe take a trip into the desert. Forget New Zealand, forget this interlude ever happened. He hasn't told Josh what he's done. Or Kate. Well, she isn't taking his calls. He can only assume she's been talking to that sister of hers. He feels bad that she had to find out. He feels bad that he did it.

FIFTEEN 'Come over,' Kate says on the phone to Lucy. 'I've got something brilliant.'

Lucy gets there after work, just as it's getting dark.

'Here.' Kate hands her a gin.

'Wow. I've never seen one of these before.'

'Shut up. The surprise is later. You have to wait.'

'Where's Toby and Mike?'

Kate makes a face. 'Don't ask. Marriage guidance.'

'What? Have they been fighting?'

'I think it's a problem with the sex,' she whispers. 'Mike told me.'

'Poor them. Is it hard for you, being here?'

'Nah. It's fine.' She notices Lucy's face. 'Oh – love. Are you all right?'

They sit at the kitchen table.

Lucy manages a grin. 'I can't believe you and Daniel – on this—'

'Would you stop it? He called again yesterday. Do you think I should talk to him?'

'Do you?'

'Not really. I'm bored of guys being shits.'

'Me too.'

'Is it really bad?'

Lucy lights a cigarette and coughs. She nods. 'Most of the time. The thing is.' She screws up her nose and sighs. 'I want him back.'

'Do you?'

'Yeah. I've thought about it a lot. I know what he's done, and everything.' She presses her lips together then says, her voice breaking, 'But I just want to be with him.'

'Oh, Lu.'

She waves Kate away. 'I'll be fine.' She sniffs and blows out a breath. 'It probably won't work out. It's a stupid idea. I just miss him, that's all.'

Kate checks outside the window. It's dark. 'Hey,' she says, pulling her friend up by the hand. 'Come and look at this.'

On a wooden box in the tiny back garden stands a tripod. At first Lucy thinks Kate's set up a camera there, the old-fashioned outside sort with a black cloth for the photographer. But as they approach, she realizes the thing on the top is part of a long cylindrical body, pointing out towards the neighbour's fence. It's a telescope.

'Where'd you get this?' Lucy says, bending forward to peer through it. 'I can't see anything.'

'Hang on. Second-hand.' Lucy stands aside as Kate adjusts the focus and sets the lens at the right angle. 'There,' she says. 'Look at that.'

Lucy puts her eye to the viewpiece and smiles. Kate is showing her the moon, large and chalky-white, pitted with shadow, a quarter of it invisible against the dark sky. 'What's on the dark side of the moon?' she asks.

'Terra incognita. Nobody knows.'

'And what are those seas called again?'

'Sea of Tranquillity, Ocean of Storms, Bay of Billows, Sea of Cold,' says Kate. 'Sea of Nectar, Sea of Rains, Sea of Fertility, Lake of Dreams.'

Lucy straightens up. 'How do you know all those?'

'I got a book out.' Kate shivers. 'Shall we go in now?'

'Wait a second.' Lucy swings the telescope round to face the east. She focuses on a large, pearl-bright planet not far above the horizon. 'I want to see Venus.'

The courier company called Daniel at eight in the morning. They wanted him to take a package for them that day. He has to be at the airport by eleven. The time now is nine o'clock.

It's not packing his bag that takes him long, or even tidying up the small evidence of his existence in Frank's flat. It's standing up on the roof, in the cold wind, looking out over the suburbs and into the city. There aren't many cars on the harbour bridge. It makes him laugh how they talk about Auckland's traffic problem when it takes you all of ten minutes to get from one side of town to the other. A ferry pulls out into the harbour, the wide train of its wake frothing behind it. The Skytower stands high and hypodermic-thin above the other buildings, like an air traffic control tower against the clouds. He should call Josh and tell him. He should go and see him. And Kate. But there isn't time. He'll send Josh the money when he gets it together in Sydney. As he thinks this he knows that he probably won't. Seagulls float on wind currents above the boats in the marina.

Nina walks out of her producer's office, her fingernails clawing crescents into the palms of her hands. She's not going to cry, she's not going to cry. She makes it as far as the ladies' where, looking at her ashen face in the mirror, she sniffs and lets a big glossy tear slide down her perfect nose. How could he be so *mean* to her?

★

'Ah,' the producer had said as she stood in the doorway, her charming-young-woman smile at the ready. 'Good. Come in.'

There was something in his tone of voice. Nina sat quietly, discarding the smile, assembling her features into serious-and-concerned.

He finally looked up from his desk. 'Let's keep this brief. You are not the producer. You are not the director. You are merely the presenter. It is not your place to improvise on the script, nor is it your place to discuss shots with the camera operator.'

Nobody has spoken to Nina like this since – when? she can't remember. A deep burning throbs inside her solar plexus. 'But I—'

'That business with the T-shirt compromised your professionalism and, by extension, that of the programme.'

The worst of it was how ordinary he sounded. Almost bored, like a father. Professionalism. Nina had always prided herself on her business-like approach. That's what made her different from her peers. That's what made her special. 'It wasn't my—' fault, she was about to say, but was smart enough to stop herself. He nods at her in a dismissive way. 'So. Personal life is for outside of the office, hmm?'

'Yes,' she says, her cheeks cold with humiliation. 'It was—'

'No need to explain. Just remember we're running a proper studio here, it's not student pranks any more.'

All right, all right, he didn't have to rub it in. Nina waits for a signal that she can leave. He doesn't give one. It dawns on her what he is waiting for. 'I'm sorry,' she says, trying to retain a scrap of dignity. 'I'm sorry. It won't happen again.'

And he smiles – oh, how like her father – in a
patronizing, not-really-seeing-her way and says, 'Good.
That's settled then. You'd better run along to – ah—'

Wherever it is that I'm going, she thinks, a forced
smile wobbly on her frozen face.

And it's only now, in the girls' bathroom, that Nina
can stamp her foot and watch her mouth turn down in
preparation for a good cry. But the hydraulic-hinged
door heaves open and the production secretary saunters
in.

'Hi,' she says to Nina, coming to the basin with her
lipstick in her hand. Is that a smirk on her face?

'Hi.' Nina smiles. Her insides twist. She focuses on
the lipstick. 'That's a nice colour.'

Lucy gets a phone call at the clothes shop.

'It's me,' says Kate.

'I'm *so* bored. Some anorexic just tried to nick off
with a shirt and I almost let her, except it'd come out of
my pay.'

'I've just been to the polytech.'

'What, with Ginny holding a gun to your head?'

'No, I found something I want to do. There's this
navigation course, they run night classes. I can roster
myself on the day shift at the cinema.'

'You're going to be a sailor?'

'Well, I don't know. I just want to learn how to
navigate first. Read the stars. Then maybe, if I like it.'

The clothing store owner, a henna-haired woman in
her forties, styled to within an inch of her life, walks
into the shop. She frowns at Lucy.

'Listen I'd better go.'

'Is that a personal call?' the owner asks, pursing her
crimson-red lips.

'OK,' says Kate, 'I just wanted to tell someone.'

'Well, I think it's terrific, babe.' Lucy doesn't take her eyes off the owner, who is looking at her watch in a pointed way. 'I'm really pleased for you.'

'It is good isn't it? I'll be able to find my way home at night when I've been chucked out of parties.'

'And you'd never be thrown overboard out of a life-raft.'

The owner puts one hand on her hip and snaps, 'Oh for heaven's sake, Lucy.'

Hang on a sec, Lucy thinks. I'm talking to my friend. And she's telling me something important. She ignores the woman.

'Then I could sail anywhere I like,' Kate is saying, 'and not have to worry about getting lost. I still might capsize though. And I'd be lonely on my own.'

'Lucy!' the owner's face is quivering. 'This is ridiculous!'

Without thinking about it, Lucy raises her hand and makes a jerk-off motion with her curled fingers, still looking the owner right in the eye. 'Gotta go,' she says to Kate, and hangs up the phone.

The owner is beside herself. Literally too, she's reflected in the specially angled full-length mirrors that stand in the corners of the shop. There are three of her, bony and outraged, gathering themselves up to give Lucy the sack.

'You can shove this lame excuse for a job up your skinny arse,' Lucy gets in first, smiling. 'Your overpriced clothes look shit on everyone who wears them. Don't worry about paying me for this week.'

And she scoops up her bag and tosses the keys down on the counter. 'Mind it yourself,' is the last thing she says as she walks out the door on trembling happy

legs, the grin still stuck to her face. It's only when she's
across the street and heading for the bus to go home that
she thinks, Fuck. How the fuck am I going to pay the
rent?

He can just about see Lucy's flat, and Kate's from up on
the roof. And over on the hill on the other side of the
city, the student radio station. The bar where he met up
with Tara again. Maybe he should have stayed with her,
he thinks. They suited each other in a way. He shut his
eyes and felt the cold air skim over his forehead. If he
was hung up on anyone, it was on Kate. But it was not
a good idea. He sneezes. Damn. Just what he needs for
flying.

He wonders if the colours of Auckland are reproduced
anywhere else: the blacky-green trees, the changing sea,
the painted weatherboard houses. When he'd first
arrived, the summer flowers were still in those small
front gardens – scarlet hibiscus and pink camellias,
flaming birds of paradise, lemon mimosa. They were all
gone now, but a million shades of green were still there,
in the oaks, the pale cabbage trees, the olive fronds of
flax. Giant bamboo, broad-leaved ficuses, the trailing
leaves of pepper trees, silver dollar gums. And over it all,
this uncanny light, ultra-defining, exposing everything
like a cut-out in front of a screen. He longs for concrete,
and streets of terraced houses, and solidity. For buildings
that have stood so long you do not question them. For
crowds, for gridlocks. For a life where crossing town
can be enough of an effort that you don't have to ask
yourself what else you are doing. He wants a daily grind.
He wants a struggle.

★

Kate has put a thick jumper on and taken her atlas out
to the back garden. She sits in a kitchen chair under the
sycamore tree, cup of coffee warming her hands, the
atlas open to the southern hemisphere on her knees. She
loves the shapes that have been drawn between the stars,
making a sense of the formations, creating a mythology.
A tiger-marked monarch butterfly lands on the top of
her telescope and a fantail hops on the grass in front of
her. Christ, she thinks, any minute the seven dwarves
will come home from the mine and find me dead with
an apple in my hand. Her throat itches. She coughs to
clear it and it turns into a coughing fit. She's doubled
over in the chair, her coffee cup fallen to the ground.
Her eyes water as she grips the atlas, gasping for breath.
Finally the spasms subside. What have I done wrong? is
her first thought, What does that mean?

When they were little Ginny had a very cut-and-
dried approach to illness: it was your own fault. Every
ache and pain had some psychosomatic cause. A sore
throat meant you'd been telling lies, earache was letting
you know you were a bad listener, and stomach ache
revealed that you were guilty about a secret. Kate and
Nina both became adept at sneaking aspirin out of the
bathroom cabinet, dosing themselves up and keeping
quiet about their annual flu symptoms. Otherwise they
were racking their brains for hours trying to think of
something they were guilty about, or a lie they had
inadvertently told. Kate remembers long nights in the
room they shared, clutching her pillow with the effort
not to cough. If Nina heard she might be sympathetic –
or she might tell their mother. You never knew. To
take her mind off the coughing she would pull back a
tiny bit of curtain and look up at the sky. Sometimes
you couldn't see anything, only dark woolly clouds.

Sometimes you could see only the bright stars and sometimes you could see the whole Milky Way. What she liked best were the satellites, like stars with motors, gently circling the earth. The glass on the window pane would be cold, and the bushes just outside her window contained demons. But the mysterious stars and the roving satellites were beautiful, so far away.

On the roof, the air really has a bite to it. Daniel says a mental Goodbye to the view. He walks back to the trapdoor to climb back down into the apartment – but it's shut. Did he shut it behind him? He pulls at the cold metal handle. It won't open. It's locked. He's locked himself onto the roof. He grabs it with both hands and tugs hard. This is mad. He looks around for something to lever it with. The broom. It doesn't work. His neck is hot despite the chill. There's nothing else up there, no pot plant that a spare key might be hidden under, nothing. He crawls to the edge, lowers himself onto his stomach and looks down. There's no way he could reach any windows from here. He's locked them all anyway. There are no safe ledges. He runs to the other side of the roof and cranes his neck to see down into the street. It's empty. What could anyone do if he got their attention? The only person with another key is Josh. He could shout to somebody to call him. But he doesn't know the phone number at the station, or at Mary's flat. He has to wait for Josh to come back here. And then Josh will see the packed suitcase in the hallway, the stripped bed and the tidy flat. Where were you going? he will ask, and what will Daniel say? Despite everything you've done for me I was running out on you? His pulse hammers at his throat. He looks down to the ground again. It's much too far to jump. His hands are prickling,

his stomach tight. This is it. He's going to miss the
flight. He isn't going to leave.

In her garden, Kate watches a bee settle on a late flower
from the clambering rose on the neighbour's fence. The
bee's body seems to be made up of a million tiny, soft-
looking hairs. She remembers reading something about
how bees only see in shades of blue, that they have
multi-surfaced eyes that give them a myriad perspective
on their world. The bee nuzzles at the centre of the
rose. It rubs its spiky black legs against the cream petals.
She closes the atlas on her knee and holds it to her chest.
It's getting cold, she thinks, blowing warm breath onto
her hands. She stands up, checks the sky for rain clouds,
climbs the back steps to her kitchen and disappears
inside.